Am

When the Heart Remembers

When the Heart Remembers

EVA ZUMWALT

DOUBLEDAY & COMPANY, INC.
GARDEN CITY, NEW YORK
1984

All of the characters in this book
are fictitious, and any resemblance
to actual persons, living or dead,
is purely coincidental.

Library of Congress Cataloging in Publication Data

Zumwalt, Eva.
When the heart remembers.

I. Title.
PS3576.U5W5   1984   813'.54
ISBN 0-385-19230-4

Library of Congress Catalog Card Number 83-20744
Copyright © 1984 by Doubleday & Company, Inc.
Printed in the United States of America
First Edition

*For Brenda, Lloyd,
Sheila, and Ron*

When the Heart Remembers

CHAPTER ONE

Slender and tanned in cutoff jeans and bright striped pullover, Sarah Wingate folded a sheer pink froth of negligee into her suitcase and straightened to look about her bedroom. This room and two of the other three in the apartment were cluttered with packing boxes, empty and partially filled. Only Sarah's roommate's bedroom was untouched by the whirlwind of packing. The living-room couch was stacked high with gift-wrapped packages. Hanging in a protective covering against a closet door gleamed a white satin gown and a misty veil.

"Sarah, when are you going to open your gifts?" A pretty, dark-haired girl with merry brown eyes handed Sarah a pile of lingerie from a drawer. "I want to see them."

"You will," Sarah promised. She pushed back a strand of honey-amber hair that had strayed from her haphazard upsweep. "I'd like for Sam to be here when I unwrap them. Oh, Kelly!" She sighed. "How am I ever going to get everything packed? Look at this mess! Everything has to be ready to ship before five today. I'll never make it."

Kelly tilted her head, dark hair curling vitally around her face. "Don't despair. I'm good at packing. But surely you don't want to pack the gifts without looking at them first. Listen, Sarah. I grew up in a houseful of brothers, and I survived two of their weddings. The groom is always a nervous wreck. He couldn't possibly care less about the presents. They're mostly household things anyway."

Sarah thought about that and nodded. For a moment she felt unaccountably tired and dispirited. "I suppose you're right. Oh well, Sam will be here soon. I'll pack everything else. If he doesn't want to help open the gifts, he can take the first boxes out as we look at the presents and list them."

Kelly came suddenly to hug her. "I'm going to miss you, Sarah! Why does Sam have to take you so far from here? New Mexico yet—couldn't he work in a bank here in St. Louis just as well?"

"I'll miss you too, Kel." Sarah's eyes misted. "But Sam's family has the controlling interest in half the banks in New Mexico. The Underwoods would not take kindly to any suggestion that Sam move away from their state."

Kelly turned away and blew her nose noisily on a tissue. "I know, I know, Sam's the crown prince of the Underwood empire. He has to be groomed to accept the throne."

"And you can come and visit—or better yet, move out there and work in my shop with me." Sarah began to place books into a carton, aware that her head ached and she had not eaten since breakfast, hours and hours ago. But there was no time to stop. The wedding was scheduled for ten the following morning, and this weekend was the first opportunity she'd had to pack. The job she'd just relinquished at Cauble Concepts, an advertising firm, had kept her running until the last moment. She had been forced to work overtime for a week to finish projects assigned to her.

"If you still have your shop by the time I can come out," Kelly murmured.

"Oh, Kelly, you're not back on that old subject, are you?" Sarah closed the box and began to seal it with packing tape. "Sam has agreed that I can try my wings in my own business, or the half of it I was able to buy with the money my mother left me, and my savings. You heard him yourself, when we blundered onto the subject last night before you left with your date. Sam understands that I can't simply clean and dust an apartment all day. He knows how I feel about having a career of my own."

"I heard what he said, Sarah, but you can't pretend he was happy about it. I really thought at one point he was going to back out on his promise about the shop. Anyone could see he was angry—"

She bit her lip and stopped, too kind to continue to criticize Sarah's fiancé, even though it was no secret between the two young women that Kelly had never liked Sam very much.

Sarah sighed. "Well, we did have that terrible argument last month about it. But you know he reconsidered and agreed I could try my hand at business. It's all settled, really it is."

"That's what he says now—" Kelly waved a hand to forestall Sarah's protest. "Sorry, hon. I shouldn't have said anything. You and Sam are going to be married, and very, very happy, and that's all that matters. Truly, I'm so glad for you."

Sarah smiled at her friend. "I know you are. You're my best friend. I always depend on your understanding."

She smothered the nagging worry that had stirred in her chest. Kelly was right about Sam's attitude toward the business Sarah had found with the help of an aunt who owned a realty agency in Las Cruces, New Mexico, where Sarah and Sam would be living.

Maureen Dwight, Sarah's only living relative, had assured Sarah that the gift shop was a viable investment. The owner, a widow of sixty-eight, wanted a partner, in order to spend more of her time traveling and enjoying semiretirement. The business needed revitalizing. For that reason the price was extremely attractive. Maureen was certain it could be made profitable with an imaginative hand at the helm.

Sarah had asked Maureen to find a small business for her as soon as she accepted Sam's engagement ring and knew she would be living in Las Cruces. It had not occurred to her to ask Sam for permission, nor had it entered her mind that he would deeply resent her plans.

"I want a wife, not an adding machine!" he'd snapped at the height of their argument over Sarah's investment.

Shocked and hurt, Sarah had stared at him for a long moment.

"Sam, I can be a good wife and have something more on my mind than one simple job at a time. But if you think I'm incapable of handling anything besides shopping lists and a vacuum cleaner, then I think you'd better look for another girl."

With that she had returned his ring, and spent an unhappy week wondering if she'd made the right decision. She missed Sam, even though his attitudes were infuriatingly Victorian.

She'd met Sam through friends, almost a year ago. He was in St. Louis on business, conferring with a St. Louis businessman who owned a heavy share of stock in the banks controlled by the Underwoods. The businessman had liked an advertising campaign that Sarah assisted with, and he had invited members of the ad agency to a party while Sam was in town. Sarah and Sam had immediately become friends, and he escorted her home that evening.

During that visit, Sam asked Sarah out twice before he returned to New Mexico. Sarah had been mildly regretful to see him go, but soon her busy life made those two pleasant dates fade from her mind.

Then in the winter he reappeared in St. Louis, calling Sarah almost as soon as his plane landed, taking her out to dinner that same night, and the next, before he had to fly back. After that he made frequent visits, sometimes for a business reason, sometimes not, but always including Sarah in his plans while in the city.

Perhaps it hadn't been the earthshaking romance Sarah had dreamed of. Sarah missed Sam when he was away, though not to the point of tears or daydreaming on the job. When he was nearby, she enjoyed his company, and enjoyed the envy of her friends of having the attention of a handsome, quite wealthy young man. It was certainly not an overwhelming passion she felt for Sam. But she was twenty-six, not a schoolgirl falling blissfully and blindly in love with the captain of the football team. Perhaps love was inevitably less exciting as one matured.

And so she had accepted his ring—and felt bereft when the relationship was severed by their quarrel. Within a week of their breakup, Sam was back. Stiffly, as if he found the words bitter to the tongue, he apologized, and agreed that Sarah could continue with plans for her business.

"But if it doesn't work out"—his voice was carefully restrained—"I hope you'll be fair enough to admit that being my wife is a full-time job."

"It will work out, Sam," she said. "I promise I'll make it work, and you won't find I'm neglecting you, or our home."

So the compromise was made, and the wedding plans went ahead. It was to be a quiet wedding, and small, only Sarah and Sam's friends in the city present. Sam's parents were vacationing in Europe. Sarah knew they'd asked him to wait until their return in the fall. It said something for his ardor that he did not agree but wanted to be married as soon as possible.

Plans for shipping Sarah's belongings to New Mexico had been completed over dinner last night, then Sam had brushed her cheek with a good-night kiss at her door. "I'll finish my business here in town by lunchtime probably," he said. "I'll be here by two to help you finish packing."

His kiss seemed absentminded, too brief. Sarah was aware of a sense of disappointment. Resolutely, she shook the feeling off. Probably, Sam was tired, nervous about the last-minute wedding preparations.

Now, as she rushed to complete the packing, Sarah glanced at her watch. Sam was forty-five minutes late, which was not like him. Usually, he was prompt to the minute. As she moved into the kitchen to finish with the dishes and glassware, Sarah was more relieved than worried. Probably, Sam's lateness was a blessing. He was not going to be pleased when he saw that she had not yet finished here.

As she passed the packages on the couch, wrapped beautifully in white or delicate pastel prints of wedding bells and flowers, Sarah bit her lip. Kelly was right—what reason was there to wait to open them? Sam would think it too girlishly sentimental that she had wanted to share seeing them for the first time with him. She resolved that the moment she had taped and labeled the boxes of kitchenware, she and Kelly would pause for coffee and open everything together.

Kelly, nesting pots and pans expertly, glanced up. "Didn't Sam say two o'clock?"

"His business must have kept him later than he expected. Let's have a coffee break, okay? And a sandwich, if I can find two minutes to eat it. I'm starving."

At that moment the bell rang, and Sarah turned toward the apartment door, nervously trying to smooth her hair, suddenly aware of what a mess she must look. "That will be Sam now," she said.

But it was not Sam. It was a deliveryman carrying a box of flowers. Sarah accepted it and stepped back inside, lifting the lid. "Look, Kel, white carnations. How pretty."

"I hate carnations—they smell like funerals," Kelly remarked, slapping a piece of packing tape on a carton.

Sarah did not hear her friend. She had opened the card, and stood staring blankly at it. The box of flowers fell to the floor, unheeded.

"Sarah?" Kelly gave her a startled glance and came to her side. "What's wrong?"

When Sarah did not answer, Kelly took the card and read it.

Sarah,
    Forgive me, darling. This marriage won't work. I haven't the courage to tell you in person. By the time you read this, I'll be on my way home. . . .

There was more, but Kelly did not read it. "Oh, Sarah," she whispered from a constricted throat.

Sarah drew a deep, shuddering breath. "Kelly, I—I think I want to be alone for a while. Do you—do you mind—"

She turned blindly, went inside her bedroom, and closed the door.

Kelly stared after her, then lifted the flowers from the floor and crammed them into the garbage container in the kitchen, then gave the can a kick for good measure. "Sam Underwood," she said aloud, "I hope your plane gets hijacked to Siberia!"

"I don't care, Sarah. Whatever his reasons, I still think he's a first-class rat."

It had been three days since Sam's defection. Sarah and Kelly had just finished mailing the gifts back. The apartment looked bare and inhospitable with most of Sarah's belongings still in boxes.

Sarah shook her head. Her gray eyes were smudged underneath from sleeplessness. "What good does it do to blame Sam? If he had doubts, it would only have been worse if he'd kept his promise to me out of a sense of duty! How could a marriage survive that way? It's much better to end it now."

Kelly rubbed her cheek, eyes anxiously on her friend. "I know you're right. It's just—the way he did it! What kind of a man would *do* a thing like that?"

Sarah forced a smile. "Sam's kind of man, I guess. I really know how to pick 'em, don't I?"

"What will you do now?" Kelly asked. "Will you go back to your old job?"

"I've been thinking about that. They may already have hired a replacement."

"They'd let you come back, I know they would. It would be hard, after all the excitement over the wedding. But it's a good job, and you were almost due for a promotion."

Sarah's eyes were wide and serious. Her face seemed to have thinned these past few days. Shadows beneath the cheekbones led subtly to the wistful line of her lips.

"No, Kelly. I won't go back to Cauble. I'm going to Las Cruces after all."

Her friend stared at her. "Sarah, you're not serious! You surely wouldn't follow Sam, after what he's done."

Sarah made an impatient gesture and walked across the room to look out the window, slender and graceful in her jeans and white cotton shirt. "It has nothing at all to do with Sam. I don't want to see him again, you know that."

She paused, staring out into the street, as if the answer to some knotty problem was written there, if she only had the wit to read it. "And I don't particularly want to be in the same city with him. But there's my half of a gift shop there, waiting. I've already signed the papers, and I'll be darned if I'll give up my dreams of having my own business just because Sam changed his mind about me!" Her mouth had a determined look now, and her chin lifted.

"But Sarah, you could sell your interest in the shop and buy into a business here, where you have friends. Why do you want to go out there, halfway across the country? You know Sam will think—"

Sarah gave a brisk nod and moved away from the window. "I know exactly what he'll think if he sees me in Las Cruces. But he'll be wrong, and sooner or later he'll see that, I guess. I can't explain to you why I want to go—call it pride, or stubbornness, or whatever you like. I just don't want to give up that little shop before I've even had a chance to try. Sam had every right to decide he didn't want me to be his wife, but he has no right to wipe out all my plans. And he can't if I don't let him."

"Sarah, please think it over!" wailed Kelly. "Oh, I was so happy you'd still be here. This is awful!"

Sarah came and patted Kelly's hair. "Hey, stop crying, or you'll have me in tears again. It's not awful at all. It's sensible. I have an idea. Why don't you come with me, Kelly? There's a good college in Las Cruces. You could do some graduate work there. And a physical therapist can find work anywhere, I'm certain. We can room together."

Kelly dropped her head and was very quiet for a moment. When she looked up, she shook her head regretfully. "I couldn't leave here, Sarah. I think—well, Dave and I are beginning to make serious plans. He's not sure he wants marriage yet, but I know he cares for me."

Sarah smiled. "Maybe if you came with me he might see things in a different light."

Kelly grinned wanly. "Sure, different light, and different girl! I'm not as brave as you are, Sarah."

"I wish you'd think about it."

"Why don't you think about it before you make a final decision," Kelly suggested cunningly. "Go back to work for a few months, and then if you still feel this way, go."

Sarah's gray eyes shadowed momentarily. "Right now, I'd really like to do that, Kel. Believe me, I would. But if I don't go right away, I might lose my nerve. Maybe I'm making a mistake. Honestly, I don't know. Somehow it seems better than sliding helplessly back into a life I've already closed the door on. To try and open that door again seems like failure. I can't quite explain it." She gave Kelly a pleading look.

Kelly sighed. "I think I understand. It's like that first year in college, when we got so homesick we thought we had to go home or die! And when we went back, it was great for a day or two. And then—"

"And then it was like trying to wear a dress you'd outgrown," Sarah finished for her.

Kelly nodded. "Then we knew we had to make the new life the familiar one. That didn't make it easier though. I remember how hard it was for a while not to think of home as the only safe, warm, protected place in the world. I comforted myself by eating. Lord, I must have gained fifteen pounds that first semester."

"And then you went on that weird broccoli and banana diet!" Sarah laughed. She hugged Kelly. "I guess that's why I asked you to come with me to New Mexico. You're like my family now, like a sister as well as my dear friend. I was clinging to the familiar, wasn't I? But this is my bridge to cross, not yours. Kelly, I've just *got* to cross it and see what's on the other side."

Kelly cleared her throat and tried to smile. "I only hope I have as much courage as you when I have to make the kind of decision you're making now."

Sarah remembered Kelly's remark the day she left St. Louis, as she caught a last glimpse of the great steel arch and the wide Mississippi from the plane window. The decision was made, the bridge was burned behind her, but she didn't feel courageous. She felt hollow and numb, and afraid that she might have made a hasty and foolish choice to leave her friends, her interesting and well-paid job, the city where she had spent most of her adult life. Perhaps Kelly had been right. Perhaps she should have waited for a few weeks, at least until she was over the shock of Sam's change of heart. Perhaps she should have waited to be sure that she was thinking clearly. In a month or so everything might look very different. The hurt of rejection, the inevitable questions would be dealt with. . . .

She supposed that her depression was natural. Reaction was only now setting in. At first, the sharpest edge of the hurt had been lost in the simple mechanics of bringing to a halt so much that had been set in motion. The minister had to be informed, with a call and then a brief note of gratitude and apology, and a small check to compensate him for time already spent. The guests must be informed that the wedding was canceled. Thankfully, Kelly had insisted on doing that difficult chore, phoning everyone who had received an invitation, answering the inevitable shocked questions with an invented excuse more comfortable than the truth: "It was a mutual decision, and both Sarah and Sam are very sorry if anyone has been inconvenienced. . . ."

The lovely, unworn dress had to be returned to the wedding shop, and gifts sent back. And then, in the wake of Sarah's impulse to continue with her business plans, there had been the last numbed spurt of packing and shipping of her belongings to be stored in Las Cruces until she found an apartment. The hardest thing had been the farewell to Kelly.

But now Sarah was aboard the plane, on her way. There were no more chores. There was no more need to simply put one foot ahead of the other. There was nothing to do, nothing to hold back thoughts and bruised emotions. Until the plane landed at Albuquerque International, Sarah was forced to wait quietly, wearing the pleasant, unrevealing expression that made her seem no different from other travelers. One must not reveal the surging turmoil of uncertainties within.

Now that she must come face to face with the abrupt change that had been made in the course of her future, Sarah longed to be somewhere alone to work through the mental postmortem of her romance and of her neatly thought out plans for her life with Sam.

It was frightening to realize, days after the fact, how severely her confidence had been shaken by Sam's decision. She sat in the comfortable seat, staring out at cloud patterns without appreciating their beauty. Fellow passengers would be seeing her as an attractively dressed young woman, outwardly poised, shining amber hair falling richly along the shoulders of her blue linen suit with the white blouse whose lace-edged jabot fell in graceful folds. Slender hands were folded in her lap. Lovely legs and ankles were accented by white high-heeled sandals. She might have been the very embodiment of the educated, well-brought-up, successful young woman.

And all the while, deep inside, she searched for the flaw that had caused Sam to reject her so suddenly. She could not escape the fact: the man who had promised to marry her had backed away from his commitment. Surely it was because of something lacking in Sarah.

CHAPTER TWO

Sarah's hands squeezed together momentarily, and perhaps some very intent observer might have caught the quick gleam of moisture in the wide-set gray eyes, moisture that was rapidly blinked away. That observer might well have wondered at the depth of trouble in Sarah's eyes at that instant.

But the moment of weakness was not allowed to last. Taking a deep, steadying breath, Sarah gave herself a fierce inward command. Sam's choice was made. And she had made a choice of her own—a good choice! She would fix her mind upon that, and she would make her new life a full, exciting one.

"Sarah Wingate, you're a big girl now!" she whispered to herself.

After landing in Albuquerque, Sarah had a very brief wait before boarding an Airways of New Mexico plane bound for Alamogordo. She wanted to drive the last seventy or so miles from Alamogordo into Las Cruces. It was an instinctive wish to—fit herself into the landscape. She had scarcely fastened her seat belt when someone slid into the seat beside her. He was an attractive man, in his early forties perhaps, a hint of silver at his sandy temples belied by the youthful firmness of his tanned skin. He smiled at Sarah with the age-old message of attraction felt by a man for a desirable woman.

"Are you traveling alone?" he asked. "I'm Brad Curtis."

Sarah regarded him unsmilingly, not really in the mood for a quick and easy acquaintanceship. He tilted his head engagingly, brown eyes good-humored, full of interest.

"Of course, if you'd rather I sit elsewhere—?"

Feeling that she had been rude, Sarah relented. Perhaps it would be as well to pass the time in conversation instead of futile thought. "No, that's quite all right, Mr. Curtis. I'm Sarah Wingate."

"Brad, please. Where are you bound, Sarah?"

She studied him swiftly, still reluctant to share too much information about herself with a stranger. Mr. Curtis looked respectable, even prosperous. His perfectly pressed gray slacks and nicely tailored charcoal and light gray check jacket had not come from a discount-store rack. There was a heavy turquoise and silver ring on his right hand, a wide gold wedding band on the left. His tie clip was silver and turquoise in the shape of a thunderbird. It looked very expensive. So did the leather briefcase he'd placed in the rack overhead. He appeared to be a successful businessman.

"I'm going to Alamogordo, then on to Las Cruces by car," she said at last.

His eyes brightened with interest. "That so? I'm from Alamogordo myself. I own a string of sporting goods stores around the state. One in Las Cruces, in fact."

Sarah smiled politely and let the conversation lapse. But her new acquaintance was not ready to allow her to return to her thoughts.

"You're planning to drive to Las Cruces?"

"Yes. I assume I can find a car rental agency in Alamogordo."

"There's a Hertz office at the Desert Aire Motor Inn. I assume you'll be staying overnight in Alamo? It will be after eight when we get in, and Las Cruces is eighty miles from Alamogordo."

Sarah's eyes went a bit frosty. His questions were beginning to sound like a classic come-on. "I really hadn't decided, Mr. Curtis."

He laughed, obviously reading the withdrawal in her tone. "Relax, Sarah. I only meant to recommend the Desert Aire as a nice place to stay. My business guests often check in there. The rooms are well kept, and the dining room serves good meals."

"Thank you. I'll see if I can get a room there."

"And," his smile was roguish, "I'd like to buy your dinner. Now don't stiffen up! I'm not asking for anything except the company of a lovely lady when I dine."

Sarah's eyes dropped with obvious meaning to his left hand, to the gold band on the third finger. Again he interpreted her silence. "Yes, yes, I'm married, but not for long. My wife and I are separated, six months now. She lives in Albuquerque. I've just been there, visiting the kids. We have two sons, eight and five. They live with their mother."

"Forgive me, Mr. Curtis," Sarah said quietly. "I'm rather tired, and I want to have dinner in my room and get some sleep."

She expected his suave good humor to vanish, and gave him points when he accepted her refusal without displeasure, merely nodding with a shade of regret. "Okay, Miss Wingate. Maybe we'll meet again. I'm in Las Cruces often. How long have you lived there?"

"I'm moving there for the first time. I've only seen the town once, when I was a child."

Brad Curtis showed signs of wishing to continue their conversation, but Sarah felt suddenly that she hadn't the energy to talk to anyone. "If you don't mind," she said, "I think I'd like to nap a bit. I really am very tired. I'm sure you understand."

He regarded her with smiling skepticism, but obligingly rose to his feet. "Sure, Sarah. I see an old friend down the aisle. Nice meeting you," he said, and left her alone.

She turned her head against the seat back and shut her eyes to discourage any other gregarious fellow passengers. She found herself thinking about that single, long-ago trip to Las Cruces. Since her engagement to Sam, and their plans to live in the southern New Mexico city, she had remembered that visit again and again, particularly what occurred near the end of it.

Sarah had been ten years old at the time. Her widowed mother had taken her to visit Maureen Dwight at Christmas. Maureen was Mrs. Wingate's younger sister. She had never married. Even then she was active in the real estate business, although she did not own her own agency until several years later.

Maureen, with her sister Ellen, had grown up in a small Missouri farming community. Ellen was already married by the time Maureen began college at the University of Missouri, at Columbia. In her third year there she fell in love with a young veteran of the Korean conflict, who had been seriously injured during his tour of duty. After his recovery and discharge he returned to school, hoping to earn his MA in education and teach math in his hometown high school. He and Maureen planned to marry as soon as he finished school.

One month before winning his degree, Carl suffered a fatal heart attack, possibly the result of some undiscovered problem arising from his combat injuries.

Maureen finished school, returned home for a time. But she was restless, even with a job in the local bank that looked promisingly toward promotions. She saved her money, bought a car, and decided to travel for a few months. She drove to California, to Oregon, then looped back across the West and Southwest. She found Colorado beautiful, Arizona tempting, but somehow New Mexico seemed to offer something she needed. She had planned to stay only a few days. Instead she toured the state from end to end, enjoying the contrasts between the deserts in all their stark beauty, the magnificent central and northern mountain chains, the vast open plains in the Southeastern corner.

Las Cruces, in the southern part, pulled her back again and again from sojourns in the other cities. She took a temporary job in a realty office and found she had an aptitude for selling, an enthusiasm for the work. After a few months she realized that she did not want to leave the Southwest. She called her parents and Ellen with her decision, stayed, and made New Mexico her home.

Maureen was a happy, attractive woman. Sarah had always adored her only aunt. During that Christmas visit Maureen often made the little girl laugh, something that had not happened much since the death of Sarah's father some months earlier. Mama was still desperately unhappy, and though she tried to be cheerful for Sarah's sake, her gray eyes, so like Sarah's, had revealed her grief.

Sarah remembered how she had felt then, how lost and frightened she was because Mama was lost and frightened. Daddy had always taken care of them. Who would do it now? Why had he gotten sick when he'd always seemed so strong? Why had he—left them?

In a part of her mind Sarah knew Daddy would never willingly have gone away, leaving her and Mama to be afraid like this. But there was a babyish, half-guilty anger in her heart that would not quite go away, no matter how much she tried to think about it in the right way. It was an ugly, tearing feeling, being angry at her father, and at the same time missing him so much.

Somehow Aunt Maureen had seemed to understand better than anyone. She helped Sarah to talk about it, without prying or pushing. It made Sarah feel better. There was still the anxiety and the sadness, but she began to enjoy the visit, to take an interest in this funny, dry country, where Christmas was almost like summer. Sarah would always remember Las Cruces by its unique landmark, the Organ Mountains rising in a starkly magnificent rampart fifteen miles to the east. It was those mountains that motivated the near-tragic adventure, the experience that marred the end of the trip and still, in dreams, sent shivers of fright along Sarah's spine.

The last day of their visit Mrs. Wingate, Maureen, and Sarah had driven out of town in Maureen's car toward the mountains, to a small town that lay where San Augustin Pass carried the ribbon of highway looping upward over the Organs' gigantic, stony barrier.

They stopped for lunch at a café in the town near the base of the pass. Sarah was not hungry, and as Mama and Maureen became absorbed in talk, Sarah wandered outside to wait for them.

It was a bright, sunny day, as warm as spring. In the ultraclear New Mexico air, the mountains seemed very close, the great, sheer stone peaks clawing at the sky. Sarah had never seen such mountains. They did not look quite real. Some of them were like pictures of imaginary mountains in a picture book, sharp towers of bare stone with ribbonlike strata of soft colors, gray and dusty rose and mauve. They held a strange fascination for the lonely, confused child.

Ever since their arrival in Las Cruces, Sarah had longed to climb one of them. She had said as much to Aunt Maureen, who merely laughed, as if Sarah had made a joke. But Sarah was quite serious about her desire to reach those mysterious crags. So—since they were only a short distance away, and since Mama and Maureen were going to be *hours* over their lunch, why not simply walk to the mountains, to the sharpest, brightest one, and climb to the top, right now?

Without another thought, Sarah went dancing unnoticed across the empty highway. Dressed in a corduroy jumper of rust brown and a white, long-sleeved cotton blouse under a light cardigan, brown school loafers and brown tights, she was like a dried leaf blown across the sandy desert floor, away from the highway and the little town.

Sarah had been disappointed not to see snow at Christmas even though Aunt Maureen explained that Las Cruces, only some thirty miles from the Mexican border, often boasted warm, dry days most of the winter. Now Sarah was glad of the warmth. It was a wonderful day for a walk up a mountain. She felt as happy as she had for many weeks as she ran, delirious with her adventure, toward the weirdly beautiful cliffs to the east.

The ground she ran across was sandy. There was little grass, only dry weeds and brittle, thorny bushes Maureen had called sagebrush, mesquite, tarbush, and creosote. There were lots of spiny cactus plants of different shapes. Sarah was careful to detour around these, after being cruelly scratched a time or two. Once it required several minutes to pick the sharp spines from the knit fabric of her tights, and her ankle stung for a while.

Sarah had been running quite a long time toward the mountains, scrambling down into dry, gravel-floored gullies and out again. Now at last she was climbing. Not the mystical, looming cliffs, but foothills covered with brush and small trees. It was exciting to be on a slope at least. Eagerly, Sarah ignored her tiredness and a skinned knee she had collected in the last gully and scrambled higher as fast as she could.

Quite by chance she found that if she walked in one of the upward winding dry slashes in the earth, that lay like deep, rocky cracks in the surface of the mountain, it was easier to hurry. And she knew she must hurry, to be back before Mama and Aunt Maureen finished lunch, or she would be sharply scolded. Sarah was beginning to be uneasy about going for her walk without asking. Still, the lure of the heights was very strong. So she climbed, breathing hard, intoxicated by the feeling that soon she might get to the very top, to stand right on the sharp edge of the softly colored stone. . . .

Glancing upward, Sarah was puzzled to see that the colors of the vast rock wall were changing. A little frightened, she halted, panting. The rock looked scary now, all reddish and lighted strangely.

She looked over her shoulder, seeing to her shock that the sun was going down, a fiery splash of brilliant light setting aflame streamers of clouds, so that they became glowing streaks across the huge New Mexico sky.

It was growing colder. Sarah had not realized it while she was moving. Her activity had kept her warm and perspiring. Now her body felt clammy and chill.

She looked again at the enormous frozen curtain of rock that rose not far ahead of her. Now it was a frightening thing, a massive weight too great to imagine, leaning over Sarah as if any moment it might shift in its ancient foundations, fall and crush her.

With a dry-throated gasp, Sarah crouched unmoving, one knee of her laddered tights resting in the dry soil of the crevice she had been climbing. It was only when she began to feel the sharpness of a pebble pressing into her flesh that she was released from the spell. Whirling, she began to run down the steep gash in the mountain. To her terror, she saw that the light was already fading from the gigantic bowl of sky. It would be dark very soon, for the winter dusk did not last long. Soon Sarah would be alone up here in the darkness, where no one could find her.

Running, sliding, grasping at thorny bushes to keep from falling right down the mountain, Sarah rushed and scrambled toward the desert floor that now seemed so far below her. She had not understood how very big the mountain was, or how much time it would take to reach the top. She was not even halfway up, yet she was terrifically far from Mama and Maureen, from warmth and lights. She was sobbing now, tears making it difficult to see where she was going, so that she fell more and more often. But the pain of bruises and scrapes did not make her stop. Panic made her get up each time and run again.

Now, comfortable and safe in the plane that carried her over the state she had not seen for years, Sarah felt again for a moment the fright of the little girl she had been. She swallowed dryly, remembering how she had fled through the gathering darkness until she could see nothing at all, and was forced at last to stop, crying and calling for help into the velvety, cold, moonless dark. She called until the sound of her voice in the blackness scared her unbearably. Then she was quiet, and there were only the cold rocks and dirt and the tremendous black bulk of the mountains rising behind her.

When help came out of that darkness, at first it only increased her fright. Again Sarah's mind made the journey back to that December evening when she had huddled weeping against a boulder, shivering, aching from her falls.

Once more, gathering all her courage, Sarah called out to her mother, one high, wavering call. But she knew that her mother had no idea where to find her, and she knew that she, Sarah, had done a very foolish thing, to come walking in this wild place alone.

And then, above the sound of her own sobs, she heard something—sharp sounds, metal hitting stone, and the rubbing of something big against dry brush and limbs. Something was coming up the gully toward her. Sarah imagined some large, hungry animal.

She stopped crying and clung to the smooth, chill surface of the boulder, wondering if she should try to run and hide. But there was nowhere to go except back up the mountain, and she couldn't do that. Even if she had not been so afraid, she was very tired. Her legs shook from fatigue and cold.

She was not even sure she could stand up. And so she held herself as still as a hunted rabbit, hardly daring to breathe. Whatever the animal was, it was still coming, slowly, with hollow, clopping footsteps. It was coming right toward her.

"Hey!" someone shouted. "Is anyone up there? Call out if you're there!"

For a moment Sarah could not get her voice to work, and when she did, it was only a wordless, rising cry of misery.

"Okay, I hear you," came a young, reassuring voice. "Stay right where you are. I'll come up and get you."

There was a long pause. Then the beam of a flashlight washed on the rocky dry walls about her. A slender, tall young man scrambled up to her niche and sank to one knee, but not too close. He seemed to understand that she was very frightened and would not want a stranger to touch her. For an instant he held the light so that she could see his face, thin, smiling, eyes that were a deep blue, friendly and kind. Finally he held out one hand. "I think you're the young lady we've all been looking for. Are you Sarah Wingate?"

"Y-yes!" Sarah cried, and flung herself into his arms.

"Hey, you're cold!" He let her cry against his chest until she could stop. Then he disengaged her arms and got out of his jacket, a denim one with a warm blanket lining. When he wrapped it around her, it felt better than anything she had ever put on in her life.

"Honey, can you walk?" the quiet voice asked. "Are you hurt? We'd better get down to the road. Your mother and aunt are going crazy with worry. They're afraid someone in a car might have taken you away."

"Yes, I can walk." Sarah wiped her eyes and swallowed. This man would think she was an awful baby. He handed her a handkerchief, clean, neatly folded, and smelling of sunshine. She felt guilty at crumpling it, and after she blew her nose, she thought perhaps she ought to have it washed before giving it back.

"I've got a horse," her rescuer said. "Hang onto my hand, and we'll get you home."

But to Sarah's dismay, she was not able to walk after all. Her legs were as wobbly as a baby's. He did not laugh. Without comment he lifted her and carried her down to a tall horse that stood tied and waiting, nibbling at dried weeds. He boosted Sarah into the saddle, leaped on behind her with strong, lithe grace, and reined his horse around to walk slowly down the mountain. As they rode he talked to her about little things, asking where she lived, about her school, about her parents. He did not scold her, or tell her how stupid her climb had been. It didn't matter. She knew it anyway.

When they got down onto the sandy flatland, he held Sarah firmly and nudged the horse into a rocking canter. She twisted about, once, trying to see her companion's face again, but his hat brim shadowed it too deeply. He was only a strong, tall shape, his chest warm against her shoulder.

"How old are you, Sarah?" he asked, and she thought he smiled, his voice sounded smiling.

"Ten." Then, shyly, "How old are you?"

"Eighteen."

"What's your name? And how did you find me?"

He laughed. "I'm Johnny Trist. This is part of my dad's ranch you went walking over. When the state police put out a call for volunteers to search for a lost ki——"—he caught himself—"girl, my dad and I and some of our men offered to ride over this area, since we know the country. Other men are searching south of the highway, and toward town."

Sarah felt a sharp new alarm. "Police? Are they going to put me in jail? I didn't mean to do anything wrong!"

He didn't laugh, but she heard the amusement in his voice. "No, of course not. They're just going to give you some hot chocolate and wrap you in a blanket and get you back to your folks. See, we're almost there. See those lights?"

Johnny Trist's arm tightened comfortably, and he spurred his horse to a fast, pounding run, letting out a lighthearted yell. Sarah realized that she was actually having fun, riding the running horse with her new friend. It made her feel more guilty than ever.

Sarah stirred from her memories and glanced at her watch. The plane would be landing soon. It was time to think of the future, not an unimportant incident out of her childhood. Still—a bit of the memory clung, even as she began to gather up her unread magazines and her handbag. It was an odd thing to think of and to regret now, but she had seen her rescuer's face only during that tiny moment when he found her. When they rode into the search command post, he had handed Sarah down into the waiting arms of half a dozen uniformed policemen and accepted their congratulations with a quiet word or two. When Sarah had tried to catch a glimpse of Johnny Trist, he had already whirled his horse away into the darkness.

Sarah smiled now as her plane taxied to a stop. She unfastened her seatbelt. It was a nice memory, at least that last part of it, her rescue and the reunion with her mother, who had been shocked out of her depression by the fright Sarah had given her. Soon Mrs. Wingate had begun to rebuild her life, to be more aware of Sarah and her needs.

Somewhere in her things, Sarah still had a neatly laundered, folded square of handkerchief embroidered in one corner with a *J* and a *T*. And for a long time as she was growing up, Sarah had occasionally thought of the improbable young knight who had ridden out of a dark and cold New Mexico night to help her.

CHAPTER THREE

Sarah found that Mr. Curtis had not exaggerated the accommodations at the Desert Aire. Her room was very comfortable, the decor appealing. After a small meal which she had sent in, and a relaxing bath, she slept better than she had in more than a week. It was after nine when she woke the next morning, and she felt eager to be on with the adventure.

Hurriedly, she showered and dressed in blue slacks and a silky blue print blouse. Coffee was delivered to her room. She drank it as she packed. Within an hour she was on the road in a rented Mercury Lynx, heading west past Holloman Air Force Base, and later, past the entrance to the White Sands National Monument.

The landscape, revealed by the hot summer sunlight, was tugging at her memory. It was over this highway that the Greyhound bus she and her mother had ridden so long ago had passed. Mauve and gray mountains with sheer stone strata lay behind her to the east, the San Andres and Oscuro Mountains were a low and distant rampart westward. Between the highway and that range, miles of astonishingly creamy dunes of sand lay in wind-sculptured fantasy, intertwined with their own oddly shaped shadows thrown by the strong morning light. The vast white gypsum deposit was like an immense ocean beach with no ocean.

Beyond the Sands the pavement ran between desert sands of less exotic hues—browns and reds and grays—studded with mesquite and greasewood and other low growths. This was land restricted to military use, the White Sands Missile Range, where testing sometimes caused the blocking of traffic on the highway until the completion of a test firing. But today there were no roadblocks. The sleek car ran smoothly along the road. Oncoming traffic was not very heavy. The long, straight highway racing to meet the distant blue rampart of the Organ Mountains invited high speed, but Sarah prudently stayed within the speed limit, reminded by a black and white state police car and an occasional olive drab military police vehicle.

At last the pavement merged into a new four-lane highway that soon was lifting in a long, easy curve into San Augustin Pass. Sarah spared as much attention as she dared to the stone spires and cliffs that formed the Organ Mountains. There were breathtaking heights, and sheer drops from summits that looked razor-narrow. Even now Sarah felt the fascination that had led her as a ten-year-old girl to try and climb to the top of those majestic rocks.

She reached the top of the pass. In moments the car swept around a curve and downward, the road dropping almost frighteningly, a curving descent into a landscape starkly grand. Far ahead there were other mountains, a distance-blued line. But below lay a desert basin running south and north. This was the famous Jornada del Muerto, fifty miles wide, a hundred miles in length, bordered by the San Andres Mountains and the Oscuros on the east, the Rio Grande to the west.

At the foot of the pass sprawled the little town of Organ, much as Sarah had remembered it—small, run-down, a cluster of buildings passed by the fast traffic in moments.

Some fifteen minutes later Sarah had reached the outskirts of Las Cruces, marked by its three tall crosses that stood to the left of the road.

Las Cruces was an attractive, modern little city beside the Rio Grande, perhaps best known for the New Mexico State University campus. Mixed with its modern, sleekly designed buildings were remnants of its Spanish heritage—low, flat-roofed buildings constructed around verdant patios.

Sarah knew from correspondence with Maureen Dwight that this town, spread with languid grace upon its seemingly limitless desert space, was an agricultural as well as a ranching center. The origins of the university were agricultural.

Maureen was almost fanatically proud of her adopted state. She had written that this productive area was known for its fine fruits and vegetables, melons, and livestock feed such as milo and alfalfa. There were wide fields of onions and chilies. The university agronomy and horticulture departments were constantly developing new varieties of productive plants.

Sarah stopped the Lynx beside the road to study a hand-drawn map sent by her aunt. Moving back into traffic, she took the El Paso exit and after a few minutes of driving, turned west into Las Cruces on University Boulevard, where Dwight Realty was located. A few blocks later she pulled into a parking space in front of a Spanish-style complex of buildings across from the campus.

Sarah stepped out of the air-conditioned car, surprised for a moment by the intense heat. She paused to look about, liking what she saw. This quadrant of the city was laid out with open spacing that retained acres of natural desert landscape between housing developments and business centers. The campus was a good example of the spacious, generous feel of the community. Great sweeps of lawn beautifully landscaped with little groves of evergreens adapted to this climate, willows, ornamental plum, and a myriad of other trees and shrubs separated the buildings. Some of the dorms and academic structures were ultramodern, some obviously much older in design. Somehow they coexisted appealingly.

The campus drew Sarah. It occurred to her that she might enroll in a class or two later, if time could be spared from her business.

"Sarah? Sarah, darling!"

Sarah turned gladly, recognizing the voice.

Maureen Dwight was a trim, small woman in her late forties, with hair cut in a short, smooth style and glowing like spun silver in the sunlight. Her ash-blondness had slid gracefully into a shining silver. Her face was still youthful, and tanned, with fine laugh lines pleasantly accenting the corners of her merry blue eyes. Here was a woman whose maturity had been made an asset. She hugged Sarah enthusiastically.

"Sarah, I've been watching for you all morning! I can't tell you how wonderful it is to have you here at last."

"It's good to be here," Sarah returned her smile. "I only hope I've done the right thing in coming. I just stepped out in blind faith, and I admit that my steps are pretty wobbly."

Maureen stood back, hands still on Sarah's shoulders, and gave her a look that seemed to read her soul. "Aha! Second thoughts. You come in and have some of my famous coffee, guaranteed to produce instant self-confidence. Then we'll go see your shop. You're going to love it, and you're going to love Las Cruces. This place has a way of growing on you."

Inside, within a roomy office, Maureen gave Sarah a chair that would not have been out of place in a comfortable home. She poured a mug of coffee that was as good as she had promised. The slim, silver-haired woman paused by her receptionist's desk, requesting that her calls be handled by another member of the firm. Shutting the office door, she sat down behind her wide, uncluttered desk.

It was an inviting office, with the cool blues and greens of carpet and drapes. Pale gold aspen paneling on two walls created a soft accent against the white plaster of the other walls and the ceiling.

"My dear," Maureen leaned forward. "I'm so sorry about—"

"About the resounding dull thud of my wedding?" Sarah interrupted with studied lightness. "Oh well, it's not every girl who can claim the experience of being left waiting at the altar. I've no doubt it will add tremendously to the development of my character."

Maureen did not smile. She hesitated before speaking. "Did you love this man so much then, Sarah?"

Sarah tried for a flippant reply, then abandoned the effort. Maureen's question had not been made from idle curiosity, nor was she seeking to pry into a painful area. Her concern was genuine. She deserved a more thoughtful answer. And perhaps it was time for Sarah herself to come face to face with the question Maureen had asked.

She met her aunt's quiet look. Somewhat surprised, she felt the corners of her mouth lifting in a rueful smile that reflected an inner uncertainty. "To tell the truth, Maureen, I don't know. I'm not sure I knew the answer to your question even before Sam changed his mind."

She paused, then continued slowly, feeling her way through her own thoughts. "I admit that it hurts to think about Sam. I was convinced that we were—compatible. He's a very pleasant, attractive companion, and I miss knowing he'll be calling. But now that he's out of my life—" She struggled to find the right words. "It's—it's a little like having a tooth pulled. Your tongue won't stay away from the empty space, and you're leery of exploring it. Now that I dare touch the place in my life where Sam used to be, it doesn't hurt quite as much as I thought it would. I believe I feel a little guilty about that. It seems so shallow!"

Her smile was shadowed with self-doubt. She sighed. "I'm beginning to think the twinges I feel are mostly wounded pride."

Maureen gave a soft chuckle. "My dear, I know precisely what you mean. I've had an experience or two in my long life."

Sarah set her coffee cup down with a determined thump. "Let's go see my shop. Suddenly I can't wait to get started."

Maureen held up a hand. "There's one thing you should know first. There's a small complication."

Sarah's fine brows drew worriedly. Seeing the look, Maureen shook her head and smiled. "No, it isn't a big problem, but the situation has changed slightly. Mrs. Bendell, who sold you half interest in the shop, has had some rather alarming symptoms of illness the past few days. She's suffered a mild heart problem for years. As you know, she intended to keep part ownership, letting you run the shop, while she retained only a token voice in the management. But her condition is such that her doctor has advised her to take a full retirement. She's decided to move to the West Coast, to be near her daughter. And she has authorized me to sell the remaining half of the business. Of course, if you want to buy it, you have first chance."

Biting her lip, Sarah shook her head. "Maureen, I can't. I've already spent half my savings. Another chunk is going to be used for redecorating and getting settled. I don't want to go into debt. I'm totally inexperienced at merchandising. I could make serious mistakes—what if the shop fails?"

Maureen bent her head thoughtfully, tapping her desk blotter with a pen. She looked up. "Yes, you're wise not to overextend. Well, Mrs. Bendell wants to sell quickly, and I think I may have a buyer. It's a coincidence—I only happened to mention it during a conversation about another matter—The only problem is, a co-owner may not want to leave full managership in your hands, and his or her ideas may not agree with yours."

Sarah nodded. "I understand that. I suppose we'll just have to work out some kind of agreement when you have a buyer."

"For now, just run the shop as you see fit," Maureen advised. "Mrs. Bendell has a girl keeping it open, but you can take over right away. As I've already told you, the place is in need of an imaginative touch, and a thorough cleanup. The premises are drab—probably, the place hasn't been renovated for years."

"It will be a challenge."

Maureen caught up her car keys. "Come on, let's go see your place of business, my girl!"

It was only a few minutes' drive. Sarah's shop lay in a tastefully landscaped setting on El Paseo a few blocks north of the university. The building was of fairly recent construction, a cream-stuccoed adobe with a red tile roof, about thirty by fifty feet in size. The parking area was spacious, which would be a real plus. A large wooden sign swung between massive posts at the street. The sign proclaimed, La Casa Encantada in deeply carved letters painted blue and white against the warm, natural brown of the thick wooden plank.

Sarah felt a tug of excitement as she stepped out of Maureen's Pontiac and walked with her aunt across the thick gravel to the quarry tile walk. There was a circular planter that held desert growths near the front of the place. Wide plate glass windows flanked a heavy plank door with large, handwrought black iron hinges and latch. As they stepped inside, a string of silver bells above the door tinkled merrily.

Unfortunately, these were the last favorable impressions Sarah gained of the present management of her new business.

A tall, sulky-faced young woman came forward, chewing gum with sober determination. "Help you?" she muttered forbiddingly.

"Millicent, this is my niece, the new owner of the shop," Maureen said. "She'll be taking over right away. I want to show her around."

Millicent shrugged and moved away to a counter that held a cash register. She sat down and began to manicure her nails. Bottles of nail color and polish remover were scattered over the surface of the counter.

Mrs. Bendell must have felt ill for a long time. It was obvious that the owner had spent little recent time and energy in her gift shop. Sarah's fingers itched to get to work. The place was absolutely grimy. Even the displays were dusty, much of the stock shopworn, none of it very distinctive or attractive.

She tilted her head. "I see the first order of business is to have a rock-bottom sale to get rid of this stuff. Just look at it! It screams mediocrity. And then I want to restock with really unique gift items." She turned around, surveying the stock. "There's nothing here you couldn't buy at any variety store. Maureen, do you think I can find some local artisans to supply me with original, handmade things?"

"What exactly did you have in mind?"

Sarah took a deep breath, a little afraid that Maureen might think her ideas impractical. "Almost any beautiful, distinctive craft item that would make an interesting gift: pottery, jewelry, art—even some fashions, if I can get my hands on a sewing machine and make up some of my designs."

"You can design clothing?" Maureen asked, her warm blue eyes interested.

"I took some courses in college, and I design most of my own things. I make my own patterns and do the sewing as well. Maybe the college crowd would go for some of the ideas I have in mind. I could try just a few things at first, to see if they generate any interest."

"It sounds like a great idea, honey. But remember that you'll have to hire some things done. You'll have your hands full just running the shop." She paused thoughtfully, fingers tapping on a dusty display case.

"I do know several students who might be able to help you find some of the items you want. I can introduce you to some local artists too. Let me see if I can't get one or two people over to my house to talk with you this evening. Now"—she glanced at her watch—"let's get some lunch and discuss your living arrangements. I want you to stay with me as long as you will."

"Of course I'll stay with you until I find an apartment," Sarah smiled, "and you're a dear to offer to put me up indefinitely. But I know you're used to living alone, and I think that's what I want too. I'm looking forward to having my own place."

"I hope you don't plan to live alone forever, my dear," Maureen put in. "You're far too beautiful to settle for that kind of future."

Sarah's eyes were momentarily shadowed, and her smile required an effort. "Did you say something about lunch? I'm starved."

They sat in a quiet little restaurant a few doors from La Casa Encantada, lingering over chef salads and coffee until past two, enjoying the chance to visit. At last, Maureen asked for the check. "I've a client due in twenty minutes. She wants to see a house I've been trying to sell for six months—mustn't upset her by being late. Shall I take you to my house, or would you like to come with me and learn how to sell a white elephant?"

Sarah considered for a moment. "Take me back to my rental car, and tell me how to find your house. I'll return the car and catch a cab."

"Oh dear, that reminds me. You're going to need a car here, Sarah. There's no bus service, and our wide open spaces are hard on the feet."

Sarah nodded. "Yes, I saved enough for that. I'll want something small, not necessarily new. Can you recommend a reputable dealer? I'm ignorant about engines, and I could kick a tire for a week without learning a darn thing. I'll be at the mercy of the first salesman who spots the Missouri pigeon trudging over his used-car lot."

Maureen grinned. "I know just the man. He wouldn't dare cheat my favorite and only niece. I'll just give him a call."

She scurried from the table, an attractive figure in her cool aqua dress, her elegantly cut hair gleaming. People at other tables spoke to her as she passed. It was obvious that Maureen Dwight was well known and well liked. Sarah felt a glow of pride for her lovely aunt, wondering why she had never married. Surely she'd had many opportunities since that long-ago lost love.

Taking unfair advantage, Sarah quickly took care of the check and joined Maureen at the phone booth just as Maureen hung up and reached into her handbag for her wallet.

"I paid for lunch," Sarah smiled.

"Sarah, you shouldn't have, it was my treat!" scolded her aunt. "Oh well, I'll make a very special dinner, as a welcome home!"

"Mother always said you were the best cook she knew. Did you reach the car salesman?"

"I did indeed, and I'm to drop you off at Brandt Ford right away. Ask for Larry Brandt. They'll have used cars in other makes, and he can be trusted to show you only the reliable ones and give you a fair price. I've asked him to provide transportation for you to my office after you've seen what they have to offer. Larry's the son of friends of mine, and I've known him since he was in rompers."

Sarah liked Larry Brandt at once. He was a blockily built young man with sandy hair and beard, and there was an appreciative smile on his plain but nice face as he shook hands with Sarah.

"So you're Maureen Dwight's niece!"

"Yes, I'm Sarah Wingate, Mr. Brandt. I've just moved to town. I sold my last car before moving. I need something small and definitely not temperamental, not too expensive. Do you have anything that fits that description?"

"Call me Larry, please. Before we look at cars, how about dinner tonight? I'll just phone my wife and ask for a divorce."

Sarah wasn't quite sure whether to be amused, until he gave her an unrepentant grin.

"That was a joke, Sarah. I'm not married—was once, but I recovered. If I'm rushing things, just say so."

Sarah sidestepped neatly. "Maureen says you won't cheat me out of my life's savings on a decent used car."

Brandt nodded with mock solemnity. "She's absolutely right. It's putting me out of business, I can tell you."

He escorted her out of the showroom to the car lot, where rows of autos were parked. Now he became all business. He showed Sarah a half dozen cars, not taking up her time with models too large, too expensive, too old, etc. There were several small- or medium-sized sedans no older than two years and in excellent condition among the reconditioned autos on the lot.

In the end, with Brandt's advice, Sarah chose a Ford Mustang, white with red upholstery, two years old.

"This one's unusually nice," Brandt said. "An oilman from El Paso gave it to his son when he graduated from high school. The kid drove it a few months, then went to Europe with friends for a biking tour, and the car was stored. The boy liked traveling—stayed over a year. When he came home, he wanted a larger, more powerful car, so we made a trade with him, just a few days ago. The car has had very little use. The tires were new when the car was stored. They've got maybe a couple of hundred miles of wear."

"It looks perfect to me. Let me drive it, and I'll make my decision."

Sarah found nothing to displease her in her brief drive. When she turned back into the lot, Brandt was waiting for her. He had someone take the car to be washed, promising to have it delivered later in the afternoon. They completed the necessary paperwork and Sarah wrote a check, happy with her deal.

"Now then," Brandt said, "can I buy you a drink?"

"Thank you, but I need to get back to Maureen's office."

"I'll drive you." He grinned engagingly. "And what about dinner tomorrow night? How's seven sound?"

Sarah hesitated, but only for a moment. If she was going to be living here, perhaps she should begin making friends. "All right, thank you, Larry. You can pick me up at Maureen's home. I'll be staying there until I find an apartment."

Sarah lost no time returning the Hertz car, and then caught a taxi to Maureen's house, a charming three-bedroom ranch-style home on Avenida del Sombra in a new subdivision on the edge of town. There were a dozen houses on attractively laid out lots, with curving streets and cul-de-sacs to minimize traffic. Young trees and new lawns were thriving. The homes were separated from other developments by acres of sand and mesquite and had marvelous views of the Organ Mountains.

Maureen's house was clean, cool, and spoke of Maureen's personality in its charming paintings, beautiful but comfortable modern furniture, pale beige carpet, and soft gold drapes at the generous windows. Sarah explored the silent house. A bright bouquet of zinnias and shasta daisies from Maureen's flower beds marked the room that was to be Sarah's.

With a sigh of weariness, Sarah set her luggage down and headed for the shower. The heat and the day's rapid pace had left her feeling sticky and wilted. Even her hair felt limp.

The bath adjoining her room was done in varying shades of blue and green, cool to the senses. Mexican tile on the wall featured a gorgeous design that resembled soft fronds of seaweed against a pale blue background. There were thick towels in plenty, a variety of soaps for Sarah's selection, lotions and jasmine-scented bath crystals.

This last persuaded Sarah to spend time in the tub instead of the shower. She sank into the luscious froth with a sigh and let the tension be soaked from back and shoulder and neck muscles. It was with regret that she removed herself from the bath, restored the tub to glistening cleanliness, and dressed in white shorts and a red bandanna-cloth halter.

Since there seemed nothing to do, she lay down to rest, letting her mind replay scenes of her journey to this city, her new home.

CHAPTER FOUR

Sarah had meant only to relax for a few moments and then get up. The next thing she was aware of was the soft sound of the door opening. She opened her eyes to find the light less hard and bright, and Maureen standing in the doorway, apologetic as Sarah sat up.

"Go back to sleep, darling. Rest as long as you like."

Sarah yawned. "I didn't mean to fall asleep. Oh, but it felt wonderful! Maureen, I adore your house, and this bed is sheer heaven. I'm ashamed that I've wasted half the afternoon. Didn't realize how tired I was."

"It's probably the heat. And so many decisions to make. Now, I'm going to make some iced tea. Or would you prefer a soft drink?"

"Tea sounds wonderful," Sarah assured her, and got up. She moved to the dressing table and glanced at her reflection. With a groan she hastily opened a suitcase and found her hairbrush. "Give me a minute to do some repairs," she said.

Maureen laughed. "It's gilding the lily. I'll meet you in the kitchen."

The tea was ready when she padded barefoot along the cool quarry tile hall to the kitchen. Sarah accepted the tall, cold glass eagerly and perched upon a stool at the wide breakfast bar. "Maureen, you're spoiling me, and I love it. It's almost like being home with Mom again."

Maureen gave her a perceptive glance, her face wistful. "You still miss her, don't you? So do I. And I love spoiling you, so get used to it!"

She smiled, and Sarah thought that her vivacious face might have belonged to a much younger woman. She watched Maureen as she moved energetically about the small, efficiently designed kitchen with its oak cabinets. Bright curtains hung at the windows, a blue flower print cut into sunbonnet girls and appliquéd on white, with an old-fashioned rickrack trim in red.

Maureen glanced over her shoulder. "I hope you're hungry. We're having the Dwight Special tonight."

"Fantastic! Uh—what is it?" Sarah tilted her head, and her honey-amber hair slid silkily over one bare, tanned shoulder.

"Steak, marinated in my own special mixture, cooked outdoors on the grill. Plus," Maureen added conspiratorily, "two attractive males to share our meal with. Unfortunately, both are too young for me, so it will be up to you to entertain them."

"Maureen, what are you up to?" Sarah's fine brows drew just a bit. Her aunt laughed. "Not what you suspect, darling. The dinner guests will be here on business. Ward Cowley is a graduate student, and a jewelry maker, and I think you might like to display some of his work in your shop. He does wonderful designs in silver and turquoise and coral. They're different from the traditional turquoise pieces you see everywhere out here. He's managed to make his designs distinctive, with a contemporary look that somehow or other doesn't lose the beauty of the traditional. He's already made quite a name for himself, and Ward knows other creative young people. His wife does some lovely weaving. Unfortunately, Charlotte had a class this evening. You'll meet her later."

"That sounds perfect. I'm so glad you invited him. But you said two men. Who is the other?"

"He's interested in buying into La Casa Encantada—you remember that I mentioned I had a prospective buyer. He called this afternoon, and he still seems interested in making the deal. But he's in town only briefly this time, so I've asked him here tonight. I really thought I ought to grab this opportunity to present the deal to him. But before I do, there's one idea I need to mention to you. I think you ought to have more say in running the shop than fifty percent ownership gives you. You'll need just that necessary little extra clout in times of disagreement on policy."

Sarah was silent for a moment, her face reflecting her troubled thoughts. "I understand, and of course I agree. But I really cannot afford a greater percentage until I'm sure the shop can pay its own way. I'm nervous about dipping further into those reserves now."

"Very wise, dear," Maureen nodded, pouring more iced tea for Sarah. "That's why I've decided to buy a ten percent share of the business myself."

"Maureen!" Sarah lifted her head sharply, protest in every line of her body. "I can't let you do that."

"Now wait, honey. Hear me out. I have every faith that the shop will be a good investment. I'll sell you my interest, say one year from now. Sooner, if you feel you can afford it."

Sarah shook her head helplessly. "Maureen, how can I ask you to do this? This business is my risk. I won't involve you."

"You haven't asked me," was her aunt's imperturbable reply. "I volunteered. I often invest in worthwhile small businesses. I seldom guess wrong, and without bragging I can say that my investments have made me very comfortable financially. I don't need your permission to buy in anyway, my dear. Now with that all settled, I can offer the remaining forty percent to John Trist."

Sarah's gray eyes widened. "Who, Maureen?"

"John Trist. He's interested in buying into a business for Shirley DeBrese." She paused, her face thoughtful, and stirred her tea. "She's the only part of the deal I don't quite like."

"Why?" Sarah asked absently. Her mind had caught at the name John Trist, and she was turning it over and over in her thoughts. John Trist—*Johnny* Trist? Was it only coincidence that the name was the same, the name of the young man who had found her when she was lost in the Organ Mountains so many years ago? Could it be the same person?

Maureen did not notice Sarah's preoccupation. She moved to open the refrigerator and take out a wide, covered bowl. "Shirley DeBrese is going to marry John Trist. At least, that's the persistent rumor. Shirley is quite a society favorite. Until about a year ago she was in line to be a very wealthy woman. Her grandparents are a prominent Texas family from El Paso, oil money from way back. Bad investments made by Shirley's father caused bankruptcy of the family business last year. Shirley is the youngest of three daughters. The other two married extremely eligible men. I suppose the DeBrese family still lives very comfortably, but the big money and social clout is gone. If you ask me, Shirley would never have condescended to having her name linked with John Trist's before her parents lost their money, though you might put that opinion down to a bad-tempered, catty female's lack of faith in the human race."

Sarah came back to the moment. "Why wouldn't she have gotten engaged to Mr. Trist?"

"Because he's not from quite the same social strata, if you follow me. The Trist family has interests in oil and cattle and horses, and farms in the southeastern part of the state as well as here. John is certainly not poor! But the Trists have never cared much about the social scene."

Maureen smiled. "I can remember years ago seeing John's grandmother driving a ranch truck through town, or strolling into a store dressed in blue jeans and cotton shirt and boots—long before jeans were fashionable! She had beautiful hair, I remember, thick and as white as mine, and she wore it braided into a coronet. Her face was as weathered as one of the Trist's cowhands, and *still* she was beautiful somehow. She had deep blue eyes, and she was always kind and serene. But if she'd been invited to join the Woman's Club, or the country club, she'd have smiled graciously and said she had lambs to shear or a branding crew to cook for."

"Perhaps her grandson is more socially oriented," Sarah suggested.

Maureen shook her head. "John's a good deal like Anna Trist. He doesn't simply coast on his father's and grandfather's hard work and business acumen. He works right along with his men, whether the work is moving cattle or baling alfalfa hay. He keeps a close eye on his oil leases and he knows every man he's hired by first name. I've done business with John often. He cares more about the land and livestock than the social whirl. Not that half the hostesses in the state aren't delighted if they can get him on a guest list."

Maureen seemed to notice Sarah's long silence. She glanced at her niece questioningly.

"Mr. Trist sounds like the strong, silent type." Sarah remarked, still wondering if this could be the John Trist she had met.

Maureen shook her head. "If by that you mean a handsome country bumpkin, I think you'll be surprised. John's nobody's naïve cowboy. He has a doctorate in animal science and an MA in agronomy. Once I overheard the dean of the university practically begging John to teach full-time. He does lecture often or present a seminar. Some of the experimental methods he's devised and is using in his own farming and horse-breeding operations are models that are being taken note of, even by foreign governments."

"I—I'm suitably impressed." Sarah felt a completely ridiculous little lurch of disappointment and loss. If this was the same young man Sarah had known long ago for such a brief, dreamlike time, then he had grown and changed into an unrecognizable person. And, of course, how could it be otherwise?

"Well,"—she stood briskly—"if we're having company, let me help you."

"You can start the salad if you like, dear."

Companionably, they worked together. The talk turned to the years that had passed since they had seen each other, of their memories of Sarah's mother, and at last, of Sarah's abortive engagement. Sarah found that it was easier to talk about it now. It was even a kind of relief.

"It was my insistence on a life outside the home that made Sam back away," she said. "Maybe if I'd been willing to wait, to put my own plans into effect—if I had given Sam time to get used to the idea, in a year or so—"

"Would it have been worth the sacrifice to your own dreams?" Maureen asked.

Sarah bent her head. Her hands stilled in the act of slicing a bell pepper. At last, she looked up with a perplexed sigh. "I don't know. Certainly, it would have been worth any sacrifice, if I'd loved him enough. But I would have resented having to give in on something so basic. Not that I don't enjoy housekeeping—I'm even a pretty good cook. Still, I'd go mad with nothing to do but dust knickknacks."

"I have to agree with you there." Maureen smiled, and sliced fresh apples into a pie shell. "My home is important, but it could never fill my life. Of course, I never had to account to anyone but myself."

She turned, opened a drawer, and took out a bright, fringed, green and white tablecloth. "Put this on the table on the patio, and I'll bring the charcoal and get the grill going. Darn thing takes forever to reach the right heat."

"What should I wear tonight, Maureen?" Sarah took the cloth.

"My stars, I almost forgot!" Maureen's vivid face lighted, and she snatched the tablecloth back and tossed it aside. "Come with me. I have a little gift for you—a welcome home gift."

She caught Sarah's hand and pulled her out of the kitchen and along a hall, into a bedroom. She slid open a mirrored closet door and lifted out a plastic garment bag.

"Wear this tonight, won't you? Oh, I do hope it fits. I got your size from your friend Kelly last Christmas. If you haven't lost too much weight, this should be about right. I hope you like it. I looked all over town for something really special."

"Maureen, what a lovely thing to do." Sarah was touched almost to tears by the unexpected gift. "You shouldn't have done it."

"Nonsense. Come on, look at it, and tell me I don't know how to pick clothes, if you dare."

Sarah zipped the bag open. Inside was a long wraparound skirt in a natural off-white linen, lined in a rich blue silky fabric with a delicate gold fleur-de-lis pattern. There was a blue camisole top with narrow, over-the-shoulder ties tipped with a little flurry of turquoise-beaded strands.

"Maureen, it's—it's fabulous!" Sarah cried. "How can I thank you?"

"You can go and make yourself perfectly gorgeous so I can show you off to my guests."

Sarah took Maureen at her word, and the next hour was put to good use erasing the strain of the past days. She had a shampoo, found her blow-dryer, and went to work on her hair, restoring it to a rich, silky gleam. She took time to apply the small amount of makeup she used, carefully darkening the thick lashes that accented her wide gray eyes, touching her lips with lipstick in a soft coral shade. Then she put on the new outfit.

She gave herself a final inspection in the floor-length mirrors on the closet doors as she slid her feet into high-heeled, natural leather sandals. Though never afflicted by vanity, Sarah had to conclude that she was not displeased with her appearance. The skirt and cool top were definitely becoming to her slender figure, and the Gibson girl hair style was good for the delicately prominent cheekbones and the wide-set eyes— even if those gray eyes looked a bit nervous now with the prospect of meeting strangers. Even now some of Sarah's schoolgirl shyness came back on occasion.

She had heard the doorbell twice, in the past fifteen minutes. Maureen's guests must have arrived. She shouldn't delay longer. Sarah took a deep breath and left her room, finding her way along the hall and out into the patio, where the sound of voices and the tantalizing scent of the steaks proclaimed that the evening was under way. Sarah opened the sliding glass door and, after a little pause, stepped through. Two men's voices hushed, and eyes turned her way.

The smaller of the men was wielding a long-handled fork at the barbecue grill with an exaggerated air of expertise. He was blond, bearded, hair falling to the shoulders of his brown tank top. His jeans were faded so pale that Sarah suspected he had worked very hard on the effect. He wore leather sandals on his large feet. His hands matched the feet in size, yet they were surprisingly graceful and long-fingered. His blunt-featured face was intelligent and friendly, and his hazel eyes rather large and appealing. He looked to be in his late twenties.

"Aha! What have we here?" he demanded, staring at Sarah, fork arrested in the midst of a jab at the steaks.

The other man leaned gracefully against the trunk of a young cottonwood tree. He was perhaps thirty-four or -five, very tall, powerful in build, yet trim and lean. Dark straight hair fell boyishly over his tanned forehead, and lay against his shirt collar just a trifle raggedly. He was smooth-shaven, and his deep blue eyes narrowed a little under thick lashes and brows that winged darkly outward as he surveyed Sarah. His wide, expressive mouth twitched as if he repressed a grin. This man was certainly not magazine-ad handsome, yet something about his rugged features was very attractive indeed.

Sarah realized that she was returning stare for stare. She lowered her eyes, cheeks warming uncomfortably as she moved across the patio.

"Ah, there you are, dear." Maureen came out with a wooden salad bowl heaped high. "Gentlemen, this is my niece, Sarah Wingate. Sarah, John Trist and Ward Cowley."

Maureen's hands were too full to indicate which name belonged to which man, but Sarah knew. Unhesitatingly, she held out her hand to the tall, dark man.

"Mr. Trist, I'm happy to know you." Quickly, he caught her fingers and, silly as it might be, Sarah felt as if she'd received a tiny electrical shock. Perhaps he sensed something as well, for an unreadable thought flickered in his eyes, and he held her hand just an instant too long, so that she had to draw it away to shake hands with Ward Cowley.

"Ward is the jewelry designer I spoke of," Maureen said, placing the salad on the bright cloth that covered the redwood table. "I think he can supply some wonderful items for your gift shop. And of course John is thinking of purchasing an interest in La Casa Encantada."

"It was good of you both to come," Sarah smiled.

"Neither of us would miss a chance at Miss Dwight's cooking," Ward said.

"It's been years since I've sampled her cooking," Sarah nodded, "and I can tell you I feel deprived. I intend to make up for lost time, so I hope there's plenty of steak."

Even while making inconsequential small talk, Sarah was thinking with astonishment, *I'd have known him anywhere!*

It was the eyes. Oh, she had never forgotten Johnny Trist's eyes, seen once in the glow of a flashlight, remarkable eyes, with depth and intelligence. They seemed to hold some amusing secret no one else suspected. Sarah remembered that other time she had looked into them. Even then Johnny Trist's eyes had been smiling with a gentle amusement at a scared little girl, lost and cold on a steep mountainside.

Sarah felt that John Trist *must* recognize her as well. The impression was so strong that she had difficulty untangling her gaze from his as she replied to a polite question about her trip to New Mexico.

How strange that sense of mutual recognition was. It was so totally unlikely. Probably this man had forgotten completely the night he had joined searchers looking for a lost child in the night-shrouded, mysterious canyons of the Organ Mountains. Even if he was occasionally reminded of the incident, Sarah could only hope that he did not look at her tonight and see a dirty-faced, tangle-haired, weeping ten-year-old!

Sarah's own thoughts confused her, and she had to gather them sternly into control, lest her woolgathering cause her to say something ridiculous. She cleared her throat, determined to contribute something intelligent to the conversation. Her pride demanded it.

"Mr. Trist, I understand you're considering buying into my shop on behalf of someone else."

He inclined his dark head lazily. "Yes. Shirley DeBrese, a—friend of mine. She's been looking for something like this. I looked at the shop a few days ago. Perhaps it would do, but I admit I have some doubts."

Sarah felt a bit stung at the implied criticism of her new business, although she could not really defend its present condition. "Have you? And what are your doubts, Mr. Trist?"

"John, please," he said. "Well, for one thing, the shop plainly hasn't been handled well. The books have shown a loss for over a year. Maureen tells me you have some ideas of your own about that." He raised one black eyebrow questioningly. His slow smile made Sarah aware of alarm bells in her brain.

Sarah felt suddenly defensive. Did his smile mean that he had brushed off in advance any ideas she might present? Was he prepared to listen politely and—indifferently? Sarah had the sensation of being a high-school freshman facing an oral exam without preparation.

Unconsciously, she drew herself up, shoulders square, chin lifted. "I think a great deal can be done to give the shop more appeal." She had to pause and clear her throat again to stop an annoying tremor. She continued more firmly. "I'd like to display the work of local artists and artisans, for one thing." She glanced at Ward Cowley, who grinned back encouragingly.

"I can put you in touch with some really creative people," he said. "Some of the students are doing fantastic work. And I work with a senior citizens arts and crafts group. You should see some of the hand-pieced quilts they've done, the carving—and there's one artist who does great miniature landscapes. He's very professional."

"Yes, those are the kinds of things I want," Sarah nodded eagerly. "I don't need things so avant-garde that the ordinary person wouldn't be attracted, nor so expensive that they're beyond the means of most people."

She turned to Cowley, relieved to escape Trist's scrutiny. Cowley's interest was warming. "Maureen says that you make beautiful original jewelry. That's one area I'd like to go into, if you can give me a selection in a wide price range, so the young wife on a tight budget can afford a tiepin or ring for her husband's birthday, or a college girl can find distinctive earrings and bangle bracelets that are wonderful quality and affordable." She warmed to her subject, almost forgetting Trist's attentive presence.

"I thought about pottery," she continued. "I'd like to find pieces that are beautiful and yet practical. I'd like handwoven ponchos—your wife creates woven originals, doesn't she? Wall hangings and colorful small rugs might sell well—"

"I think you've got the right idea. In fact, you've given me some ideas for my own work." Cowley had apparently gotten so interested in the conversation that he had abandoned the steaks. Maureen took the fork from his unknowing hand and began deftly to test and turn the meat.

"Don't forget," Cowley said, "sometimes it pays to have a few special display items that are more expensive, but so distinctive that they give tone to the other displays, and bring in the folks who can afford something out of the ordinary."

"Yes, I'd thought of that," Sarah nodded. "The first thing I have to do is clear out all that dime store junk that is lying around the shop catching dust now."

"Excuse me," Maureen laughed, "but could you two hold off on planning long enough to eat?"

A little embarrassed that her enthusiasm had made her forget everything else, Sarah accepted the plate Maureen handed her, and in a few moments she was seated on a padded redwood lawn chair eating the most delicious steak she could remember.

"Maureen, this is wonderful," she said. The men murmured fervent agreement.

"Can you teach Charlotte the secret of this steak?" Ward pleaded. "I hate to think I may never taste it again."

As Maureen began to discuss her recipe with Cowley, John Trist came to refill Sarah's wineglass, carrying his plate in one hand.

"Your aunt is quite a lady," he remarked. He folded his long body into a nearby chair, and cut a bite of steak.

"She's marvelous," Sarah said. "I can't tell you all she's done for me. She made my move out here as painless as possible, and found the shop for me. Maureen's my only relative. I'm lucky that she's my dear friend as well."

"Your parents are not living? No brothers or sisters?"

She shook her head. "My father died when I was a child, and I lost my mother two years ago. I was an only child."

"Do you think you can learn to like our 'Land of Enchantment'?" John watched her steadily. The color of his eyes was unusual, deep and sparkling. They were also disconcertingly direct.

"I like it already," she said. "It's very different from where I grew up, but I find it a fascinating area. The spaces are so tremendous! It's hard to make the mind take them in. It's an experience just to drive through all that empty, uncluttered country. And the air is—different somehow, lighter, exhilarating."

He smiled, and his face became younger. "It's the lack of humidity, and the elevation. Wait until you've visited our high country. We have marvelous skiing—Sierra Blanca isn't much more than a hundred miles from here, near Ruidoso. Or you might like riding or hiking in the White Mountain Wilderness Area, or the Gila Wilderness Area—or the Sangre de Cristos. New Mexico has some wonderful mountain country. There are some surprising contrasts here. Even the climate can be radically different within a space of a few miles, from a high valley to a desert floor for instance."

For a moment Sarah felt that she could almost see the vistas he described. "Do you live here in the city?" she asked.

"I keep an apartment here, for business reasons, but my ranch, east of here, is home. My land runs this side of the Organ Mountains and south toward El Paso. I stay at the ranch as much as possible. I confess that my heart is out there."

"And—Miss DeBrese? She lives here in town, I take it. I understand that she is your fiancée."

"Where did you hear—ah," his glance touched Maureen, and his thoughts seemed to move inward for a long moment. He turned back to Sarah, his face inscrutable. "Shirley thrives on city life. She firmly believes there is nothing to do in the country." He smiled slightly.

"But I suppose when you're married, she'll move to your ranch?"

He studied her gravely, and she felt her face warming. Had she asked something too personal? "Bridges should be crossed when one reaches them," he said.

She sought to amend the mistake she had apparently made—"I wondered if she would be near enough to come in to the shop regularly, in the event that she becomes a partner. This is all very new to me. I'm not quite certain what to expect, or how active the co-owner will be."

He set aside his empty plate and leaned back comfortably, long, booted legs stretched out. "Shirley probably wouldn't be on hand—or underfoot"—he grinned lazily—"on a daily basis. You'd probably see a lot of her at first. She's excited about becoming a businesswoman." He lifted his wineglass, as if in ironic salute. "Frankly, I doubt if her enthusiasm will be very lasting. Shirley has a great many interests, various clubs and organizations, and she frequently models for fashion shows."

"I—see," Sarah murmured, wondering if he was making a comment on all women who imagined themselves capable of running a business. Or perhaps John Trist was simply hoping that his wife-to-be would soon consent to accept her rightful place—in the Trist kitchen. Was it another case of a man's resentment of his fiancée's plans for a career?

Sarah heard the coolness in her own voice. "If you feel that Miss DeBrese is not genuinely interested in business, why are you thinking of buying a percentage of La Casa Encantada for her?"

He favored her with a penetrating regard that said she definitely had ventured a bit too far into his private territory, and she braced herself for a sharp reply. It was surprisingly mild. "I don't believe you quite understand, Miss Wingate. I am not proposing to make Shirley a gift. It will be a loan, a straight business deal. Shirley has requested my help with the financing. But she wanted at least a half interest in a business. I'm not certain I can persuade her to settle for forty percent."

"And as you mentioned, you're not yet sure that it's a wise investment." Her voice carried an edge.

He shrugged broad shoulders, and there was a disturbing power even in that small movement. "As to that, any investment is a gamble. This one is so small I won't lose sleep over it."

Sarah felt rebuffed and angered for no clear reason. "I'm sure that a gift shop must be very small potatoes for someone like you, Mr. Trist, and it must seem very trivial indeed that I—and presumably your fiancée—could find this business a challenging and a worthwhile test of our abilities."

He gave her a startled glance. "Oh, now wait, Miss Wingate. I didn't mean—"

"Please excuse me." Sarah stood quickly, slender and tense in the cream skirt and blue camisole. She was unaware of her appeal in that moment, temper heightening her delicate coloring, wide gray eyes stormy, lips struggling to keep an indifferent set. "I really must speak to Mr. Cowley," she said, and moved away from John Trist.

CHAPTER FIVE

She crossed the patio, setting her empty plate on the cart, taking her half-full wineglass with her as she approached Maureen and Ward Cowley, who were now examining a rosebush covered with red blossoms that sprawled over the six-foot-high adobe wall separating Maureen's property from the next lot.

"I've sprayed the darn little pests," Maureen said gloomily, "but every time I look there are more aphids. They must multiply like rabbits."

Cowley grinned within his beard. "Be thankful they aren't the same size. I'll speak to Professor Cline in the horticultural department and pass on his advice to you. I read somewhere that you can put onions in a blender and spray the resulting soup on the bugs. At least it might make their eyes water."

Smiling at his nonsense, Maureen turned and took Sarah's hand. "I think this girl wants to discuss business with you, Ward. I'll fetch the dessert. But let's have it inside, shall we?"

The party adjourned to the living room for dessert and coffee. At Maureen's suggestion Ward Cowley brought from his car a small case containing examples of his jewelry. Maureen had not overstated the excellence of his work. Highly impressed, Sarah spoke for several pieces on the spot and asked to see more.

"I'll bring them to the shop tomorrow. Will you let me provide my own display case, Sarah? If my designs are seen to their best advantage, they sell better," he said. "I build my cases myself, from lumber I bought when an old barn was demolished. It's a wonderful silver-gray, the softer grain of the wood weathered away. I use black velvet as a backing for the silver and turquoise, and coral."

"It sounds eye-catching," Sarah nodded. "But I'd like to see it before I decide, to be sure it will fit with the general decor I have in mind."

Unoffended, he tilted his head. "You know, I think you may have quite a head for business, Sarah."

At ten-thirty John Trist glanced at his watch and stood to go. Maureen rose to see him out. But John turned to Sarah, who sat at one end of Maureen's blue couch, legs curled under her. "Perhaps Miss Wingate would walk out with me?" he said smoothly. "There's something I'd like to discuss with her. An idea for the shop."

Surprised and a little flustered, Sarah got up. He bent to kiss Maureen's cheek and thank her. Sarah followed him to the foyer. He opened the door and politely stood aside for her to step onto the porch. He closed the door behind them, and they stood for a moment in silence as a car passed on the quiet street. Then he inclined his head, his strong features softened by the porch lighting.

"Have I said something to offend you, Sarah?" he asked bluntly.

Taken off guard, she gazed at him, eyes widening. "What makes you think that, Mr. Trist?"

He made an impatient gesture. "Call me John," he commanded. "And please do me the courtesy of simply answering my question. Did I offend you? If so, I can only say I'm sorry. It was not my intention."

She bent her head, then looked up, meeting his look squarely. "It was only—I thought you sounded patronizing about Miss DeBrese's interest in going into business. I know most men don't want to believe a woman can handle business decisions—"

"Where the devil did you get that notion?" he broke in, running long fingers through his thick dark hair. He put on his wide-brimmed western hat and tugged it down sharply. The irrelevant thought passed through Sarah's mind that of the great many men she had seen in the Southwest inclined toward western dress, Trist seemed most naturally suited to it. Perhaps it was the weather-tanned skin, the little lines at the eye corners made by narrowing his eyes against the strong sunlight of New Mexico.

She brought her jittering thoughts back into line. "I've had some experience with men who—"

"Oh, have you?" he interrupted what she'd been about to say, thus twisting the meaning of her intended statement. "I wonder what kind of experience made you think all men consider women decorative morons?"

"I didn't mean that, precisely. But you seemed so sure Miss DeBrese would soon lose interest in the project. Surely that isn't quite fair."

"You really needn't defend Miss DeBrese to me," he pointed out coolly. "Perhaps I know her as well as anyone."

Sarah could not answer that. She was too honest to try to defend an indefensible position. Abruptly, the corner she'd backed herself into struck her sense of humor. She found herself laughing softly. John Trist quirked a black eyebrow, his face so puzzled that it made Sarah's laughter bubble up irrepressibly. She controlled herself with an effort and cleared her throat.

"Forgive me, Mr. Trist. I suddenly realized how hostile I was being, without reason. Please put it down to the times. Women have developed a 'stick together' syndrome. But honestly, don't you think that Miss DeBrese should be allowed to prove herself?"

"She has no need to prove anything to me," he replied, but his slight smile signaled a cessation of hostilities. He moved with long-limbed grace down the steps to the walk and looked up at her, his eyes shadowed by his hat brim. "I'll be on my way now. We'll be seeing each other."

"Yes, of course," she said, and offered her hand.

But he did not shake it, as one businessperson to another. He simply held it for a moment, his fingers powerful, vital around hers. He stared at her with disturbing intensity.

The night was so still that Sarah heard her own deep, unsteady breath and was alarmed at the way this man's touch affected her. It must be some new vulnerability caused by the shock of her suddenly broken engagement. It was something she would have to be on guard against. She told herself firmly that what she felt was merely heightened chemistry, the warmth and strength of a man's handclasp conjuring an illusion of something that did not exist. John Trist had no possible interest in her as a woman. He already had plans for his future, and he was in love with a girl to whom he had pledged that future.

Sarah drew her fingers away. He turned to go, then swung back quickly. "You know," he said with a crooked grin, "you've changed."

With that he was gone, long legs carrying him to the four-wheel-drive vehicle parked at the curb.

Astonishment held Sarah staring after the Jeep until it vanished around a curve in the street.

"He *did* remember!" she whispered.

A sudden breeze made the ceramic wind chimes hanging nearby stir musically.

The door behind her opened. Ward Cowley stepped out, thanking Maureen for a pleasant evening. He turned to Sarah, smiling. "I'll bring my wife to meet you tomorrow. She'll like you."

"Thank you. And thanks for your advice about the shop."

As he left, and Sarah stepped back into the house, she forced her mind back to the reality of the moment. But though the breeze had vanished and the wind chime melody ceased, still in her mind that gentle, tantalizing, random sequence of notes underscored a quiet amused voice: *"You've changed—"*

Sarah helped Maureen put the dinner dishes in the dishwasher. She tried to dismiss the moments with John Trist from her mind. It really wasn't so mysterious that he knew Sarah was the grown-up version of a small girl whose foolish act years ago had caused a great deal of difficulty for a great many people. Obviously, Maureen had recalled the incident and mentioned it to him at some point.

Sighing as she scraped a dish, Sarah almost wished she had not found an explanation. That moment of recognition had been magical, had brought a small, wondering lift of Sarah's heart, an unexplainable instant of delight. Now she saw that she had overreacted. So she had met John Trist once before, and he had been reminded of it—so what? It meant absolutely nothing.

Sarah gave herself a severe mental scolding and made a resolution. She was not going to become one of these women who fall for every handsome face and imagine some interest where there could be none.

After all, she had a great many absorbing matters to occupy her mind and her time. Perhaps one day she would meet someone special and there would be a new awakening in her heart. Now was definitely not the time.

The next day began with a flurry of activity. Maureen showed Sarah three apartments, but because of their location none of the three proved suitable. Maureen promised to check into several other listings. Before noon Sarah was trying out her car along the busy streets of Las Cruces. It was a little difficult finding her way about the unfamiliar town, and she spent some time familiarizing herself with the streets. She was pleased with the Mustang. It was smooth-running and solid, an attractive and well-kept car.

At last, turning into the parking space before La Casa Encantada, Sarah noted that the lot was almost empty of cars. She frowned, mentally assessing sales. The business had been allowed to deteriorate almost to nonexistence. It would take some work and ingenuity to change all that.

Before going inside, Sarah stood thoughtfully tossing her car keys in the palm of her hand, looking over the shop's exterior, the landscaping, the large, hand-carved sign: LA CASA ENCANTADA, The Enchanted House.

She liked what she saw until her eyes fell on the window display once more. It was just so ordinary, so totally uninspiring.

As she stood there, a van pulled into the parking lot and two people got out. It was Ward Cowley and a young woman with a thin, sensitive face and long pale hair braided down her back in one plait.

"Sarah," said Ward, "this is Charlotte, my wife."

Sarah moved over to them, hand outstretched. At once she liked Charlotte's kind, honest expression and her quite beautiful brown eyes. "Charlotte, hello! I hope you've brought some of your weaving to show me. I'm desperate for something with style for the shop. Come inside, and I'll show you what I'm up against."

Ward lifted a large carton from the van and followed the girls inside. They had barely begun to look around the place when Charlotte giggled sympathetically. "I see your problem, Sarah. This is a shame. Someone has turned it into a bad copy of a Woolworth's variety store."

Cowley grinned and thrust his hands into his jeans pockets. "There's one consolation. Anything you do will be an improvement."

The sulky-faced clerk approached, saw that they were not customers, and turned away. Sarah called after her. "Oh, Millicent, may I speak to you for a moment?"

The woman turned, waiting. Her unpleasant expression made it easier for Sarah to tell her that she would not be needed after the standard two weeks' notice.

Millicent shrugged. "If it's all the same to you, I'd as soon quit after today. The job is dull. No one ever comes in."

"That's fine, if you prefer it. I'll give you your wages now. You may go at once." Sarah turned toward the office. While she was computing what she owed the woman, Ward and Charlotte moved around the shop, talking. Through the glass partition Sarah could see Charlotte gesturing toward a rack of postcards here, a display of cheap costume jewelry there, and an impulse struck.

As soon as she paid Millicent, Sarah went back to the Cowleys. "Charlotte," she said, "I have no idea what your schedule is, or if you'd be interested at all, but—would you consider coming to work for me? You can choose your hours, to fit your class schedule."

Charlotte turned to her, braid swinging. Her intelligent eyes were surprised. "You want to hire me?"

Sarah gestured at their surroundings. "I need someone to help me get this place into shape. We'll get rid of this junk somehow, a sale to begin with, I suppose. Then we'll close up shop and clean and redecorate. We'll make a totally fresh start."

Charlotte tilted her head consideringly. "Well, I only have two classes during this session, but of course in the fall I'll have a full schedule. I might work here until then, if you think that would help. I have to tell you, I've never worked as a clerk."

"Then your experience exactly equals mine. We'll learn about it together. Believe me, just your expression is an improvement over Millicent! I hate to ask, but could you possibly begin today? I want to mark this stuff down and get it moved out, even if we have to give it away. And then we'll bring in some really good stock."

"Well—I suppose I could begin now. In fact, it might be fun."

"Would you like to see some of Charlotte's work?" Ward asked, grinning at his wife with undisguised pride. "She won't tell you so, but she's an artist with her weaving."

Sarah's exclamations of pleasure were genuine as Charlotte lifted several things from the carton Ward had brought in. There was a variety of handwoven pieces, in warm and lively colors, made of hand-dyed, hand-spun wools. Sarah especially liked two ponchos, a fringed vest, some decorative wall hangings, all with original designs. They were bright and imaginative and appealing.

"These are exactly the type of thing I'd like to display," Sarah said briskly. "We'll have a small fashion department. I have some clothing designs of my own in mind, if I can get someone to make them up for us."

Charlotte was pink with pleasure at the compliments to her work. "I have a friend who's a whiz of a seamstress. If you have some designs ready, I'll take you to meet her, and we'll see if she can put some things together."

"Great!" Sarah felt a rush of excitement. "Well, what are we waiting for? Here, pack your weavings away to protect them from dust. I'll buy all of these. I'll have to get a mannequin or two—and clothing racks—oh gosh, I can't wait to get started!"

Smiling at her enthusiasm, both Charlotte and Ward went to work, Ward lettering signs and slashing prices, while Sarah called the newspaper to place an ad about the sale, together with some information about the business being under new management, soon to blossom into something exciting. Then she joined her new friends, and together they worked into the afternoon. Sarah tried to shoo the two of them out to eat. Cowley merely grinned and phoned an order for pizza to be sent in, and they worked on.

Sarah soon left the changing of prices to her helpers. She plunged into a frenzy of long-overdue cleaning, careless of her blue shirt and white jeans. She didn't need to worry about offending a customer with the whine of the vacuum cleaner she found in a supply room, for there were no customers all afternoon. Beginning to dust the displays, she paused to call a window-cleaning service to send someone out next day.

She removed all the shopworn displays in the windows and began to get rid of dust and cobwebs. She had just stepped out of the window, dust smudged over the tip of her nose, her hair more than a little bedraggled and adorned with a wisp of cobweb. The bell over the door tinkled, and a tall form blocked out the sunlight for a moment as John Trist stepped in. He paused in mid-stride, taking in the sight of her dishevelment.

Instinctively, Sarah put up a hand to brush back her sagging hair, and a corner of his lip twitched but was quickly controlled.

"Ah—the boss lady, I believe." He bent his dark head with a suggestion of a sweeping bow to royalty.

Sarah was irritated at being caught looking as dusty as the uninspiring wares her shop displayed. Nor was she in a mood to tolerate his badly hidden amusement.

"Is there something I can do for you, Mr. Trist?" she asked with a hint of asperity.

"It's John, remember? Yes, there is something you can do for me. I'd like to see the shop again, and hear some more of your plans, if you have time." Something flickered in his eyes, something mischievous, boylike. "I think it would help me make up my mind about the deal."

She felt a sudden undefined suspicion, sensing that he had not said quite all he was thinking. But she had no excuse to refuse. She nodded courteously and set down the armload of nondescript articles she had gathered out of the window.

"I understood you were leaving town last night," she said.

"I did. Drove out to the ranch. But I had a business conference with my attorney and Shirley this morning here in town."

Sarah brushed past him, very conscious of the contact of her arm against his, since he did not bother to move over in the constricted space where she must pass. "Come this way, and I'll show you the whole building."

CHAPTER SIX

John looked around him. Were his eyes narrowed critically? Immediately, she was spurred to a defense of her new business place.

"I know it doesn't look like much now, but wait until I get rid of all this stuff, and restock." Enthusiasm began to warm her voice as she listed the ideas she had for fresh paint, new carpet, and a much more spacious layout of displays instead of the cramped, crowded effect the place gave now.

As she talked, and led him from area to area, he was quiet, attentive. Each time she turned to him, she found his eyes upon her, and she was not sure he had even glanced at what she'd been discussing. It was disconcerting. She found herself growing increasingly nervous.

She moved from the showroom into the office. "All this room needs is a good cleaning and some organization," she said, and started to leave the room.

Surprisingly, he shook his head, casually barring the doorway. "You're wrong, Sarah. This place is inefficient. He grinned at her surprise. "Look at it. You have insufficient filing space, the desk is too small, that typewriter is practically an antique. You need a place to keep catalogs and samples. And if you plan to design fashions, don't you need a drawing board and such? The room's too small. I suggest you knock out that wall and incorporate some of your stockroom space for office use."

She blinked. "How did you know I intended to try my hand at designing?"

He shrugged. "Maureen said something about it. A good idea, if you ask me."

"Why—thank you," Sarah said faintly.

"I've decided to loan Shirley the money to buy into the business," he said abruptly. "I'll make an appointment with your aunt for the signing."

"I'm sure Miss DeBrese will be pleased," Sarah murmured.

"And you?" He gave her a quizzical look. "I assume the transaction will be a good one for you as well."

"I'm sure it will be." She smiled brightly. "I'm looking forward to meeting your fiancée."

His lips parted as if to say something. But as she waited politely, a look of frustration crossed his face. "I—I imagine she'll be in tomorrow. Now, would you let me buy you a cup of coffee?"

"Thank you, but I think I'd better get on with the work here. There's so much to be done before we can have the new opening."

"Then you can use some help." He took off his summer-weight western-style suit jacket, removed his tie, and began to roll up his shirt sleeves.

"No, John, I couldn't think of letting you—"

"You can't prevent it. I'm great with a push broom," he grinned. "I think I could even manage a mop. I wonder which year that stockroom was cleaned?"

Sarah's crew made rapid inroads on the chores of cleaning the building and arranging the present stock as attractively as possible. At five-thirty Sarah called a halt, beaming at Ward, Charlotte and John with a smudged and happy face.

"How can I thank all of you? You've accomplished more than I dreamed was possible. Charlotte, I promise you that after we get things in gear, your work won't be such drudgery."

"We really did make a difference, didn't we?" Charlotte smiled. "We're ready to have the sale, and once that's out of the way, you can begin the renovation, and then restock."

"Oh, gosh"—sudden fright gave Sarah's voice a tremor—"if only I can have enough stock on hand to open!"

"We'll do some checking with artists and craftsmen around town, and I guarantee we'll find all you can use within a few days," Ward reassured her. "And if you would like, I'll make a buying trip to Juarez and pick up some nice things."

Sarah brightened. "That's a wonderful idea, Ward. I'll pay you for your time and expenses, of course."

"And I'll be in tomorrow morning after my eight o'clock class to help with the customers," Charlotte promised.

Impulsively, Sarah gave her a hug. "I think we're going to be great friends."

Charlotte's delicate face colored, and her smile was warm. "I know we will."

Charlotte and Ward left as Sarah waved from the shop doorway. She turned to face John Trist, finding him disconcertingly close, looking down at her thoughtfully. Something leaped into her throat, quivering there, and she had to swallow before speaking.

"It—it was good of you to help with the cleaning," she said.

"My pleasure." He grinned briefly. "You're going to need painters and carpenters in a few days."

Sarah sighed, realizing suddenly how tired she was. "Yes. And I'll have to get some estimates on carpeting. This is very worn."

"I had some work done on my home a few months ago. The contractor I hired is good, and charges fairly. I think I can get a good price for you on the work you need, and we might get the materials wholesale through a friend of mine who owns a builder's supply company."

Sarah pushed her hair back, frowning doubtfully. "I really don't like imposing upon you further—"

He gave an exaggerated sigh. "Please, Miss Independence! I'll have money committed to this venture. Isn't it to my advantage if your initial outlay is as small as possible, so the profits start to flow sooner and Shirley can repay me?"

She couldn't refute his logic. "Very well, John. Thank you."

He shrugged. "Now, may I take you to dinner this evening?"

On the point of accepting, Sarah remembered that she had promised the evening to Larry Brandt. But even if she had not, could she have agreed to a dinner date with John? He was engaged to be married. Or was that an outdated taboo?

"I'm sorry," she said. "I already have a date this evening."

Did she imagine the sudden withdrawal in his eyes? She could not be sure, for he was turning away, going to pick up his jacket and tie. "I see," he said evenly. "I wasn't aware that you had—friends here in town."

"I haven't, not really. That is—" She drew rein on her tongue, annoyed at her compulsion to explain. She owed no explanation to anyone.

He turned suddenly to look at her, knotting his tie. "But I was forgetting. You were engaged to a young banker who lives here."

"How did you know that?" Quick resentment edged her tone.

"It was in the papers. Sam Underwood is one of the big catches of the area. Anything that occurs in the Underwood family is news."

"And you recognized my name, fancy that! I'm terrifically flattered. But if you're asking whether it's Sam I'm meeting, it's not."

He could not have missed the chill. "And of course it's none of my business. I'll be going."

Quickly, he caught up his hat and left the shop.

Sarah had won the exchange. Why was the small victory without triumph?

Larry Brandt arrived early for their date. Sarah, wearing navy fashion jeans and a pink, long-sleeved shirt with white daisies embroidered on the pocket, hurried from her room, still fastening her hair back with a hand-carved wooden barrette. She had slipped her feet into soft suede ankle boots.

From his expression Larry enthusiastically approved of her appearance. "Lady, you do light up a room! How do you feel about Mexican food? Or have you tried any? No? Well, it's time you were introduced to enchiladas and burritos and—"

Unable to get a word in, Sarah let Brandt lead her to his car, a Thunderbird. He helped her in, got behind the wheel, and broke speed limits for driving and for conversation all the way to a cozy, tiny restaurant in Mesilla, the picturesque old Mexican settlement now virtually a part of Las Cruces, where curio shops and a historical old church were set around a tiny square of park.

The café lay in a narrow side street. Larry parked where there seemed barely space for a bicycle—with a quick swerve and a series of expert backing maneuvers that made Sarah shut her eyes, waiting for a crunch of metal.

Larry laughed. "You can relax. We've landed."

As he helped her from the car, he lifted her fingers to his lips quickly. "Come on, beautiful. You'll dazzle the regulars."

The café was dimly lighted, the tables small, and all filled. Evidently, this was a very popular place. Sarah and Larry managed to snare a table just as a couple left it. A pretty girl with dark eyes and hair came quickly to clear the used dishes and take their order. Sarah asked Larry to choose for her. He read off the melodic Spanish names from the menu and ordered a bottle of red wine.

By the time the food arrived, steaming and sending out wonderful, spicy aromas, Sarah realized that she was enjoying herself. Larry was good company—attentive, witty, carrying the conversation until she felt like joining in, and then leading her to talk about herself.

"You think you'll like it here, Sarah?"

She nodded without hesitation. "Yes. Everyone has been so kind. My aunt is an angel, and I've met Ward Cowley and his wife, and John Trist—"

"Trist, eh?" Brandt's eyebrows rose.

"You know him?" Sarah asked, and cut a forkful of rich, saucy enchilada.

"Everyone knows Trist. He's bought several ranch trucks and at least one of his cars from us. Great guy, right?"

Sarah carefully kept her expression noncommittal. "I'm sure he's a nice man."

Larry chuckled. "Honey, if that's the only effect John Trist has on you, he must have changed in the last few weeks. There are dozens of attached and unattached ladies here in town, not to mention college girls, who would give their eyeteeth to get cosy with Trist. Not only is he wealthy—though you wouldn't know it to talk to him—but he's not exactly hard on the eyes. And you admit he's 'nice.' "

Sarah made an effort to change the subject. "What is the sauce on our enchiladas? It's wonderful."

Before Larry could answer, another voice broke in. "Well, well! If this isn't a surprise."

Startled, Sarah looked up to find Sam Underwood standing at her shoulder, one hand on the back of her chair. His expression as he looked down at her might have meant anything.

"Hello, Sam," she murmured, hiding her dismay.

"Friend of yours?" Larry Brandt said with a frown. He rose to his feet.

"Larry, this is Sam Underwood. He's an old friend. I—met him in St. Louis."

"And I was under the impression that you were still living there." Sam edged around as if to cut Brandt out of the conversation. A glance at Larry's face made Sarah uneasy. He looked tense and ready for some action.

"I'm busy, as you can see, Sam," she said hastily. "If you want to talk to me, why don't you call me at my aunt's home."

"I think I'd like an explanation now," Sam persisted. "What are you doing in Las Cruces? I tried to call you in St. Louis two days ago. I guess this explains why I couldn't reach you."

"Mister, you're interrupting our dinner," Larry snapped. "And you're bothering my date. So if you would just leave us alone, we'd appreciate it."

Sam flung a look over his shoulder at Brandt, and Sarah recognized the signs of his quick temper. "Who are you anyway, bud?" he asked. "Sarah, is this what you're replacing me with? And why did you follow me here?"

"Sam, please!" Sarah begged, low-voiced. "Of course I didn't follow you. I came to take over the business I'd bought. Did you think I'd simply forget about that? Now please go away and leave me alone. You're creating an embarrassing scene!"

"You heard the lady." Larry caught Sam's elbow, and for a moment Sarah was sure Sam was going to swing at him. Larry was taller and heavier than Sam, and perhaps it was the difference in size that made Sam hesitate. Angrily, he shrugged loose from Larry's grasp and moved away, leaving the restaurant.

Larry sat down. Sarah let out an exasperated breath. "I'm sorry about all that," she said.

"Who is he?" Brandt's face was still rigid with displeasure.

Sarah sipped her wine and sighed. "He was my fiancé until a week or so ago."

"You broke the engagement?"

Sarah felt a hysterical laugh rising and hastily checked it. "Not exactly. He decided he didn't look forward to being married after all. Left me waiting at the altar, so to speak!" She poked at her food, realizing that she'd lost her appetite. "I think he was just surprised to see me here. I suppose he imagined I came here to be near him."

"And you didn't?" Larry asked. "If this guy is important to you, I won't horn in."

Sarah swallowed annoyance at his question. Perhaps he had some right to ask, since Sam had staged his awkward little scene in Larry's presence. "What can I say? It takes time for every remnant of feeling to die. But I did *not* follow Sam out here. I didn't want to give up my plans to go into business. It's just that simple, and there were no overtones to my decision to move to Las Cruces." She picked up her small handbag and stood. "I'd like to go, if you don't mind."

Larry was instantly repentant. "You haven't finished your meal! Come on, sit down. At least let this hungry man have his dinner." He gave her a comically pleading smile.

Reluctantly, she sank into her seat again and toyed with her food until he was finished. She forced herself to make conversation on innocuous subjects, but the evening was ruined. As they left the café, Larry proposed a movie, but Sarah asked to be taken home, pleading tiredness after a day of cleaning the shop. Without argument he drove her to Maureen's home.

She slid from the car quickly, before he could complete the quick slide of his arm about her shoulder. From the curb she flung him an artificially cheery good-night.

But he caught up with her at the steps, where last evening she had stood with John Trist. Sarah had a moment's vivid memory of the tall man, and it made her a trifle inattentive to Larry, who was grasping her hand, smiling at her beguilingly.

"Hey, honey, I know I said the wrong thing at dinner. But you didn't give me a chance to apologize, and I think you'll have to admit that we were having a fine time until your former fiancé turned up."

She nodded. "None of this is your fault, Larry. It was just bad luck that Sam found me there. I'm sure it startled him too. He isn't usually so rude."

"Then you won't hold one lousy evening against this innocent car salesman?" Larry laid his hands over her shoulders and drew her uncomfortably close.

"Of course not." She lifted his hands away, but could not quite dodge his kiss. Her quick turn to the door made it little more than a brush of his lips across her cheek. In a moment she was inside the door, standing very still to let a feeling of regret for the less than successful evening drain away. She was glad that Maureen had already gone to bed. She was in no mood for rehashing the date.

She went to her room and prepared for bed. Switching off her lamp, she lay under the sheet watching moving lights and shadows on the ceiling made by an occasional passing car.

She sorted out her feelings and laid them neatly in a row, trying to disarm them in the interest of sleep. Surprisingly, the uppermost discomfort of her mind was not sadness over her lost relationship with Sam, but embarrassment, and perhaps a pinch of guilt. The encounter with Sam was not something she could have foreseen, or prevented. And it was simply silly to tell herself she should not have come to the town where Sam lived and worked. Her motive was clear in her own mind: the following up of a legitimate business deal. Nor had she wished or attempted to meet Sam again.

Yet perhaps she should not have reacted so strongly to Larry's natural indignation at having the evening interrupted, and his probing into her reasons for moving to Las Cruces. It must have been upsetting. Understandably, he had questions.

Nevertheless, the comfortable friendliness she had begun to feel for Brandt had been short-circuited. It was not his fault. If he called and asked for a second date, it would be only fair to give him another chance, though the prospect was not very appealing at this moment. Ah well, she smiled to herself in the dark, Larry had not exactly enjoyed himself tonight. Perhaps he would not be eager to date Sarah Wingate again!

Feeling better, Sarah turned over and began to relax. Mercifully, the uncomfortable evening slipped out of her thoughts, to be replaced with plans for the shop. Heaven knew that would provide plenty to occupy her mind. Mentally, she cleared out the present display racks, saw the floor recarpeted and the walls attractively repainted . . .

At that point in her daydreaming somehow John Trist slipped into the mental scene looking as he had today, sleeves rolled up over brown arms, careless of his expensive clothing, cleaning the supply room of the shop, helped by Ward Cowley. Sarah remembered that once the two men had laughed like boys.

She drifted into sleep, wondering what John and Ward had been laughing about—and wondering why the sound of that laughter lingered so in her mind.

CHAPTER SEVEN

The next days were crammed with activity. Maureen found Sarah a charming apartment in an old but well-maintained complex, overlooking a patio complete with pool and shady plantings. After a hectic sale day at the shop, Sarah arranged for her belongings that had been shipped from St. Louis to be hauled to the apartment. She and Maureen arranged books and dishes and a couple of treasured paintings in the comfortable one-bedroom apartment. By the time the desert sun had set, Sarah had a home.

Maureen stayed for dinner: hamburgers and soft drinks delivered by a smiling young man who flirted outrageously with Sarah as she paid him. Maureen left soon after eating, professing a sudden craving for her bed after the day's activity. She hugged Sarah almost tearfully.

"My house is going to seem very empty without you."

"I'll be underfoot so often you won't know I'm gone," Sarah assured her. "And if you don't drop in here or at the shop at least every other day, my feelings will be hurt dreadfully."

Maureen held her away, tilting her silver head. "Sarah, are you glad now that you moved here?"

Unhesitatingly, Sarah nodded. "I don't know why I agonized over the decision. It's tremendously exciting to be getting my business underway. Do you realize that since we had the last unsold stock carted away to the Salvation Army, the workmen can get in to start the renovation tomorrow. They said it would be a two-day job on the showroom, perhaps two more enlarging the office. And then the carpeting can be laid—why, by next Monday I can begin to put out our new displays. The stockroom is filling up with things I've bought or taken on commission from Ward's friends and acquaintances and a dozen people good at making craft items who heard I was buying and came by to show me their creations. The loveliest things, Maureen!"

She continued briskly, "And I'll set up a sewing machine here tomorrow. I want to turn out a few of my own designs—Sally Quinn is doing a half dozen of my originals already—you know, the girl Charlotte recommended—"

She paused for breath. Maureen nodded soberly. "That's all wonderful, Sarah. But you haven't been out socially since that evening with Larry Brandt, though I know he's called twice."

Sarah shrugged. "Well, there just hasn't been time and energy really. I explained that to Larry, and he'll call again after I have the business in hand. Speaking of that, I keep wondering when I'll meet Shirley DeBrese, and what ideas she'll have. You"—she hesitated and turned to adjust the fold of a drape—"you haven't seen her, or Mr. Trist, have you?"

"Not since the papers were signed. I believe John is at Roswell, or Clovis perhaps, baling hay at one of his farms, I think he said when he called."

"He called?" Sarah turned too quickly, forgetting to hide the sudden glow in her gray eyes.

"Well, yes, a day or so ago, just a business call. Our realty agency has some rent property he owns listed. Oh, by the way, can you make time to meet with Max Gamble, tomorrow perhaps? He can explain the legal details of your partnership, how expenses and profits are to be divided, all about tax matters and such. He's a good attorney even though he's young. And he can recommend a competent accountant to help you keep everything straight."

Sarah sighed, feeling suddenly tired. "Yes, of course. Would you make the appointment? You'll go with me, won't you?"

"If I can. I'll call Max first thing in the morning."

She patted Sarah's cheek and left the apartment.

Sarah turned, feeling suddenly lonely and strange, missing her now familiar room in Maureen's house, and the kind, lively company of her aunt.

But it really was a very attractive apartment, and with her own belongings set here and there, the impersonal atmosphere had almost been dissipated. If she added masses of plants at the south window and in the bright little kitchen, it would be very nice.

Perhaps it was only that she was a bit overworked. Somehow Sarah was having difficulty convincing herself that she was not lonely.

There was barely time the next morning to give instructions to the carpenters and painters John Trist had arranged for and see the first of the old display racks hauled away before driving to her appointment with Max Gamble. Maureen had called at the last moment, unable to make the meeting.

As Sarah was shown into the lawyer's ultramodern office, the attractive young man rose to meet her, hand outstretched. He was of average height, well built, with thick blond hair and a neatly clipped mustache. His smile was warm, his dark eyes alert and lively. Sarah reflected that his good looks and his charisma must be a definite asset to his law practice.

"Sarah, Maureen just called to say she had an important client arrive unexpectedly from out of town—"

"Yes, she called me too," Sarah nodded.

"I can give you all the information you need, I believe. By the way, I'm happy to meet you. Maureen's spoken of you often. She's one of my favorite clients."

Sarah sat in the chair he indicated. "My aunt recommends you highly."

"That's good of her." Gamble's attractive smile widened, and he gave her an all-encompassing look. "And good of her to give me the opportunity to meet her beautiful niece."

Abruptly, he shuffled some papers on his desk and became so businesslike that she could hardly be certain he had complimented her on a somewhat personal note.

By the conclusion of their meeting, Sarah was both impressed by his competent grasp of her business matters and grateful that he would be available for advice while she was learning the ropes. He also gave her the phone number of an accountant.

Sarah returned to La Casa Encantada, which now bore a "Closed for Renovation" sign plastered across the door. There was a red Datsun sports car near the planting of yucca and other desert growths in the center of the parking lot. Also in the lot were two pickups with a Williams Construction Company logo on the doors.

Sarah stepped inside the shop, to be confronted by a startling scene. A young woman, crinkly red hair to her shoulders, sleek in white fashion jeans and a pale green gauze shirt embroidered with bright flowers, was shouting at a man in coveralls and cap who was painting the ceiling —or at least, he had been painting the ceiling. Now he and three other men were standing about uncertainly.

"Why wasn't I consulted about the color?" the girl shrieked. "I hate that! Plain white, for heaven's sake! What kind of decorating is that? What kind of imbecile chose *white?*"

Sarah stepped forward. "Excuse me, were you looking for me? I'm Sarah Wingate."

The woman whirled, her wide blue eyes shooting sparks of temper. "Oh, so you're the one!" She tossed her rather overwhelming mass of hair back from her face. She was an unusually beautiful woman but could have been more so without her outraged expression and pouting mouth.

Sarah gathered her shattered wits and smiled. "You must be Shirley DeBrese. I'm glad to meet you."

Shirley rejected the peaceful overture. "I just bet you are!" Again she tossed her hair. Apparently, it was a favorite gesture. "You probably hoped I'd never show up, so you could simply run things to suit yourself."

At the moment Sarah could not truthfully have denied that statement. "Shirley, why don't we go have some coffee and discuss this out of the way of the workmen."

The girl, taller than Sarah, drew herself up explosively. "Oh, sure, so these—these gaping idiots can finish and be gone before I have a say in anything!"

She seemed close to angry tears, and Sarah wondered how she was going to handle this situation. It made her feel frantic for the painter and carpenters to be stopped in the work they were doing, delaying the opening with every minute that passed.

As she hesitated, Shirley's threatened tears appeared, trickling artistically down her cheeks, not even disturbing her mascara. Sarah wondered with irrelevant fascination how she did it. Struggling for a grip on the problem, she smiled with determined friendliness. "Shirley, how could I ask for your opinion when you weren't here and hadn't contacted me? I don't have your phone number—it's unlisted, I believe." An inspired lie presented itself. "I did ask Mr. Trist if he had an idea what you'd like, and he agreed that a white ceiling might create an atmosphere light and carefree—like your own personality!" she improvised recklessly. "And then the paneling was carefully chosen. See the red-gold tints? It's not far from the shade of your hair."

Ruthlessly, Sarah quashed guilt at the blatant con job she was attempting. She would not have been surprised if Shirley had burst into contemptuous laughter. Sarah was sure her transparent flattery wouldn't fool a child of five.

But to her relief Shirley's tears were drying up and the furious lines magically disappearing from her face. "John chose that? Well, why didn't you say Mr. Trist decided on the color?" Shirley turned, ordered the dumbfounded painter to get back to work, and returned her attention to Sarah. "Of course, if John made the decision, then it's perfectly all right. I would trust his judgment in anything!"

Sarah made a mental note to try and cover the tracks of her deception with John Trist later. That would be awkward. Ah well, one problem at a time.

"Oh yes," she said, treading firmly deeper into falsehood. "He was very particular in checking into my own plans for the shop to be sure they would dovetail with yours before he agreed to the deal, Shirley. Now, how about that coffee? Let's go to Sambo's. Shall we take my car?"

"I'd rather take my own."

"Fine. It's a lovely car," Sarah agreed.

Within minutes they were ordering coffee in the bright, busy restaurant on El Paseo. Making as much mileage as possible while Shirley was in a better mood, Sarah began to outline the plans she'd made, describing the type of gift items she had in mind, shamelessly dropping Trist's name as endorsement here and there. After all, he *had* approved of the plans, hadn't he?

Unfortunately, even the magic of John's name began to backfire.

Shirley narrowed her round eyes thoughtfully at Sarah. "You seem to have done a great deal of planning with John about all this," she broke in suddenly. "A great deal more than should be necessary, it seems to me. Could it be that the new girl in town is more interested in an eligible bachelor than in business? Honey, in case nobody told you, John Trist is taken!"

Hastily, Sarah shifted gears.

"Do you honestly think I could compete with you?" she asked.

Shirley tilted her head, giving the matter intense thought. She tossed her bright hair back, like a battle flag. "Probably not," was her conclusion.

Illogically, Sarah was pleased that there was a small element of uncertainty there.

With fingers crossed in her lap Sarah smiled at the other girl. "Now then, why don't you tell me what ideas you have in mind for the shop, and maybe we can incorporate some of them."

Shirley looked startled. "Ideas? Uh—like—what we should sell, you mean?"

"Yes." Sarah waited attentively, her gray eyes fixed on Shirley's face.

"Oh." Shirley bit her lip. "Well—"

Sarah gave her some help. "What do you think about the jewelry I spoke of, original silver designs by Ward Cowley?"

Shirley brightened. "I have several bracelets Ward Cowley made. One of them cost five hundred dollars. It was a gift, from one of my friends. It's really the 'in' thing now to wear Cowley jewelry, you know."

"Then you think a selection in our shop will be a good thing?"

"Oh, sure." Miss DeBrese glanced at her watch, apparently apprehensive about further questions. "Listen, I have a style show at two, so I have to run."

"I'm sure I'll be seeing you at the shop," Sarah murmured in spite of the dread in her spirit.

"Oh yes. I naturally want to be there to show all my friends around when they come in. I'm spreading the word. Of course, I wouldn't want to really *wait* on anyone. Like a clerk."

"No, of course not," Sarah agreed gloomily, and returned the wave Shirley gave as she made her way happily out of the restaurant. Picking up the check, Sarah paid, so absorbed in her thoughts that she almost forgot her change.

Outside, she realized that Shirley had left her without a ride. She called a cab and waited outside, meaning to go to her apartment. But when the taxi driver turned east on University, an impulse made her redirect him onto the NMSU campus. She stepped out, paid the driver, and began to walk aimlessly about on the wide lawns, under the shady trees.

It was a typical southern New Mexico summer day, ninety-five degrees and cloudless, a dry breeze fanning the trees now and then. Everywhere she looked, she saw summer students dressed in shorts or cutoff jeans, and wished she were as casually dressed. This climate called for as much bare skin as the conscience allowed. At least Sarah was becoming accustomed to the heat. The lack of humidity made the air less heavy than Missouri's.

For an hour she strolled along the walks, finally dropping into the registrar's office, where she asked for a catalog, in case she found time later to enroll in a course or two. She found a shady bench and leafed through the catalog but found she could not fasten her mind to the information in the text.

She thought of her encounter with Shirley and smiled ruefully to herself. She felt like someone who has escaped, but only temporarily, some catastrophe. For the moment, Shirley DeBrese was mollified, even disarmed. Perhaps she would not create another spate of fireworks in the shop. But how could one be sure? Oh, how right Maureen had been when she arranged to keep Shirley the minor partner. Sarah was the managing partner, with the right to override Shirley if necessary. The actual financial arrangements, distribution of profits after expenses, would be computed by the accountant Mr. Gamble had recommended. But personality clashes could not be guarded against, and Sarah could not take it for granted that each time Shirley's feathers were ruffled they could be as easily smoothed as today. Not even—she felt wicked laughter bubble inside—if she continued to use Trist's name as a talisman. She had overdone that today, triggering a jealous reaction in Shirley.

"Oh, John, I owe you an apology," Sarah murmured, standing to walk to a nearby phone booth and call a taxi. The remarks Trist had made on Sarah's first evening in town, to the effect that Shirley's interest in the business might be only fleeting, seemed much more reasonable now. In fact, they shone as a ray of hope!

As Sarah slid into the taxi and gave her home address, she wondered what new surprises this day could bring.

She was preparing a light meal—salad and a broiled chop—when she learned the answer to that question. The phone respectfully demanded attention. Sarah reached for the receiver, and divided her attention between it and the broiler.

"Yes?"

"Sarah, it's Sam. Please don't hang up."

For a moment she could not reply, her mind taking refuge in the judicious and unnecessary turning of her lamb chop.

"Sarah?" The phone transmitted the uneasy rising of his voice. She sighed, shut the oven door, and turned off the broiler.

"Yes, Sam, what is it?"

"I—I want to apologize. For the other night."

"All right. No hard feelings. Now, you'll have to excuse me. I have an appointment—"

"You're going out?"

Annoyance kept Sarah from replying directly to his question. "Sam, it was nice of you to call, but I really must go now."

"Is it the same guy? Brandt?"

Sarah was human enough to feel a slight, quickly squelched sense of pleasure at the naked jealousy in his words. "Larry Brandt and I are acquaintances," she said evenly. "It really is no concern of yours, as I'm sure I needn't remind you. By the way, how did you get my number?"

He was silent for a moment. "I persuaded your aunt to give it to me."

"I see. Well, I'm very busy, so I'm going to have to hang up, Sam. Thank you for calling." She ruthlessly ignored his splutter of protest and laid the receiver in its cradle. The phone rang again almost immediately. She lifted the receiver, broke the connection, and laid the receiver aside. Probably Sam would have too much pride—and anger—to try again tonight, but she had no wish to have her dinner interrupted again, just in case.

The rest of the week was hectic and challenging, as the renovation was swiftly and competently completed by the workmen. Attractive new display cases were moved in, shelving installed, and the beautiful new merchandise was brought out of the supply room and arranged. The office was still a mess but taking shape rapidly, and Sarah was delighted with the extra space she would have. Thankfully, Shirley DeBrese did not reappear. Charlotte found time from classes and studying to assist Sarah, so things went as smoothly as possible.

Sarah's time was filled to overflowing. She scarcely bothered to eat. Maureen suggested that she hire someone to clean the apartment twice a week, because she feared Sarah was overdoing. Secretly, her niece continued to do most of her own work at night, because she was too restless to sit and too tired to go out.

Larry Brandt called regularly, and Max Gamble had asked for a date far enough in advance that Sarah had no real excuse to decline. She was to attend a small dinner party with him on Saturday night, to Maureen's pleasure.

"Darling, he's one of the most popular young bachelors in town. He's respected in his profession, and he's being mentioned as a possible candidate for the state legislature. You ought to feel flattered at his interest. He's what we used to call a catch!"

Sarah had smiled and nodded. "He seems very pleasant. I'm sure I'll enjoy the evening."

But deep down she was not really so sure. Not that she did not find Max Gamble attractive. He was a handsome man, well dressed, successful. He was undeniably intelligent and on his way up in the world.

To be honest, Sarah was uneasy about dating anyone just yet. The evening with Larry Brandt had certainly not turned out well. And perhaps her uncertainty was caused in part by fatigue. The rush of work necessary to get the shop ready left little time for rest.

At least the shop seemed to be coming together quite well. Already she had bought a great many handcrafted items, in every category. To her pleasure she would even be able to display several of her original fashion designs for evening and sports wear. Charlotte had rounded up not one but three seamstresses, one of whom proved a genius at capturing the original sketches in patterns. The final results were so good that Sarah was delighted.

Sarah even managed to make one of the designs herself, during a night when she could not sleep. It was a caftan, solid white, a heavy, silky fabric bordered at the hem in bands of turquoise and black, the wide sleeves similarly trimmed. It was simple and quite stunning.

Sarah had ordered labels—Originals from Sarah—to be sewed into every garment. She was proud of the perky mannequins she'd purchased, one of which now wore Sarah's design in white sailcloth shorts and red halter piped in white that featured one bare shoulder. Among the other fashions ready to be shown were several bright, cool tops; shirts to be worn tails-out with jeans, caught in with charming bright belts; and two skirts appliquéd with bright flowers. There were two evening outfits that were young and casual enough to appeal to the college crowd: long, cotton-blend skirts with flounced hems, and bodices that combined a demure country-girl look with something more sophisticated. The window would display one of these in a diminutive blue and green print and white eyelet lace. The puff-sleeved bodice was tucked and eyelet trimmed, with an off-the-shoulder ruffle. One of Ward's necklaces, natural nuggets of turquoise strung on an intricately twisted, heavy silver chain lay upon the mannequin's neck.

In the same window display were a hand-knitted fringed shawl in baby-soft yarn of a corresponding blue. Next to the mannequin a new volume of photographic works in color, done by a famous Southwestern photographer, lay open upon an antique piecrust table Sarah had found at a secondhand shop and had hired a student to refinish.

The other display window held two small paintings, several hardcover books, both fiction and nonfiction, and a hand-painted ewer and basin by a senior citizen who did exquisite china painting.

The showroom of the gift shop held the treasures Sarah had been able to collect, but they were uncrowded, carefully displayed to offer the best advantage to each.

Sarah's ads, something she had worked on with all the experience she possessed, were running in the Las Cruces *Sun-News* beginning today, announcing the opening of La Casa Encantada under new management.

By Friday noon Sarah's work was done. The shop was ready. Though she nervously racked her brain and paced about the showroom again and again inspecting everything, she could find nothing more to do.

With something like disbelief she realized that the afternoon, marvelously, was hers to use as she wished.

She lunched with Maureen, after showing her what work and imagination had wrought with the store premises. Her aunt's approval of the new look of the shop was wholehearted.

At their table at Sambo's, Maureen lifted her iced-tea glass in beaming salute. "Here's to the future of La Casa. May you know all the success you deserve, Sarah!"

Sarah felt a thrill of excitement that made her breathless. "Thank you. Oh gosh, it's scary, now that the shop is ready to open and I'm about to find out once and for all if I've guessed right."

"I'm certain you have. There are never any guarantees in business, but I'll be very surprised if your beautiful craft items don't sell tremendously well. I don't know of any store in this town that offers items that are more imaginative and creative. And you have a distinct advantage in knowing the advertising game. By the way, your ad for the opening is very clever."

Sarah smiled, then bent her head, pretending interest in her salad. "Maureen," she began, hesitated, and at last looked up, gray eyes darkening with unreadable thoughts. "Have you heard from John Trist?"

Maureen's eyebrows raised. "My dear, that's the second time you've asked that the past week. Do you need to contact him? I thought all his legal arrangements in connection with the shop were completed before he left town."

"Oh yes, of course." Sarah grasped for a logical excuse. "It's just that I need to find Shirley DeBrese. She came in a few days ago to the shop. But I haven't seen her since. I really think she should know about the opening. I don't know where she lives, and her number is unlisted. I'm sure John would have it."

"Oh, I see. Well, I haven't talked to him, and I'm not sure if he's here or still in the southeastern part of the state. But you can get Shirley's number from Max Gamble, I imagine. He should have it."

"Yes. I hadn't thought of that. I'll call and ask him." Involuntarily, she sighed, feeling foolish that she had inquired about John Trist like a schoolgirl with a crush. *Why* must he haunt her thoughts? At night, trying to sleep, she found herself comparing him, as an eighteen-year-old, with the man that he had become. Mentally, she replayed each of their conversations, embarrassed at remarks she had made. She must have made a very negative impression on John Trist. Certainly he'd made no effort to see or get in touch with her in days, and that should be ample evidence that she was no part of his thoughts. And why should it be otherwise?

John Trist was a very busy man. With the responsibilities of his ranch, his farm businesses, his lecture schedule for the university, and of course with his relationship with his fiancée, why would Mr. Trist spare more than a passing thought to Sarah Wingate, scarcely more than a casual acquaintance? It made Sarah more than a little exasperated with herself that she must continually try to submerge reminders of the tall, quiet-voiced man she had met only a handful of times.

CHAPTER EIGHT

Finishing her light lunch, embarking determinedly upon a different topic of conversation, Sarah resolved once more to be more in control of her subconscious. Maureen insisted on paying the check. On the way out of the cool restaurant, she asked how Sarah planned to spend her rare afternoon of leisure.

"I have an appointment to have my hair done." Sarah fished in her handbag for car keys. "It's the first time I could spare an hour in weeks. And then—I think I'll relax at home with a book."

Maureen nodded approval. "Do you a world of good. Well, I must get back to the office."

Sarah drove to the salon, in a downtown shopping center. She sank into the chair, enjoying the luxury of the hairdresser's expert attention to her long hair. The beautiful, friendly girl, Mercedes, trimmed Sarah's hair swiftly. She washed and blow-dried it, and deftly arranged a softly waving style that fell past Sarah's shoulders, caught back on one side with a jade-inlaid comb that was a recent luxury Sarah had bought. It was an uplift to her spirits to see the pleasing results in the mirror.

Sarah lingered a half hour longer in the shopping mall, splurging on a pair of shoes and a new dress, a crisp cotton sundress in sunlight yellow with a short jacket piped in white. The cheerful color would strike the right note at the opening tomorrow.

Stepping out of the shadowed interior of a department store into the glaring afternoon sunlight, Sarah made her way across asphalt so hot it felt soft and slightly sticky underfoot. She walked quickly toward her car, pausing only to let a Volkswagen pass. Shifting her packages, she moved to the row where her Mustang was parked.

"Hello, Sarah."

Sarah glanced up, startled. Leaning against her car, hat tilted to shade his eyes, arms comfortably crossed, was John Trist.

Sarah felt a thump of some nervous reaction in her throat at sight of him, obviously waiting for her, seeming perfectly at home in the heat. She took a deep breath and tried to squash down the gladness that kept welling up in her chest. She felt unsteady, but perhaps it was the shock of the sun's power after the refrigerated air in the stores. At the sight of John she had halted. Now she made herself move briskly toward him. He straightened, and pushed his wide-brimmed hat back, his attention so closely upon her that she felt surrounded, pulled toward him.

"Why, John," she said with careful lightness, "how nice to see you. Why are you standing out here in the sun? You'll roast."

"Didn't want to miss you after I finally located your car," he said, his smile doing perfectly catastrophic things to her composure. "Besides, I'm used to the heat." His deep blue eyes were so warm and direct that Sarah's breath shortened. She took refuge in a search for her keys, embarrassed when two of her parcels slithered from her grasp and hit the pavement.

Quickly, he picked up the things she'd dropped, holding them silently until she managed to unlock the car door. But she thought she could feel his amusement.

"You—were looking for me?" she asked inanely.

"Yes. I called Maureen. She made a guess that you'd still be here at the mall. I found your Mustang, but I was sure if I tried to locate you inside, you'd escape me."

"Escape?" Sarah struggled against a sudden foolish happiness that made her thoughts race off in ridiculous directions, pursuing images and fantasies that included this man and herself. She grasped at her wobbling sense of reality and began again. "What did you need to see me about?"

He looked down at his boot toe thoughtfully, as if expecting it to supply an answer. His head swung up, eyes unreadable under the hat brim, revealing only a sparkle that might have meant anything in the depths. "Maureen says your shop is opening tomorrow. I'd like to see it."

She could not conceal her pleasure at his interest. Her eyes lighted with enthusiasm. "I'd love to show you. Would you care to follow me there now?"

"I'd follow you anywhere," he grinned, and her heart rocked alarmingly. She warned herself sternly not to reveal the effect this man had upon her.

"Wait," he said. "Leave your car here and come with me. I'll bring you back to your car later."

Agreeing, she locked her parcels in the trunk and walked fast to keep up with his long stride along the rows of vehicles, startled a bit when he caught her arm strongly and pulled her against his side as a pickup roared past.

John stopped before a white, open-topped Porsche.

"I thought you drove a Jeep!" She stared at the sleek little sports car.

"Usually. This trinket was a gift to me, believe it or not. My older sister is married to a Texan who has difficulty spending all his money, and he's fantastically generous. My brother-in-law has been encouraging me to get what he calls 'classy' transportation. I didn't take the hint, so he presented me with this, last Christmas. It's about as impractical as a car can be, and I confess I love it. The men at the ranch kid me about getting too 'uptown' for my own good. One of them fastened a gigantic pair of long horns he bought in Juárez, Mexico, on the front grill. Darn near pulled the car over on its nose. I had a time getting the things off, while my men stood around laughing like fools. Here, jump in."

Sarah slid into the bucket seat. He came around and got in. The engine started with a deep, smooth purr. Expertly, he backed and whirled the powerful, sleek little car out of the parking lot.

"I met your fiancée," Sarah said abruptly.

He jerked a glance at her, unsmiling. He looked back at the street, passed a car before replying. Then his tone was casual. "So Shirley finally made an appearance."

Sarah nodded ruefully. "Yes. I'm afraid she was—a trifle upset."

"Yes? What exactly was the problem?" She noticed that he did not seem surprised.

It was difficult, Sarah found, to condense that scene into a brief form. "I suppose the main point was that she felt white paint on the ceiling was too ordinary. She complained that she had not been consulted about the decor."

"I see," he murmured expressively. "Did she wreck the place? I'll pay for any damage."

"Of course not! You're joking, aren't you?" She studied the side of his face, but he seemed perfectly serious.

"Her feelings were hurt, I guess," Sarah continued. "I managed to soothe her. But I think I ought to confess something to you. I told her a —a small fib."

He swung the car into the parking lot of La Casa Encantada and stopped near the quarry tile walk.

Lazily, he turned toward Sarah and regarded her with interest, eyes lingering on her face so long that she felt warmth rising to her cheeks. Casually, he lifted her hand, turned it over as if examining it, stroking her palm gently with his forefinger. A shiver of delicious feeling moved in a languid current through Sarah's arm and slid down her spine, shivering outward in circles, like a whirlpool that drew her down, and down . . .

"What fib was this?" he asked.

She cleared her throat. "I told her that you had approved the color of the paint and had matched the paneling to her hair."

He gave a startled choke of laughter. "Her hair? You little witch! That was quick thinking. Did it solve the problem?" He ran the tip of his finger down one of her fingers, up the next.

Sarah's breath was unsteady. "More or less. She let me buy her a cup of coffee."

"I'm sorry if she gave you trouble. I'm beginning to wonder if I did you a disservice, loaning Shirley money to buy into your business."

"I'm sure we can work everything out. Actually, I rather liked Shirley." Somewhat to her surprise, Sarah discovered that it was true. She had a feeling in her bones that Shirley was going to be the proverbial fly in the ointment sooner or later. But there was something appealing about her. Even her unconscious snobbery had no real malice in it. Her combination of temper and naïveté was original, at least. She was rather like a spoiled child who nevertheless possesses an irresistible personality.

"I don't think she's basically unkind," she mused, and was embarrassed to realize that she had spoken her thought, and that it could be construed as a criticism of the girl John loved.

"Not basically unkind. That's perfectly true." John's grin was wry. "Neither is a cyclone. But it has certain powerful effects on whatever happens to be in its path. I'm glad you like her, Sarah. Shirley can charm birds off trees, and she's certainly one of a kind."

"She's beautiful too. You're to be congratulated." Unaccountably, she felt her spirits droop. She pulled her hand away from the warmth of his. "You wanted to see the shop. Let's go in, shall we?"

Not waiting for John to come around and open her door, she slid out of the car and hurried to the entrance, pushing the key into the lock. The door opened on cool dimness. The windows were still covered. Sarah was nervously aware of John's presence, just behind her within the doorway. She switched on lights and moved briskly farther into the shop.

"Well, what do you think?" she asked, and turned to watch his reaction.

He was smiling as he looked around. "Sarah, you've amazed me. I can't believe the transformation in this place. You've done a tremendous job. Where did you find all these beautiful things? They're a far cry from the junk I saw here before."

Basking in his praise, Sarah watched as he moved among the cases, nodding approvingly at a display of hand-tooled leather purses and belts, giving a small whistle of respect at Cowley's selection of jewelry. He paused before a landscape of the Organ Mountains that Sarah had fallen in love with. It held a place of honor on the east wall. Hands on lean hips, long legs apart, he studied it.

"Sarah, I want that," he said. "Is it permitted to buy before the opening?"

She was taken off guard. "Why—I suppose so. I really hadn't expected that to sell, you know. It's here on commission from the artist, and I'm afraid it's frightfully expensive."

"I'd like to buy it—unless you don't think it's worth the price tag?"

Sensing that hidden amusement, she regarded him suspiciously. "Certainly it's worth it. I think back East it would bring more. It's a wonderful painting. I'd love to own it myself."

"With a recommendation like that, how can I resist it?" John brought out a checkbook and quickly wrote, handing the check to Sarah. She gazed at it, bemused.

"Well, what are you waiting for, lady? Let's see you ring it up."

Self-consciously, Sarah took the check to the sales counter. "Shall I wrap the painting for you?" she asked uncertainly.

"No, no. I'll leave it here on display until you have something to put in its place, shall I? I wouldn't want to ruin the effect you've achieved on that wall. Just put a 'sold' sticker on it."

"Thank you, John. You have the honor of being our first customer. This is very kind of you."

He frowned, and she was under no illusion at all that his annoyance was not real. "Kind! Sarah, don't be silly. I like the painting. What I want, I do my utmost to have."

As she came out from behind the counter, expecting him to step aside, he stood his ground. He had taken off his hat, laying it aside on a display table, and his dark hair fell vitally over his forehead. He put his hands on her shoulders, and she was arrested in mid-step, looking up at him. She was suddenly intensely aware of the strong bone structure of his thin face, the sun lines at the corner of his eyes, the quiet inner amusement always lurking in the depths of those eyes.

Sarah told herself that she should move firmly past him, push his hands away, stop this insane consciousness of his lean, strong body so near. She knew that it would be asking for trouble to linger under his touch. This moment did not belong to her.

But some strong, sweet spell controlled her. Here in the quiet shop, its windows screened away from the passersby, the traffic noises muted by thick adobe walls, it was as if they two had ventured into a place where such rules did not apply. At this moment there was no world outside the shop. And with John's big hands firm on her shoulders, and that recognition, that *question* in his look, there was no room for thought of Shirley DeBrese.

Breathless, entranced, Sarah stood still, unable to look away from his eyes. She knew before Trist bent his head that he was going to kiss her. She wanted that kiss so much that she rashly thrust all other considerations and cautions out of her mind.

Time slowed. John's mouth was firm, gentle yet demanding, coaxing her lips apart. His arms slid with aching slowness about her, pulling her hard against his tautly muscled body.

Sarah could have struggled. The voice of her conscience sounded a feeble protest at such reckless submission, but that voice was drowned in the surge of intense longing that was like nothing she had ever experienced, blocking all inhibitions for the moment the kiss lasted.

However, the moment was abruptly shattered into bright, echoing fragments. The slamming open of the shop door and an angry clashing of the little bells over it broke into the enchantment with the suddenness of an explosion.

Sarah jerked away from John to stand blinking helplessly at Shirley DeBrese, who glared at them from the doorway, hands clenched at her sides.

Shirley was dressed in brief red shorts and a minuscule halter. She looked very young, her perfect tanned legs long and slim. She let out a screech that might have been heard blocks away. "Why you—you sneaky little cat!" she cried, running to clutch at Sarah's hair, and actually getting a painful grip on it before John grabbed her hand and forced it open.

"Shirley, stop it!" he ordered, and to Sarah's astonishment and resentment, he was chuckling.

"I—I'm sorry, Shirley," Sarah began helplessly, John was struggling to hold Shirley away from her. Shirley was hissing and spluttering, shrieking accusations at Sarah.

"Just what I should have expected!" she shouted. "The minute I turn my back, you try to move in on my property, you floozy!"

" 'Floozy'?" John laughed outright. "Where did you learn a word like that? Shirley, settle down! I think it's time and past you did some explaining—"

"Explain?" shrilled the redhead. "She's the one who should explain. I knew it—the first time I looked at her deceitful, conniving face I knew what kind of person she is—" Abruptly, Shirley stopped struggling and produced those remarkable, on-cue tears.

Seeing that she had subsided, John let her go. She stood rubbing her wrists, eyeing Sarah balefully through the moisture spilling from her blue eyes.

"There's something you'd better understand, Shirley," John said quietly. A new severity in his tone made Shirley swing around to face him, looking suddenly penitent and alarmed. The furious red was leaving her face, to be replaced by mottled white. "I'm not property." John said. "Shirley, I want you to apologize to Sarah, and I want you to tell her—"

With odd haste Shirley interrupted, words bubbling urgently from her lips. "All right, all right! I'll say I'm sorry. I shouldn't have overreacted. I'm sure what I saw was—was just a friendly kiss." Fresh temper flared and was quickly subdued in her eyes. The tensely poised young woman seemed ready to explode again, but she kept her voice humble. Sarah was sure this was as artificial as the tears. "Isn't that right, John? It was just a friendly kiss, wasn't it?"

Sarah was speechless with embarrassment and remorse, and neither was lessened when Shirley suddenly burst into loud wails of distress and flung herself into her fiancé's arms.

Quickly, Sarah caught up her handbag and left the shop.

"Sarah, wait!"

Ignoring John's command, she ran across the parking lot. Trembling, she hurried to the street and began to walk rapidly in the direction of her apartment. Her car was many blocks distant, in the shopping center parking space. The heat was oppressive, the concrete walk hot even through the soles of her shoes. But perhaps the walk would help her to swallow the awful dismay that kept lumping into her throat, and the shame that overwhelmed her.

The moment she had shared with John Trist meant nothing. But how could she have been so foolish as to let herself be drawn into a situation so potentially explosive? True, who could have guessed that Trist's girl friend would appear out of thin air and observe the embrace? Yet that was really no excuse for Sarah's behavior. It was wrong and stupid to become even minimally involved with a man who was already committed to another girl. It was one rule Sarah had never broken—until now.

After a couple of blocks taken at a fast walk, Sarah felt slightly better. The New Mexico sun blazed down from the pale turquoise bowl of sky as if nothing out of the ordinary had occurred. Traffic rushed by, shoppers came out of stores with their purchases. Everything was so relentlessly ordinary that it began to soothe her agitation. She felt almost in control of her feelings when she started to step off a curb and was halted by John Trist's sports car as it swept around the corner and stopped in front of her.

CHAPTER NINE

John leaned over and opened the passenger door, ignoring the honking of a disgruntled motorist who was forced to swerve around the Porsche. Sarah, rooted to the curb, stared helplessly at him, confused by his easy smile.

"Sarah, get in, please," he said.

"No thank you." She regained her poise. "I like to walk. My apartment is only a few blocks—"

"Get in. We're holding up traffic."

She opened her lips to protest further, but his smile made her feel that she looked foolish, arguing like a thwarted child. After an instant's hesitation, she slid into the seat, looking straight ahead.

"You shouldn't have followed me, John," she said evenly.

"What kind of man do you think I am, Sarah? Did you think I would let you walk in this heat when you were with me, by my invitation? Give me credit for more consideration than that."

"Your obligation is not to me, but to Shirley." Sarah was horrified to feel her eyes filling. She drew a deep breath, staring out at the scene the car slid past—commercial buildings, parks, homes—until the unwanted tears evaporated.

"Listen, honey, I'm really sorry about what happened back there," John said. "I wish Shirley hadn't said those things. I feel like kicking myself for putting you in an awkward situation. I had no idea Shirley would walk in."

"And if she hadn't walked in, would everything have been all right?" Sarah tried to keep her voice calm. "I can't blame Shirley for being angry. I had no excuse—" She faltered and bit her lip.

"To be in my arms?" he asked with startling matter-of-factness. "If I wanted you there, it seems to me you had every excuse."

It was very difficult to resist the things John's slow, reasonable voice did to her convictions, but Sarah made the effort.

"John, Shirley certainly should be able to expect—"

"Oh, love, please don't lecture me again on Shirley's rights!" There was submerged laughter in his voice now, and it made Sarah resentful, because she could not understand how he could laugh about something so serious.

"It shouldn't be necessary to lecture you. You should be aware of her rights."

"Oh, believe me, I am. It's impossible not to be aware of Shirley's rights. She would never permit it! Please, could we talk about this later? Shirley has some things she's promised—some things she wants to say to you—"

Involuntarily, she let out a groan, and lowered her face into her hands. "Yes, I'm sure she has! But I assure you, she can't say worse to me than I already have said to myself."

"Don't jump to conclusions. The thing is, I can't really talk about—" He stopped as if searching for a way to express himself. "Oh, damn!" he muttered at last. "To be fair, you'll have to hear what she has to say first. I know that seems—I'm not making a lot of sense. Listen, could we just table it for today?"

She glanced at him, puzzled again by the lively, if exasperated, amusement in his eyes.

"Well?" he said.

She was hopelessly confused by now. "What difference can it make? If you'll just take me to pick up my car—"

"Later. First, I want to kidnap you for a few hours. I'd like you to see my home."

Did surprises never end with this man? Sarah, who had been paying no attention to the turns he made and the streets they had taken, saw now that they were on the edge of town. John braked, then turned east, toward the Organs.

"John, no. I really ought to go home—"

"Nonsense. It will do you good to get away for a few hours. Stop worrying, Shirley knows I'm taking you to the ranch. In fact, she plans to drive out later herself. She had a meeting this afternoon. I promise you there is no deception involved."

Sarah stared at him. "Are you telling me that she approves, after seeing—" She could not finish.

He grinned crookedly. "Seeing our kiss? Didn't you hear her? She understands that you and I are just *friends*. She knows I like to show my friends the piece of ground that I love more than any spot on earth. We are friends, aren't we, Sarah? Old friends?"

He met her eyes in a long look, and for a dismaying instant her will was once more dissolved in a slow, sweet surge of feeling that left her heart pounding.

Quickly, she looked away and tried to regain a sense of equilibrium. "You're speaking of the time when you found me, lost in those mountains." She raised her eyes to gaze at the ramparts that rose above the highway several miles ahead and formed a gigantic barrier to the desert. At this time of day the colors of the massive cliffs were muted, but the stone spires were still awesome, reaching hungrily skyward. "I was surprised that you even remembered that event. So long ago, and it must have seemed all in a day's work for you," she said lightly.

"Was it all in a day's work for you?"

She shuddered. "No." She swallowed. "I still have nightmares about those few hours of darkness, when I was all alone up there. Why I did such a foolish thing, I'll never know. I can't tell you how frightened I was."

"But that's all you remember. You didn't remember the name of the raw college kid who happened along to take you back to civilization. Well, you were probably in a state of shock. No one would expect a scared little girl to hang on to details like that, years later—"

Neatly, he trapped Sarah into a betrayal of reserve. "Not remember? Of course I did, John Trist! Even a little girl can be grateful."

"Sure," he murmured, watching the road meditatively. "But after all, I was just a boy who rode out of the night, a face you'd never have recognized three weeks later."

"That not true!" She was indignant at the suggestion. "I remembered your face, though I only saw you for a moment. And of course I remembered your name, and I thought of you often as I was growing up—"

He shrugged. "Well then, you see."

"See what?"

He did not smile, but the smile was there in his eyes. "If you remembered, why wouldn't I? It really wasn't quite every winter night that we were called out to search for a lost child. I got lucky enough to find her, a little, scared skinny girl with big gray eyes, clutching a cold boulder as if it were her only friend.

"You can't imagine how worried all of the searchers were. We knew what those mountains are like. It had only been months since a college student tried a weekend of climbing. He stumbled, sprained an ankle— nothing more than a sprained ankle, Sarah! He wasn't found for two days. He was dead. Exposure—hypothermia. And that was a healthy, athletic man of twenty. He had a coat and proper boots—but the nights were colder than usual, and we found him dead."

John cleared his throat roughly. "So when we heard that a girl of ten was lost up there, you'd better believe every one of us took it seriously. We were praying you'd be found before it was too late. When I heard you, just a little, thin sound that might only have been the wind, I nearly jumped out of my skin! I was afraid I couldn't locate the source of that sound. Some lost kids are so frightened they'll even hide from the searchers. Then you answered my call—God, what a feeling!"

He turned to look at her again. She could see the wonder of that long ago moment in his face.

"And there you were, trying to be brave, assuring me you could walk, when you could barely stand. Somehow," his grin flickered, "you stuck in my mind. In fact—"

He hesitated, and she studied him, wondering what was going on in his mind. He slowed the car and turned off the highway onto an unpaved road that paralleled the mountain range, southward. "The truth is, Sarah," he continued slowly, "you changed my life more than a little."

She tilted her head, memorizing his face in profile, liking the strength of it, the shape of his jaw and the tanned column of his neck.

"I'm beginning to see that it wasn't an ordinary experience for you," she said. "But how could it have changed anything for you?"

He laughed shortly. "You'd have to know something about my life at the time. I'd lived always on this ranch, working with my dad's cowhands, working stock and repairing windmills and fencing, working the farms in summer alongside Dad's men. I was a college freshman that year and I'd drifted into the usual round of partying and skipping classes. Dad was worried about my grades. He talked to me about settling down to make the most of my classes."

"You were very young." Sarah defended the boy that he had been, and he smiled at that.

"Sure. And pretty damned foolish. But not too foolish to know my father was right. Still, there was the pressure of all my buddies, and the fun of dating one pretty coed after another—no thought of the future. I knew I needed to put on the brakes, spend more time studying. It was just so easy to go along with the fun, and so hard to make the effort to turn things around.

"Then that evening—I was home during that Christmas vacation, of course, though it was unusual for me to be having dinner with my family instead of out with my friends. Dad got news that a kid was lost in our area."

"And you found me," Sarah said unsteadily. "I wonder if I ever thanked you?"

"You didn't talk all that much, but your arms around my neck when you decided it was safe to trust me expressed your feelings quite adequately."

He reached to take her hand and squeeze it, and it was as if that long-ago boy and girl had touched once more.

John braked for a rough place in the road, his left hand steady on the wheel, driving with an easy confidence that seemed automatic with him. "The funny thing about it," he mused, "I'd never felt so good in my life as I did that night, bringing you back to safety. I guess I felt that I'd finally done something worthwhile. I liked that feeling. When I went back to school the next month, I chose my classes carefully, and I began to put my mind to work. Some of my friends wrote me off. They couldn't understand my change of attitude. But I made new friends who had some idea why they were working toward a degree. And I got interested in questions that I'm still trying to find answers to today. So," he smiled, "it's really not so remarkable that I remembered the little girl who made me straighten out my life."

"I—I don't think I know what to say." Sarah laughed. "When Maureen mentioned your name, I wondered if you could be the same person. I knew as soon as I saw you that you were."

"Don't tell me I haven't changed!"

"Don't tell me *I* haven't!" Their laughter was warming.

The car was approaching a grove of trees, the only large trees Sarah had seen since passing through Organ. As they drew nearer, she could see a house, whitewashed and roofed in red tile, a big square comfortably backed against a hill. John swung the sports car into a drive and stopped in front of the entrance, a wide porch and a door built of heavy, carved wood that looked very old and very solid.

The windows were protected by lacy iron grillwork, and there was a patio gate set into the wall midway along the width of the house. Sarah learned later that the house was built around this square of patio.

"It's a charming place," Sarah exclaimed.

"The exterior hasn't changed much in a hundred and fifty years, since a Spanish hidalgo from Mexico built it," John observed. "His son sold the land, the herds, and the house that had sheltered his large family and a lot of servants to my great-grandfather. Señor Chavez wanted to go back to Mexico—too many gringos in the area. It was still territory then, hadn't been granted statehood. But cowmen and settlers were pouring in from other states. My own family came from Virginia."

He held open the door; Sarah stepped inside the house, her heels clicking on the terrazzo floor. Adobe walls, which John told her were several feet thick, insulated the interior amazingly well against the dry afternoon heat. The entrance hall they stood within was shadowy and comfortably cool. John walked to an archway and shouted down a hall. "Melba, we're home!"

Immediately, her happy voice preceding her, a tall, attractive lady of perhaps sixty, with thick, graying blond hair in a twist at the top of her head, came hurrying toward them. She was dressed in jeans and a plaid shirt, and her neat figure showed that here was a healthy, active woman.

"John, I didn't expect you until tomorrow! I'm so glad you're back. Did you have lunch, dear? I can get something ready in a jiffy—"

"No, no." He laughed. "We will have dinner here." He ignored Sarah's gasp of protest. "Shirley will be joining us," he added hastily, with a sidewise glance at his companion. "Melba, this is Sarah Wingate, a friend of mine. Sarah, Melba Cellars, my housekeeper and friend. Melba, I'm going to show Sarah around, but if you have some iced tea or lemonade—"

The smiling woman came forward with hand outstretched and greeted Sarah warmly. "So you're Sarah! Well now, I'm thrilled to meet you!"

Surprised by the welcome, Sarah glanced at John and was in time to catch a faintly sheepish look in his eyes.

"Why, thank you, Mrs. Cellars," Sarah managed.

"John, I declare she's just a lovely as you—"

John interrupted her a trifle loudly. "Did you say you have some tea, Melba?"

"Oh—why certainly, John. Take Sarah into the *sala* and I'll bring it right away."

She hurried back along the hall. Sarah turned thoughtfully frowning eyes on her host, wanting to ask why his housekeeper seemed to have recognized her name. But he was already leading her by the hand toward a door that opened into a large, rectangular room with a huge open fireplace at one end and double glass doors leading onto the patio. These last were of modern design and must have been added long after the old house was built.

Trist glanced at Sarah. "Well, how do you like it?"

Sarah looked around at the room, which held an attractive mix of well-styled modern couches upholstered in rust crushed velvet and antique chairs and tables whose massive wood frames must have been painstakingly constructed and carved by Spanish workmen long ago. There were bright Navajo rugs on the polished terrazo floor, and hung here and there on the white plastered walls. Heavy beams stretched across beneath the ceiling, and they too were charmingly carved with stylized vines, flowers and birds. These carvings were painted blue and green and yellow, faded and softened by time. Beautiful paintings hung on the white walls, a variety of styles and subjects.

"It's a charming room, John. I see why you love this house."

"Mi casa, su casa," he said, with a sweeping gesture of one long arm.

Sarah smiled. "I beg your pardon?"

"My house is your house," he translated. "It was the standard greeting to guests among the courtly old Mexicans."

"What a charming custom." She went to look out into the sunny patio.

He followed and swung open the door, so that for a moment she stood with her back touching his broad chest. Nervous at his closeness, she stepped out, down two shallow steps and onto the thick, well-kept grass. There were flowers of every color here, both annuals and perennials, and they had been tended by a loving hand. Oleanders bloomed beside the outer gate. When Sarah complimented the flowers, John gave Mrs. Cellars the credit.

"She's been our housekeeper since before my mother died, ten years ago. She helped nurse Mother. And she was here when Dad's plane went down in Mexico two years ago. I don't know what I would have done without her. She's more than an employee; more than a friend. She's like a member of my family."

Sarah could hear the sadness under John's words when he spoke of his parents. She was grateful when Mrs. Cellars appeared and his thoughts were brought back from the past. Melba carried a tray with a pitcher of amber liquid and frosty glasses filled with crushed ice.

"Thank you, Melba," John said, taking the tray from her. "Didn't you bring a glass for yourself? Get one and join us out here."

She patted him fondly on the arm. "No dear, thank you. I've got a project that needs tender loving care in the kitchen, and I promised Miguel I'd come by and read to old Mrs. Samora later. You know she gets lonely, with Roberto and Juan at Ruidoso Downs with your horses."

"All right, Melba. Give Mrs. Samora my love."

Mrs. Cellars flitted away after one more smiling, frankly curious glance at Sarah.

They sat in lawn chairs near a climbing rose covered by deep scarlet blossoms. The tea was delicious. Sarah leaned back and willed herself to relax. It was easier than she might have expected, for this quiet, peaceful place lulled the senses. There were birds happily busy in the cotton-woods high overhead, and a light breeze disturbed the leaves, making them slap softly against one another. Melba's flowers lent a seductive fragrance to this enclosed space. It was a refuge, safe from the world.

For a while they talked quietly of commonplace things. As if by unspoken consent they avoided any subject that might be provocative. John seemed different somehow, here in this place where his family had lived and worked for generations. Sarah thought the influence of those people from his past was almost tangible enough to see and touch within these very old adobe walls that had sheltered them all.

As the afternoon faded into evening, John showed Sarah around the old house, through rooms that had scarcely been altered throughout a century and a half. The Trist women had wisely kept the best of the antique pieces of furniture, and had added other fine examples, turning to more modern furniture where comfort could be added.

They paused before yet another wide, carved door. "This is my suite," John said. "I hope Mrs. Cellars has done her usual magician's act restoring order in my rooms since I slept here last."

He ushered her inside a comfortable sitting room that apparently doubled as an office, judging by the big desk at one side, filing cabinets attractively concealed by custom-made cabinets in woods that matched the other furniture in the room. The desk was mahogany, far from new, and looked much used. The room opened onto the patio, and another door opened into John's bedroom, where a massive, carved bed frame dominated the room. The drapes and bedspread were a deep gold, heavy, woven cotton. The color was picked up in a large painting that portrayed autumn foliage of cottonwoods and salt cedar along a desert barranca, or gully. It was an excellent painting, tastefully framed.

Sarah stood before the painting for several moments. She could almost feel the hot sun, the desert breeze that lifted the red sand in a spiral of dust. She turned away, still bemused by the painted scene.

Somehow the room was not what Sarah would have expected, though what that might have been, she could not have said. It had a feeling of masculine austerity, yet the gold spread and painting lent warmth and comfort, as did the well-filled bookshelves, the bright rugs, the cosiness of the little whitewashed, rounded corner fireplace.

"Did you choose the decor of these rooms?" she asked John, who leaned against the doorframe, watching her lazily.

"First tell me if you approve," he grinned. "If you do, I might take the credit. I picked the furniture actually, but Melba found the drapes and spread. I bought that painting in Phoenix several years ago."

"It's a good room, very restful." She crossed the room to the door. "I sense that same feeling throughout the house, as if one might slow down here, might be—patient for whatever life can bring."

She started to pass him. He stopped her, placing his fingers under her chin, tipping her face up as if to see her more clearly. "That's interesting, Sarah." Soberly, he studied her. "It's exactly how I feel about this place. It's why I come back to it, always, to rest after my skirmishes with the world."

Sarah's breath quickened at his touch, and she stepped hastily away. "I'm sure Shirley loves the place too, doesn't she? It's like being snatched completely out of the world, yet in reality you are near enough to the city to commute easily."

John's mouth twitched, as if something she had said was comical. "Actually, she's not particularly fond of the ranch. In fact, you might say she considers it the end of the earth. I'm a little surprised that she volunteered to come out here this evening."

Sarah's lips opened on a question. Shirley had 'volunteered'? But wasn't she invited? Resolutely, she avoided voicing her curiosity. None of that was her business. She turned to cross John's sitting room to the hall door.

"Running away again?" he asked, with heartstopping tenderness.

She half turned. "I—I don't understand what you're talking about," she said.

She wondered if he intended to touch her, to take her into his arms again, and hated herself for wishing he would do just that.

But he merely stood there, looking at her as if memorizing her features, every detail of her face. "Yes, you understand," he laughed softly. "You're running from yourself, and from me. Can't you see it won't do any good? Some things are meant to be."

Sarah found it difficult to catch her breath. "John," she began uncertainly, "this is not—I can't—"

Unwilling, she turned her head, met his eyes. His look was a caress, and she wanted to step nearer to him. Resolutely, she stayed where she was, her mind filled with conflicting thoughts that darted and flashed like swallows at dusk. Could this be happening? In spite of all her best intentions, all her precautions, was she falling in love with this man, even though he belonged to another woman?

Surely it was only a rebound from her broken engagement. Even as she thought it, she knew it was not true. When had Sam ever made her feel like this, made her helpless before her emotions, with this roller coaster sensation? When had Sam made her long for him so—so crazily!

But it was all wrong. She could not allow herself to be drawn into this kind of relationship, no matter how hard her unruly heart and body struggled to be set free from the restraints of conscience.

"John," she said desperately. "This can't happen." She felt incoherent and foolish.

"Sarah, there are things you don't understand," he said slowly. "Things about me, about my life. But this much you can believe. When I set my heart on anything, I don't give up."

He touched her hair lightly, and she felt a tiny, explosive shock throughout her innermost self. She could not speak.

"I don't allow anything to stand in my way," John said softly.

CHAPTER TEN

Abruptly, he moved past her to the sitting-room door. Sarah followed, to step into the corridor. She could not look at him directly, and she tried to ignore the magnetism of his nearness as he held the door open for her.

John led her along the corridor and outside by way of a side door.

"Where are we going?" she asked as he helped her into the Jeep.

"We still have time before dinner for you to see the stables."

"Oh yes, I'd like that. I love horses."

He climbed in and sent the Jeep over a lane that led a short distance from the house to a sprawling complex of metal corrals and large buildings of sheet metal painted white with a red trim. They passed pens that held cattle, and one with sheep. The Jeep moved past these to the last building.

John brought the vehicle to a stop and came around to extend his hand to Sarah. She was already on the ground, looking around her with curiosity. A man in jeans and plaid shirt and Stetson rode past on a big dun horse, and he tipped his hat and called a greeting.

They walked inside the wide central door into the stable. There was a corridor that ran completely through to a similar door at the far end. At either side there were stalls, and from several, horse's heads extended curiously. At this end of the building there were tack and supply rooms where saddles, blankets, all kinds of complicated-looking bridles and hackamores, ropes, and horse blankets were kept.

Another room had a refrigerator for medications, and shelves and boxes of preparations for the treatment of horses. Through another door Sarah glimpsed an area that John explained was used by the veterinarian for dressing complicated wounds and even surgery, with a tilting operating table to which a horse could be secured while on his feet, then lifted into position for treatment.

"We have our own resident vet," John said. "He's away today."

Sarah was glad to leave the clinic. "Are your horses ill that often, that you must have full-time medical care for them?"

"We raise registered quarter horses, some for racing, others for show or stock work. You'd be amazed how many ways highbred horses can find to injure themselves and how many varieties of disorders they can develop. In the long run it saves money as well as discomfort for the stock to use preventive medicine and have help nearby in case of emergency."

"That makes sense."

"And then the mares in foal are a delicate lot. I lose considerably fewer foals now that Bob Dyke is with us. I depend on his good judgment so heavily that it makes me uneasy when he's away for any length of time. He's been on vacation in Alabama this week. Fortunately, none of the mares are due for a while, and before I left the ranch myself this time, we'd had only the usual sprains and strains from the practice track to deal with. Any of my horse handlers can do first aid on something simple."

They stepped into a room that was comfortably furnished, even carpeted. The furniture was shabby and evidently much used. There was a television set, bookshelves, a soft-drink machine. Magazines lay on tables. This was where members of the crew could spend spare time or coffee breaks or evenings when watch was being kept periodically on foaling mares. One wall was covered with glassed-in shelves displaying trophies and ribbons the horses had won in the past. On the other walls were hung large photos of horses, some after victorious races, wearing blankets that were prizes of those events. John stood with the jockey in some of these photos. In one or two appeared an older man and woman. It was not hard to guess their identity even before John spoke softly behind Sarah.

"My parents, a few years before Mother died. Dad had only been building up his racing string for a few years then. This was his first winner. I'll never forget how proud he was that day."

Something in his voice as he came to a sudden halt in his speech warned Sarah not to look around him until he had recovered himself. How he must have loved them, the sweet-faced woman, beautiful in late middle age, and the strong, tall man who was very like John.

Sarah moved silently to another photo. This one featured a magnificent dark chestnut stallion. A tall, laughing, dark-haired girl held the lead of his halter and proudly displayed a purple rosette. One of the Trist horses as winner of a halter competition, and even Sarah's untrained eye could see why this beautiful horse's conformation had won the competition.

"That's my sister, Eileen, and Bar Tristan, one of our best herd sires.

You'll like Eileen, she's special. Married now, and living in Texas with the crazy gent who gave me the Porsche."

"She looks so friendly. I hope I have the chance to meet her," Sarah said.

"She's going to be crazy about you. Wait until I tell her you're the wayward waif I snatched off the Organ Mountains. Eileen's a total and complete romantic. She'll understand—" He stopped with a low chuckle that said he'd warned himself away from something he'd been about to say.

The door of the room swung open. Two men, dressed in the inevitable dusty jeans, stepped in. "John!" The elder of the two stuck out a big, callused hand. He was a balding, freckle-faced man, and he removed his hat immediately at sight of Sarah. "Casey said you were back, John. You'll want to see how good that Reveille Bar colt's coming along. He's got a lot of speed. Can you come out to the practice track in the morning?"

"I'll be there," John promised. He turned to Sarah. "This is Carter Bell, my head trainer, and Joe, his son. Boys, this is Sarah Wingate, a good friend of mine, from Las Cruces. I'm showing her the plant."

The two cowboys murmured polite greetings, shyly courteous. But Sarah was disconcertingly aware that they studied her with very inquisitive, definitely friendly, eyes.

"You like horses, Miss Wingate?" Mr. Bell asked heartily. "John's got some beauties, good as any in the Southwest."

"I do like horses, but I confess I don't know a lot about them," Sarah smiled.

"I'm about to introduce her to some of my favorites before dinner. Have you boys eaten yet?" John asked. "Come up to the house with us. Melba's got something special cooking."

"Thanks, but we just came from the staff kitchen. We wanted to check on the bay two-year-old. We put a new sweat on that foreleg this afternoon. Swelling's down some. He ain't limping today."

"I'll look at him. You two go get some rest. José and Ramón are on duty now, aren't they? If the bay needs anything, they'll help me with him."

The two men went out, the younger one glancing back over his shoulder with a knowing grin that was obviously meant only for John, but Sarah could not help seeing. It made her self-conscious, wondering what these men must think of her presence with John. They knew that Shirley DeBrese would soon become the boss's wife. She hoped that they would accept John's explanation that Sarah was a friend, interested in the workings of the Trist horse farm.

"Let's go see the horses," John caught her hand. "I'll look at the bay first, and then I'll show you the others we have here. When I've been away for a few days, I have to come and get reacquainted again. Sometimes I wish I could concentrate solely on the horses."

"Why don't you?"

He grinned. "To be honest, the horses are something of a luxury, or at least it sometimes seems that way. We could make more money with less aggravation almost any other way. But I wouldn't part with them unless I'm forced to."

"And I had the impression you were a hardhearted businessman!" Sarah laughed up at him.

"I am! I insist you believe it." He bent to kiss her quickly, fleetingly. Sarah's heart turned over, and she had to pretend that his lips had not touched hers, plunging into lighthearted comments on nonprovocative subjects.

John found that Ramón had already tended to the young gelding with the strained tendon. New bedding had been spread in his stall, and fresh hay in his feeder. The leg was improving, and John clapped Ramón on the shoulder with gratitude. The young man grinned and went away to other chores.

One by one Sarah was introduced to sleek and spirited animals who thrust their heads out from their stalls at the sound of John's voice. With pleasure she ran her fingers over satiny, arched necks. John led out two of his favorites, turning them as if they were fashion models on parade, explaining to Sarah the good points of their conformation, answering her interested questions without impatience. She saw that he enjoyed talking about his fine animals. Sarah fell promptly in love with the beautiful geldings and mares she saw.

At last John glanced at his watch and gave a guilty whistle. "Uh-oh! I've made us late for dinner. Melba will be struggling to keep it from ruining."

"Will she scold us?" Sarah asked, trying to match his long stride as he left the stable.

"It has been known to happen," he admitted.

"Then perhaps we'd better run," Sarah suggested, but she was startled into laughter when John took her at her word, grabbed her hand, and ran along the central aisle of the enormous building. Sarah felt like a little girl again, carefree and happy.

John boosted her into the Jeep, and in moments they were bouncing along the road to the ranch house.

But it was not Mrs. Cellars who appeared upset at their tardy appearance. It was Shirley. The red-haired girl was pacing about the *sala*, nervously puffing a cigarette, very near the edge of another display of temper.

"I thought we agreed to meet here at seven-thirty, John," she remarked with ominous sweetness, her blue eyes narrowed, giving her small face a feline look. She wore a white jump suit of a clingy jersey material, trimmed with a golden sunburst of sequins on the left side of the bodice. Her hair was a fiery mass that quivered with her every movement or breath, as if with a life of its own.

"Did we?" John asked innocently, and to her dismay, Sarah detected that submerged amusement again, and waited hopelessly for another blast of fury from her business partner.

For some reason, Shirley chose to be magnanimous. She rearranged her threatening expression, and shrugged one elegant shoulder.

"I suppose you were out with those damned horses, weren't you?" She tapped the ash from her cigarette into a jade bowl that was not meant for an ashtray, and gave an indulgent laugh. "Sarah, John forgets everything when he's with his four-legged darlings. I've learned to expect it. Oh, I want you to meet Charley Corbett."

For the first time, Sarah realized that there was someone else in the room, a slender young man, very blond, with a soft beard. He was dressed in white slacks, a white turtleneck pullover, and a lightweight jacket in a blue that matched his eyes. His vinyl loafers were white. All in all, he was rather a gorgeous creature, with his regular features and practiced smile. His hair had been styled to lie across his forehead with a boyish look.

He had been sitting in a corner chair, but now he stood and came affably forward to shake hands with Sarah and then with John. Trist welcomed him as warmly as if he'd been invited. For an instant a frustrated look crossed Shirley's face.

As John was making polite conversation with his surprise guest, Sarah spied Melba in the next room and slipped away from the group to ask where she might wash her hands and face.

The motherly housekeeper showed her to an ultramodern bath at the end of a short corridor. Sarah heartily approved of the Trist break with the past in this area, and she admired the beautifully tiled room with one entire wall mirrored, soft carpet underfoot. It was stocked with every possible need that a guest might discover. Melba opened a cupboard to point out towels and scented soaps, even new toothbrushes kept for guests who might decide at the last moment to stay over at the ranch.

"Now, you just take your time, dear. Dinner will hold nicely," she said, and left Sarah to herself. Sarah closed her eyes for a moment, grateful for privacy and silence and a few moments to gather her thoughts.

She was aware of tension in her neck and back, the beginnings of a headache.

Sarah could not truthfully have said that she had not enjoyed these hours in John's company. At the same time, the emotions his nearness stirred up, and which she must continually fight, were exhausting. Somehow, she did not anticipate that dinner would be a very congenial meal. All in all, she found herself longing for her own quiet apartment.

Sighing, she renewed her lipstick and makeup quickly. She brushed her hair and tucked the comb back in place, then wiped dust from her dark blue slacks. Thankfully, her white shirt was not too crumpled. She gave herself a last, doubtful inspection in the mirror. She could not hope to achieve anything approaching Shirley's stunning appearance, but perhaps she was presentable. With a rueful grin at her reflection she went out to join the group.

Shirley gave a pointed glance at her watch as Sarah appeared, and a soft sigh of exasperation that made Sarah want to slap her. "Shall we go in?" Shirley caught John's arm, but he gently disengaged her hand.

"You're neglecting your date," he reminded.

"Charley? He's not—oh well—" With a less than gracious look she moved over beside the blond young man. John ushered Sarah into the dining room and seated her.

Sarah was so confused by this time as to what her proper place might be on this particular evening that she could only let herself be directed by her host. But she was very conscious of Shirley's hot stare between her shoulder blades.

Sarah was seated on John's right, and Shirley took the place at his left, so that Sarah could scarcely glance up without encountering Shirley's resentful, smoldering look.

The only relief she had came when Shirley turned her attention away and abruptly began a teasing, almost intimate conversation with Charley Corbett, seated beside her. Sarah was surprised that she would behave so, in John's presence, until she realized that Shirley was attempting to make John jealous, as she herself had been made jealous. Sarah felt her already unsteady sense of confidence slide another notch downward. Could that be the meaning of John's attention, the reason that he had insisted she come here with him? Was he trying to teach Shirley a lesson? Perhaps Shirley had been too difficult about his plans to continue living here after their marriage. . . .

But if that were so, what had John meant by his remarks earlier, that Sarah was running from him, and from herself, and that he would let nothing stand in his way . . . ?

She felt herself flushing and could not resist a quick glance his way. She found him watching her, with that suggestion of—knowing, in his eyes. He seemed completely unperturbed by Shirley's increasingly provocative remarks and suggestive movements against Charley Corbett's arm, even when she leaned over and kissed the blond man.

If John saw the kiss, there was no more than a flicker of amusement in his face. He must be supremely sure of his promised bride, Sarah thought with confused resentment.

"What's wrong, Sarah?" John asked softly. "You haven't eaten very much."

"I'm not hungry," Sarah murmured, and managed a bright smile that meant to say all was right with her own private world and this miserable evening could not touch her.

"Melba will be scrambling for new recipes," John predicted. "She was hoping to impress you."

Nothing else he might have said would have encouraged her to pay more attention to the delicious meal before her: tender roast beef, asparagus in a delicately flavored sauce, scalloped potatoes, hot rolls with a lovely, unusual flavor. Sarah bit into one of these and made a comment as to its excellence.

"Melba calls it ranch bread," John said. "I don't know anyone else who makes it, not even the crew's cook. Melba sends down enormous batches of these rolls to the boys every few days. They'd all quit if she didn't."

Sarah managed to make a respectable dent in her food, and by the time the dessert had arrived, marvelous apple pie topped with real whipped cream, she felt a little more in command of her situation.

A white wine had been served with the meal. Sarah noticed that both Shirley and Charley refilled their glasses often. The atmosphere lightened as Shirley became mellow and friendly to all, seeming to forget the pique she had displayed earlier. She even began to talk to Sarah and for minutes at a time was pleasant.

John was watching Shirley's friend with a faint frown between his dark brows. The man was becoming more than a trifle drunk. Surely he had not achieved this state on the dinner wine. He must have been well on his way when he and Shirley arrived at the ranch.

At last, they all left the table, and Sarah could not prevent a small sigh of relief. She pretended not to see the quick, amused glance John sent her way, and she did not walk beside him, but followed the others out onto the patio, where Melba was serving coffee. Charley staggered a bit. Shirley caught his arm, laughing up at him. Apparently, the elegant young man did not realize that he had had enough to drink, for he asked the housekeeper if she would give him brandy instead of coffee.

"That will be all, Melba," John intervened smoothly. "It was a great dinner, and we're all in your debt. Let Sally and Georgia clear up."

She gave him a fond smile, left the coffee tray on a table, and went back into the house.

Shirley had been whirling gracefully to music coming from the house. She had switched on the stereo as she passed. She stopped now, tilting her head like a kitten planning mischief.

"Are you forbidding your guests to make inroads on your liquor supply, Johnny darling?" she purred. "That's not very nice. You don't want Charley to think you're stingy. Never mind, Charley, I'll get it for you."

She hurried back into the *sala,* as if emphasizing her intimate knowledge of the place, and her special rights here. John did not look particularly pleased when she brought back a bottle and several glasses.

"Shirley, your gigolo has had enough," he said so quietly Corbett could not have heard. "He has to drive you back to town, don't forget."

"Don't be silly, I'm driving!" she retorted with brittle gaiety. "And if it worries you, I won't have anything more to drink. But let Charley have his fun. Don't be such a spoilsport, John!"

"Would you care to pour the coffee, Sarah?" John turned away from his fiancée, and his expression was hard to read.

Nervously, because surely this symbolic task ought to have been Shirley's, Sarah complied. She filled four cream and brown ceramic mugs. Only three were used, however, because Charley seemed happier with the brandy bottle.

Sarah wondered when she might gracefully ask to be taken home. It would not do to interrupt the evening for the others, if John should insist upon driving her himself. Perhaps if she suggested it, one of his employees could do that chore. Pondering the problem, she sipped her coffee, wishing she had her own car here, bracing herself for whatever the volatile Shirley would think of next.

But Shirley was behaving circumspectly now. She drank only coffee, and for the next half hour made uncontroversial conversation. Only an occasional nervous flicker of her eyes betrayed any inward tension.

Yet the tension was there, in Sarah if not in Shirley, and at last she felt that she could bear no more of it. She stood, setting down her cup.

"John, forgive me, I must be getting home. Tomorrow will be very busy, and there are still some things I need to do tonight. Could you have someone drive me back to Las Cruces to pick up my car?"

"I'll take you back, of course." He stood quickly.

"Why not ride back with me," Shirley offered. "Charley is out of it. I think I'll let him sleep it off here, if you don't mind, John, and I hate to go back alone."

He hesitated, glancing at Charley, who had leaned back in his chair and gone to sleep, snoring softly. "He can stay, of course, and I'll send him to town in the morning. But I'd prefer to drive Sarah back myself."

"John, it's silly to take two cars," Shirley insisted. "Besides"—she gave him a look that seemed to carry a message—"it will give Sarah and me a chance to talk."

"I don't think—" he began, but Sarah interrupted, accepting Shirley's offer. She had the feeling that if Shirley was thwarted in this, she would stage another scene, and it seemed too much to face after a difficult evening. If she allowed John to drive her home, Shirley would be sure her suspicions were correct. Somehow this explosive atmosphere that existed between Sarah and her business partner must be diffused.

There was no further chance for private conversation with John. Perhaps Shirley saw to that, though her chatter and her friendly, girlish linking of an arm through Sarah's seemed completely innocuous. In moments they were seated in Shirley's car, whirling along the graveled drive, with only one last touch of John's fingers on Sarah's—a businesslike handshake when Sarah thanked him for showing her the ranch house and stables—to be held warmly in her mind and remembered.

As soon as they were on the road, traveling too fast for the rough surface, Shirley's chatter ceased, and she was silent. Sarah would have been grateful to leave it that way. She was confused and tired. Today she had been thrust this way and that emotionally. She felt exhausted. Closing her eyes, she could see John's face. His words sounded over and over in her mind: "When I set my heart on anything . . ."

Shirley's voice, high and brittle, suddenly burst in on her thoughts. "I suppose John told you that I—that I want to talk to you."

Sarah sighed, and tried to prepare herself for what she knew was coming. "Yes, he did. But first, let me apologize for what you saw at the shop. I have no excuse. I don't know how that happened. I can only say I'm sorry—"

Shirley gave a laugh that sounded on the edge of hysteria. "Oh, that's funny, Sarah. You really don't know 'how that happened'? She took a curve with an uneasy slide of the sports car and seemed not to notice. "I think I can tell you how it happened, since you're so innocently bewildered about it all. You just kept throwing yourself at John until he took you up on it. What man wouldn't?"

Sarah drew in a sharp, aching breath. This was going to be even worse than she'd feared. "Shirley, please. That isn't true. I know how it looked, and why you would think that, but it wasn't that way. I can only repeat, I'm sorry."

Shirley was silent for a long moment, and Sarah felt that she was struggling within herself. Knowing the hurt the other girl must be feeling, she felt torn between her own distress and Shirley's. And behind it all, John loomed in Sarah's mind, their closeness and fun this afternoon. It was all too much!

Shirley tossed her hair as if with sudden, defiant decision. "John wanted me to talk to you," she said hoarsely. "He insisted that I clear all of this up with you."

"It isn't necessary. Of course, you have a right to say what you like to me. But why should *he* suggest that we talk?"

Shirley shifted gears violently as they turned onto the pavement. The car spurted westward through sparse traffic. "Oh, it's really very simple," she said in a high, strained voice. "He realizes that no man is proof against a determined campaign by someone like you."

Sarah turned her head in amazement, staring at the other woman, whose face was dimly illuminated by the dashboard lights. "That doesn't sound like John Trist to me," she snapped, her patience worn out. After all, she had apologized, even though the fault was not wholly her own. "You seem to be suggesting that John has asked you to protect him against me!"

"Oh, well—" Shirley's voice was small, defensive, as if she realized how ridiculous it was, put that way. "Well, believe what you like." She rallied to the attack again. "He did ask me to talk to you. He wants—" She hesitated, and the hesitation had a puzzling tension in it. Sarah got the impression that Shirley was making up her mind about something. When she continued, it was in a determined tone of voice.

"He wants me to tell you the kind of arrangement we have. He's got this stupid sense of fairness, even though whatever you get for trying to come between us is too good for you, as far as I'm concerned. It's like this, Sarah honey!" she sneered "Pay attention, and learn. John and I are going to be married. You can't stop that, even if you try. But he's a man, and he'll take what's offered. He and I agreed long ago that we would have a completely open relationship. I don't like it very much. I'm very possessive. But I did agree, and I'll stick to it. If John wants a little fun on the side, that's all right. But you'd better know it won't mean anything. I don't see why you deserve an explanation, but John thought you should understand the ground rules, since you and I are in business together."

Sarah was stunned. Surely the girl was lying. If John had wanted to put across such an insulting idea, why hadn't he said so himself? He didn't seem the kind of man to speak through someone else.

Yet he *had* mentioned that Shirley wanted to talk to her, implying that he couldn't say more until she had done so. In effect, he had endorsed what Shirley intended to say. And then during that few minutes in the bedroom, the things he'd said . . .

Could he have been suggesting the kind of arrangement Shirley was describing? Could he have been hinting that he would not deny himself an intimate relationship with someone he felt attracted to, even though he fully meant to marry another girl, who knew about and condoned her fiancé's casual encounters?

Sarah felt sick. What she was thinking did not fit with the impressions she had received from John, or the pleasant afternoon they had spent together. It did not sound like the kind of man she had believed he was. Could she have been so totally wrong about that? Had she been so completely misled by the flattering look in a man's eyes, the electricity of his touch?

Sarah fought against her own disbelief, reinforced by the image of John Trist, strong and vital in the shadows behind thought, those intent eyes sliding effortlessly past all her defenses. She would certainly not be the first woman to be beguiled by an experienced man. Somehow she must face this with open eyes. Anything else would be begging for heartbreak.

CHAPTER ELEVEN

Shirley's voice penetrated Sarah's aching thoughts. "Well, I just hope you understand now, Sarah. I can't stop you from making a fool of yourself. I suppose it was only fair to warn you, even if you don't deserve that much consideration."

She swung her car into the nearly empty shopping-mall parking lot where Sarah had left her car.

Unable to speak, Sarah jerked open the door, stumbled out, and went to her car. Without waiting until Sarah had unlocked the Mustang and gotten safely inside, Shirley accelerated out of the lot and into the stream of traffic.

Sarah slid into her car and sat for a moment, tears blinding her, holding tightly to the wheel. She felt incapable of the simplest decision, of movement.

But she could not sit here all night. She wiped her eyes, fumbled the key into the ignition, and started the engine. The drive of a dozen blocks seemed hours long.

Sarah was unlocking her apartment door when she heard her phone. She stepped inside, wishing the phone would stop. She hesitated, almost decided not to answer. But the pealing bell was insistent. At last, she picked up the receiver and was jerked into confusion at the sound of John's warm, quiet voice.

"Ah, you're home. I wanted to be sure. Shirley drives too fast. I really would have preferred to take you home myself."

Sarah swallowed, made her voice indifferent, cool. "We arrived without incident." (Except that I feel as if I'd been caught in an earthquake, and I'm wondering how I could have been such a fool.) "You needn't have been concerned. Good night, John." She started to put the receiver down.

"Sarah, wait!" He paused a moment, as if trying to understand something. "I seem to detect a frost warning in your voice. Have I offended you?"

With the matter thus bluntly in front of her, Sarah's tired mind presented her choices. She could embark upon a frank discussion of the entire matter, thus baring her own feelings and the extent of her emotional involvement. That seemed appalling. Or she could evade his question and simply remove herself from the field of battle for now. But that would only bring a short reprieve. It was better to end it now, surely, while she could still hope to retreat from the situation with some dignity.

"Mr. Trist," she said, "Miss DeBrese and I had the talk you—you requested, and now the situation is very clear to me. So you'll understand if I don't prolong our conversation. Good night."

Quickly, she hung up, knowing she had done the right, the honorable thing. Even if Shirley had not spelled out John's peculiar set of rules about his relationships with women, inevitably the time would have come when she must avoid any but the most casual contact with John Trist, because of his prior commitment to Shirley. It was silly to feel so unhappy now.

Sarah would not let herself give way again to the weak tears that kept trying to spill over. With an icy grip on her emotions she showered, took two aspirin tablets, and got into bed.

But sleep was long in coming. She could have blamed it on the streetlight filtering softly through the blind, although it had not disturbed Sarah on other nights. Or perhaps she was restless because the day just past had been hectic and unnerving. Indeed, the past weeks had been anything but peaceful and restful.

Sarah was too honest to lie to herself. These factors perhaps contributed to her sleeplessness. But they became insignificant before the one overwhelming factor. Sarah had been warned about John Trist too late. The feeling was already well rooted and growing in her heart. She might readily admit that it was wrong, and extremely foolish, to love this man. The fact was inescapable. She was in love with John, and there was no way to deny it to herself. Looking toward the future, she knew that it was going to take time to recover from this foolish attachment.

At last, toward dawn, she slept. When the alarm rang, she was unrested, and the memories of the night before were too painful to probe. But this was opening day for the shop, and she must put personal unhappiness aside for the moment. The thing to do was take a cool, stinging shower, drink a cup of strong, hot coffee, and try to rebuild her resolution.

The opening was an unqualified success. Sarah's carefully planned ad campaign bore gratifying fruit, as the shop was visited by an even greater volume of customers in the first day than she had hoped. For hours the crowd was constantly replenished by new, curious people enjoying the folk group she'd hired, registering for door prizes, and lining up for doughnuts and coffee in the parking lot. So many sales were made that she realized she would have to replenish stocks quickly.

Shirley attended the opening, wearing a pink dress. She might have stepped out of a stylish New York shop. Her earrings were small, natural gold nuggets swinging from fragile gold chains. Probably, Sarah reflected, it was word-of-mouth promotion among Shirley's friends that accounted for more than a few shoppers, and Sarah tried to be grateful for that. Shirley proved, surprisingly, to be a charming and persuasive salesgirl, even though Sarah suspected the other girl hardly realized she had stepped into that role. She seemed to enjoy people, the bustle of the crowd, the music—and one might have thought from her air of complacent pride that she was personally responsible for it all.

Sarah had deeply dreaded seeing her business partner after the events of the evening before, but from Shirley's behavior today, the rancor she had exhibited last night, her shattering revelation about John's views of love and life, might never have occurred. She was amazingly cheerful, even friendly. Sarah did not know quite how to respond to this new facet of Shirley's personality. For the moment, she was simply grateful for the pause in hostilities. It was more than enough to have to fight her own fatigue and depression.

With a determined smile, Sarah moved among the well-wishers and customers, making conversation which she prayed was sufficiently coherent to escape critical notice.

Maureen paused by Sarah for a moment at midafternoon, her eyes glowing proudly. "Darling, you've really done it. All these people will remember La Casa Encantada the next time they shop for a gift—or for something exciting for themselves! I bet half the things you've sold today will stay with the buyer. Especially the fashions—Sarah, they've cleared you out in that corner."

Sarah smiled. "I know. I have my seamstresses working on other things. And I have a new source of handmade vests and skirts, really clever designs. A high-school girl and two of her friends make them, and they have some ideas for scooter skirts. They're bringing in several things Monday."

"Don't neglect your own designs," Maureen advised. "You could have a career in designing alone, I believe."

A man paused near them, holding a small girl by the hand. "Pardon me, is one of you ladies the owner of this store?" He was looking at Maureen, who grinned mischievously.

"Well, yes," she began, as if she were about to claim the honor, then she gave a pert nod of the head toward Sarah. "This is the lady you're looking for, my niece, Sarah Wingate."

The man continued to look at Maureen however, approval in his nice brown eyes behind steel-rimmed glasses. He was graying at the temples, his unruly fair hair rumpled above a wide forehead. A big nose and a really charming smile completed his oddly attractive face. He was tall, burly of shoulder, and wearing a short-sleeved blue sports shirt and neat, beltless slacks.

Amused by his obvious interest in Maureen, Sarah supplied her aunt's name. "This is Maureen Dwight," she said. "May we help you, Mr.—"

"Cornelius, Paul Cornelius," he nodded. "And this is my granddaughter, Kim. Kim was hoping to find one of the Frontier Lady dolls you advertised. I promised to buy her one for her doll collection."

"Oh, come with me, Kim," Sarah smiled. She took the shy child by the hand and led her to the shelf where the little figures, dressed in handmade cotton dresses and sunbonnets, had been displayed. But they were gone, and Sarah was momentarily at a loss.

"They must have sold out. I'm sorry Kim. Let me think. I could order one specially made for you and have it in a few days. Would that be all right? You can even choose the color of the dress, if you like."

Kim was looking disappointed, but she nodded. "I guess so. Could I have a pink dress?"

"You certainly may."

"That will be fine." Paul Cornelius had followed, with Maureen. "I'll come in and pick it up myself. But it will have to be ready within three days, because Kim is visiting from Montana, and she and her parents will be going back Tuesday."

"I'll have it here Monday," Sarah promised, and went to her office to call the Mesilla housewife who dressed the dolls in exquisitely detailed costumes. She specified a pink dress for the doll, and asked the woman to rush one to the shop by Monday morning. Flattered at the popularity of her creations, Jackie Welch readily agreed.

When Sarah came out, Maureen and Mr. Cornelius were still chatting, and the interest in his eyes as he watched Maureen seemed more than casual.

Sarah reported to Kim that the doll maker would have a Frontier Lady in a pink dress ready by Monday morning. "Would it help if I deliver it to your home?" she asked Mr. Cornelius. "If you will be at work, perhaps your wife could take delivery."

He smiled, but there was a sad look in his brown eyes. "My wife died two years ago. I live alone. I'll bring Kim here to get her doll. It will be no problem. I'm retired from the Army. I was stationed at White Sands for several years, and this area became home to me."

"Then we'll expect you Monday."

Cornelius turned to his granddaughter. "We'd better be getting home, honey," he said.

"Wait a moment," Sarah said. She hurried to the display window, took out a copy of a new children's book about horses, full of bright illustrations. She brought it back and gave it to the little girl.

"I'd like you to have this, Kim, to make up for having to wait for your doll."

"Oh!" Kim clasped the pretty book to her chest, gazing up at Sarah with shy pleasure.

"That's very nice of you, Miss Wingate. Kim loves to read," Paul said. "Listen, could I interest you two ladies in coming to dinner this evening with a crusty old captain and his family? Be mighty glad to have you."

"I'd love it," Sarah said quickly, "but I have a dinner date tonight. Perhaps Maureen isn't busy."

She turned and gave her aunt a mischievous wink, which Maureen studiously ignored in an effort not to laugh at Sarah's obvious machinations.

"Why, thank you, Mr. Cornelius." Maureen said with dignity. "I would like that. May I meet you somewhere?"

"No indeed." He gave a slight, courtly bow of his head. "When I take a lady out, I call for her at her home."

"Well, I haven't any parents for you to make conversation with while they check you out, but here's my address."

Sarah slipped away, pleased at the glow of anticipation on Maureen's face. It would do her good to have an evening out with a nice man—a very attractive one too.

The rest of the day flew by, a total success by any standards. Sarah had barely time after closing to help Charlotte count the receipts, make a list of stocks that would need to be replenished immediately, and run the vacuum over the carpet before it was time to rush home and prepare for the evening.

As Sarah relaxed in her tub for the brief time she could spare, she wished that she had not promised Max Gamble that she would go out with him tonight. She really could have used a quiet evening alone. But then, she reminded herself, she would only find her thoughts turning unhappily to John Trist, wondering again if she had done the right thing in making it clear she did not wish to hear from him. And she had made it *very* clear, she knew, feeling a sudden constriction of her throat. He had called the shop during the opening today. Charlotte had answered. Sarah had asked her to tell him that she was too busy to come to the phone. Shirley had overheard, and snatched the phone away. He would not call Sarah again.

She swallowed the lump in her throat and made herself abandon that train of thought. He would not even be in town for a time. After talking to John, Shirley, smiling like a kitten lapping cream, had mentioned that John had been asked to go to Africa, a last-minute replacement for a professor in the agricultural college of the university. It was a conference having to do with the growing of food crops in underdeveloped countries. Shirley had seemed a bit put out that he had not invited her to accompany him.

"But I suppose he didn't want to expose me to rough conditions and such, and all those dreadful diseases they have over there," she had concluded. "John is *so* protective, the darling." She gave Sarah an oblique glance.

All in all, Sarah told herself firmly, leaving the comfort of her tub and wrapping a beach towel about her slender body, it was a very good thing that John was going out of the country. It would give her time to get her mind straight where he was concerned. It would give her time to forget him. Ruthlessly, she crushed down the pang that followed on the heels of this thought and began to dress for the evening.

Max had invited her to go with him to the home of a prominent judge and his wife for a dinner at which two other couples would be present, a local newspaper publisher and a state senator and their wives. Sarah consulted Maureen as to what might be best to wear.

"Hmm," Maureen had mused, smoothing back a strand of silver hair. "I know Judge Dayton and June. The judge has a grim hold on vanishing youth, runs every day, eats health food—but don't fear that's what you'll get for dinner. June is a sweet, jolly gal, and she cooks when they have guests, although they employ a cook. I've had her ham casserole—wonderful! She actually enters baked goods in the Dona Ana County Fair and wins. She has an entire wall of their study covered with her ribbons. You'll like June." She tilted her head. "I think you'd better be fairly formal—but not overdressed. I have it! That new caftan you made."

"But I intended it for the shop," Sarah protested.

"What better advertisement for your fashion designs than to wear one of your originals where several women prominent in local society will be present?" Maureen had overruled her.

Slipping into the caftan, Sarah was glad she had finally agreed with Maureen. The white garment, hem and sleeves banded with black and turquoise, was perfect with the turquoise nugget earrings she had bought from the Ward Cowley collection at the shop. She wore her hair in a Gibson girl upsweep. The total effect, with a touch of mascara and eye shadow to accent her eyes, was satisfactory—or even better than that, if she was truthful. She rather thought she would not totally disgrace Max Gamble before his friends.

When her date rang the doorbell, she was ready. She answered the door promptly.

The attractive young lawyer lifted his eyebrows and gave a soundless whistle at sight of her. "Fantastic! Did I choose the right lady for this evening!"

Her spirits lifted at the compliment. "Thank you, Max. Would you like to come in for a few minutes? May I offer you something to drink?"

He glanced at his watch. "We'd better be on our way. Judge Dayton is a bear on promptness, and I don't want to upset him. He's making sounds that could indicate he might persuade some of his powerful friends to back me for the nomination for the state senate. Abel Swift is stepping down soon, and he'd like to have a hand in choosing his successor. Or that's the rumor. You'll meet Abel and his wife Prissy tonight."

Suddenly, Sarah felt very nervous. "Max, I didn't realize that tonight was important to your political future. What if I somehow detract from your image?"

"Obviously, you haven't looked in the mirror, honey. You're exactly the kind of woman these people admire: smart, beautiful, an up-and-coming businesswoman! Come on, stop worrying. Max Gamble always knows what he's doing!"

Torn between natural pleasure at his compliments and a nagging uneasiness over his reasons for inviting her tonight, Sarah picked up her small handbag and went with him.

Max's car was big and expensive, luxurious in the extreme. Soft music came from the tape player, and the air conditioner kept the hot desert night out. Sarah tried to relax against the plush upholstery and prepare herself to be a suitable companion to this dynamic, politically ambitious man tonight.

Max did not make the mistake of talking about himself during the rather lengthy drive out of town to the judge's estate.

"How did your opening go?" he asked, and his glance seemed to hold genuine interest.

"Very well. We had crowds, and made lots of sales. I suppose it remains to be seen if we can build on that promising start."

"Of course you can. It just takes imaginative promotion, and you certainly have the knack for that. You write your own advertising, don't you? Maureen said you'd worked in an ad agency."

"Yes, and I think that experience will come in handy."

He gave her a smiling look. "It will do more than that, Sarah. Don't you know the true value of promotion? It's simply the difference between success and failure, as I see it. I know it will make the difference in my own future. I grew up in a politically oriented family. My dad was mayor of my hometown. He'd have gone on to bigger things but for the heart attack that killed him when I was fourteen. One of my uncles was a state representative. I learned a lot at his knee, believe me. He drilled it into me that it was the voter's perception of the candidate that made or would break him. And that takes positive promotion, shaping an image that the people will remember and believe in."

"But there has to be something of value to promote before that's valid," Sarah remarked, and was startled into a smile at the indignant look he shot her way. "No, no, I wasn't speaking of your political worth, Max. I was thinking of promotion in general and my business in particular. Unless I can manage to offer good quality items the public finds distinctive and desirable, all the advertising in the world won't help."

Max grinned. "Just so you aren't saying this hopeful item on the political market is all flash and dazzle and no substance."

"I wouldn't think of suggesting such a thing." Sarah's look was pure innocence. "After all, I have no special knowledge of what goes on behind that attractive display window."

He chuckled. "Well, lady, I intend to remedy that. And meanwhile, you are definitely an asset to me tonight."

She stirred uneasily. "I do wish you wouldn't keep saying that. It makes me feel that too much depends on my performance, and I'm not at all sure what you're expecting of me, Max."

He reached and patted her hand. "Nonsense. All I expect of you, you've already fulfilled. It's the way you look tonight, and those big, intelligent eyes."

Sarah sighed, not greatly reassured. "Thanks—I think."

Max merely grinned at her again and turned his Buick into a curving drive that led from the highway into a sprawling estate of well-kept lawns and towering trees, formal flower beds and masses of blooming shrubs. They followed the drive to the portico of a large brick home, built in the style of a century ago.

"Such a charming little cottage," Sarah breathed.

"Yes, the judge lives very comfortably. I sincerely hope to do as well someday, when my ship comes in."

"Your political ship," Sarah commented.

"You bet."

Gamble parked the car, got out, and came round to let Sarah out. She walked nervously beside him as he mounted the shallow steps and walked across the broad terrace to ring the entrance bell. They were admitted at once by a maid, an attractive young woman who led them into a lovely room and out onto a patio, where the others were gathered.

"Are we late, Judge?" Max held out an eager hand to a trim, compact, white-haired gentleman who moved toward them.

"No, no. Right on time. Everyone else was early. Ah, introduce me, Max!"

"Sarah Wingate, Judge Dayton. And this is June, Sarah, the best cook this side of the Mississippi. That gentleman is Senator Swift, Mrs. Swift, ah—Barney Widdey and Marianne. Barney is publisher of the Las Cruces *Sun-News.* Marianne is a professor of English at NMSU."

Sarah murmured a greeting to each of the new faces, struggling to remember names. But it was not so very difficult after all. Everyone present except for Mrs. Swift, a statuesque blond woman years younger than her genial, round-faced, balding husband, was cordial in the extreme. Priscilla Swift, on the other hand, possessed a glacial, ultraproper brand of courtesy that daunted Sarah. June Dayton took Sarah's hand and offered to show her around.

"I always like to show new guests the house the first thing," she confided chattily. "I know when I'm in an unfamiliar house I hate having to ask the hostess where the bathrooms are."

She gave Sarah a warm smile. "I'm so glad Max brought you tonight, dear. He mentioned you before and the gift shop you've taken over. I've noticed your ads, and I mean to drop in the first time I'm in town."

"Thank you, I'd like that," Sarah said. "You have a beautiful home, Mrs. Dayton."

"Oh, please call me June, dear. I grew up on a central Texas ranch, and I'm still a country girl at heart. When the judge starts putting on airs, I remind him that he started his career as a runny-nosed six-year-old in a one-room country schoolhouse on the plains. His daddy and mama lived in an unplumbed frame house for years until their ranching business got on its feet. Don't let this big ol' house fool you, honey. We're still just the plain folks we were, in spite of all the fancy things the good Lord saw fit to make us a gift of. Sometimes I wish this big house would shrink, so I could take care of it myself. It would be grand to take my shoes off without getting caught looking undignified by a maid or the cook!"

Sarah was immediately at ease with this voluble, motherly little woman who showed her the kitchen, obviously her favorite room, and let her stir a sauce while she checked a casserole in the oven.

Mrs. Dayton straightened with a sigh, one hand to her back. She was wearing a fragile white silk blouse and a long denim skirt with rows of old-fashioned rickrack around the bottom. Her nice, slightly blued gray hair fluffed around her face.

"Well, I've got to get back to our guests. Ella," she waved an admonishing finger at her cook, hovering in the background. "You keep an eagle eye on that meat. You can serve in"—she consulted her diamond encircled wrist watch—"in twenty minutes."

Sarah followed her from the big, magazine-perfect kitchen. In the hall June dropped her voice. "Lord, I'd rather stay in there and cook than make silly conversation with Prissy Swift. I declare, she's so afraid a smile will crack her face!"

Startled, Sarah giggled and bit her lip. June Dayton gave her a shrewd glance, laughter in her eyes. "Now then, take my advice. Don't you let Prissy give you a chill. She's really a dear girl when you get to know her. She's terribly shy, and she covers it with that concrete wall of proper manners. Her mama taught her the *right* way to do everything, you see. It was an awful mistake!"

They found the others in a book-lined study, where the judge and the other three men had fallen into an intense discussion of the political scene and the candidates the local powers would be most likely to back in the next election. Mrs. Widdey sat leafing through a magazine.

Wondering if Mrs. Dayton could be right about Prissy Swift being shy, Sarah moved over to the woman who stood neglected, pretending to admire a painting over the mantel.

"Mrs. Swift, have you lived in New Mexico all your life?" Sarah groped for a topic of conversation.

The woman turned, and for a moment her icy expression made Sarah wish she had not attempted an overture. But then the woman's lips relaxed, and for a wonder, she seemed to welcome someone to talk to.

Sarah found that Mrs. Swift was an interesting person when she began to thaw. She had lived in Europe as a child, the daughter of a diplomat and his Boston socialite wife. An only child, Priscilla had received the best in education and everything considerable wealth could give her. She had not found romance, however, until she met Abel Swift on a cruise ship, two years after the death of his young wife. Prissy was thirty when Abel proposed. They had been married, apparently quite happily, for six years.

"Wasn't it hard for you to adjust to New Mexico after all your travels?" Sarah asked, beginning to like this unusual woman.

"Yes," Prissy nodded, and her eyes wandered to her husband with unmistakable warmth. "But I don't regret a moment of our life together. Abel is so good to me."

And Sarah was to see with what courtly tenderness Senator Swift treated his wife as he led her into the dining room. For a moment it made Sarah long for that kind of devotion, something more than just physical attraction, something designed to last a lifetime.

CHAPTER TWELVE

It was a delicious meal, served at a charmingly set table with a center-piece of daisies and nasturtiums arranged with attractive results in com-bination with feathery mesquite branches in a brown pottery bowl. It was evident that June Dayton was an individual, with a unique creative bent that made this big, expensive house a home rather than a show-place.

Sarah was grateful that the round little woman and Marianne Wid-dey steered the table talk away from politics, though once or twice it veered that way. Sarah was drawn kindly into the conversation.

"That's a stunning caftan, dear," June commented. "Did you buy it here or in St. Louis?"

"I designed it myself," Sarah said. "I'm trying to add a line of fash-ions at the shop."

Marianne regarded her with admiration. "You actually designed that yourself? I wonder if you would consider creating one for me? It would be perfect for some of the campus social functions."

Sarah flushed with pleasure. "I'd be delighted to, Mrs. Widdey. Shall I sketch some ideas and send them to you? You can choose one, and I'll have it made up at once."

"Max, you picked a classy filly this time," Abel Swift mumbled to Sarah's date quite audibly. Sarah was slightly discomfited at the chuckle that spread about the dining table, but she felt that she had passed some unwritten test. Max squeezed her hand under the table and grinned at her with undisguised approval.

All in all, the evening must be counted a success. On the drive back to Cruces, Max was almost bouncing with excitement.

"Sarah, I'm almost certain the judge and Swift will back me if I decide to run," he said, jubilant. "You were a great help, darling!"

Sarah should have been gratified. His comment was pleasant to hear, of course, yet something about it was very slightly annoying. She moved abruptly in the luxurious car seat, turning to study her companion in the glow of the dash lights. As if he felt her attention, he flashed her a smile and took her hand. She let him hold it for a few moments, for it seemed impolite to snatch it back.

"Max, please don't give me credit for the impression you made on those men tonight and the impression you must have made in the past. After all, your record in your profession and personally—those are the things Judge Dayton and Senator Swift must be looking for. I suppose the kind of girl you ask out might have some minor effect, but—"

"Not the 'kind of girl I ask out,' " he mimicked gently. "*You.* You and your intelligence, your charm, your ease among strangers. Swift was right, baby, you're a winner!"

She felt exasperated. "I'm not out to win anything," she said lightly. "But I did enjoy the evening. Mrs. Dayton is lovely. I'd enjoy knowing her better. And Mrs. Swift and Marianne Widdey were very kind and interesting. Prissy Swift is surprisingly warm and human under that rigid exterior."

Max looked disbelieving. "Really? I always wondered why Abel Swift married such a cold fish. Of course, she has money of her own, and I guess she'd be the same ultracorrect wax figure if she were presented to royalty. No chance Mrs. Swift would make a social blunder. She's like something from the last century."

"Mrs. Dayton says it's the way she was brought up, in a diplomat's family. I feel sorry for her. I think she must never have been allowed to be a little girl—to be herself."

"At least she'll never put her foot wrong, say the wrong word to the press, embarrass her husband."

Sarah's vague annoyance grew. "And you consider that an asset?" she asked, carefully controlling her voice.

He shrugged. "I wouldn't like to be married to it, at least in the form of Prissy Swift, but I've seen promising political careers set back and even ruined when a wife had a couple of drinks and said something cute in the wrong company."

"Well, there must be something in between being a robot pro- grammed with all the right responses and being an undisciplined mess!" Asperity edged her words in spite of her restraint, but he merely laughed.

"Yes, there is something in between, and you're it. You're the perfect type as far as I'm concerned."

Fortunately, they drew up before Sarah's apartment complex just then, and she was prevented from making a remark she might later have regretted.

Max walked her to the door and obviously would have liked to come

in. She made the honest excuse that she was exhausted after the opening
and the evening, but she did not protest when he said he would call in a
few days.

There was so much to be thought about that Sarah felt she could not
possibly sleep. But the near-sleepless night before, coupled with the
day's stressful events, had truly taken their toll. She was asleep minutes
after her head touched the pillow.

Thankfully, Sarah was able to sleep in on Sunday. When she rose at
nine and indulged herself with a prebreakfast swim in the patio pool,
she found herself feeling rested and ready to tackle the challenges that
yesterday's successful opening had given her. After a light breakfast of
grapefruit and coffee, she tidied the apartment, drove to meet Maureen
at a church near the campus, where they attended the morning service.
Sarah spent the afternoon making lists and plans for the coming week.

She was thankful for the crush of details that she must decide just
now. It helped to push all thought of John Trist from her mind—except
perhaps for a *stray* thought or two, wondering what kind of landscape
surrounded him now, far away in Africa, wondering when he would
return, wondering if she ever entered his mind . . .

Late in the hot afternoon, Sarah drove to the shop, turned on the air
conditioner, and made a quick survey of the condition of the showroom.
It could do with some light cleaning, and all the remaining stock in the
back must be put out. Thankfully, other items were promised from
Sarah's suppliers, and in the morning Ward was bringing in some things
he'd found in Juárez.

She took a pad and made notes of items that she must order. Cowley's jewelry display was down to two bracelets and a set of earrings.
The Frontier Lady dolls had gone over well. Perhaps their maker might
add another character or two to the line—Spanish costumes or authen-
tic Navajo or Apache figures, for instance.

There was another idea that had been simmering in the back of her
mind, something that had occurred to Sarah just this morning. On
impulse, she picked up the office phone and dialed Ward and Charlotte's
number. Charlotte answered almost immediately.

"Char, forgive me for disturbing you on the weekend, but I wanted to
bounce an idea off your superior instinct and see what you think."

Charlotte laughed. "After that, would I dare deflate your new bal-
loon? Listen, why don't you come on over. Ward and I are just lounging
around the backyard making hamburgers on the grill."

"No, Char, I wouldn't want to intrude—" Sarah began.

"Silly, we'd love to have you! Ward wants to show you some new pieces he's working on."

Sarah wrote down Charlotte's directions to the house on Albert Avenue and in fifteen minutes was parking her car on a shady street where rows of neat, small stucco homes were set among lush lawns.

Charlotte came trotting along the side of the house to meet her. "We're back here. I'm so glad you came."

Sarah followed Charlotte to the backyard, where Ward was poking at some ground meat patties on a grill. The scene reminded Sarah wrenchingly of that first night at Maureen's, when she had stepped out on the patio to be introduced to Ward and John Trist. For a moment the sudden lump in her throat made it hard to respond to Ward's happy greeting.

"Hey, lady, come and grab something cold to drink. Soft drinks or beer, take your choice."

Sarah smiled, swallowed, and recovered her emotional balance under cover of selecting a grape drink from a Styrofoam chest filled with ice. She sat down in a lawn chair after being told there was absolutely nothing she could help with.

"Ward's fanatically proprietary about his outdoor culinary arts. He won't even let me touch the onions for the burgers," Charlotte said. "It's great. All I have to do is lie back and encourage him with remarks about how marvelous it all smells."

Sarah relaxed in the friendly atmosphere of the Cowley backyard, and in a few minutes she was able to shake the shadows of that other evening from her mind. Or at least to push it back, out of sight, and almost out of touch.

"Now then," Charlotte said, sitting down near Sarah."What's this fantastic idea you wanted to tell me about?"

"Well, here it is. I think it might be good—please tell me honestly what you both think. It will be a display of greeting cards, but with a big difference. They'll be personalized."

Charlotte tilted her head. "How do you mean?"

"They'll be made to order, on the spot. I want to find a commercial artist—someone who uses watercolor or acrylics. I need someone who can sketch in little illustrations quickly—softly focused scenes, somewhere between realistic and impressionistic—am I making any sense?"

Charlotte's eyes narrowed thoughtfully, and her delicate features brightened with enthusiasm. "I see what you mean, and I think it will be fantastic. I can probably find someone for you in the art class I'm taking. There's a graduate student who's really talented, and I think she might be willing. Tell you what, I'll call her right now. If she's free, maybe we can get her over here."

Unfortunately, Betsy Hobson was on her way out on a date when Charlotte called, and the best Charlotte could manage was an appointment for Sarah to see Betsy the following day.

Ward had the burgers ready. Sarah found her appetite enhanced by being made so welcome by these good friends.

She left their home by ten, after an evening of enjoyable conversation. As a bonus, she had Ward's and Charlotte's promises of a dozen pieces of jewelry and two of Charlotte's wall hangings for the shop.

When Sarah reached La Casa Encantada next morning, she found Shirley already inside, shifting merchandise about. Of course, it was to the girl's credit that she was taking an intelligent interest in the business. Nevertheless, Sarah could not quite see it as a good omen.

Shirley was at her most engaging today. She seemed to have completely forgiven Sarah for earlier unpleasantness between them. She was still bubbling with enthusiasm about Saturday's opening.

"It was really fun, wasn't it? I felt like a real businesswoman, showing things to my friends. They were impressed with our stuff."

"They wouldn't be today," Sarah said. "We'd better get restocked in a hurry. I've just talked to Jackie Welch, and she's sending over three dolls. Oh, if Mr. Cornelius and Kim come in while I'm gone, give Kim the Frontier Lady with the pink dress. Ward's coming later to refill the jewelry case and bring the Mexican things. Tell him to leave a statement and I'll write a check and give it to Charlotte when she comes in after her two o'clock class. Now I'd better try to replenish our supplies."

She consulted her list, dialing a number quickly as Shirley walked around the office, picking up things and setting them down, like a suddenly bored and restless child.

"Hello," Sarah said into the receiver. "Is this Annie? Oh, Mrs. Carnes, this is Sarah Wingate. Do you know if Annie and Susan have the vests and scooter skirts ready for me? Wonderful! I really need them today. . . ."

She made two more calls, ordered three sets of ceramic mugs and several sets of wind chimes.

As she hung up and glanced at her watch, she saw that there was barely time to make it to the campus and her engagement with Betsy Hobson. Reluctantly leaving the shop in Shirley's care, she drove the few blocks through midmorning traffic.

Betsy Hobson lived in one of the newer dorms on campus. She had a private room, and it was bright with examples of her art. From the moment Sarah let her eyes roam about the room, she was appreciative of the girl's talent.

Betsy was a tall, slender black girl, with a smooth complexion the shade of creamed coffee and eyes like a doe, sparkling and intelligent.

"Here's what I have in mind." Sarah accepted a chair and a glass of iced tea. She explained her concept of greeting cards created on the spot from the customer's own ideas. "They'll sell for five to ten dollars, depending on the amount of work. We can do all the standard greetings, plus some more personal things, love notes perhaps, or get-acquainted bids. We'll have hand-lettered messages that say exactly what the sender wishes. What do you think?"

The pretty girl ran slender fingers through her Afro and frowned thoughtfully. "Something like this, you mean?"

She turned to her easel and worked for a few moments with watercolors on a blank square of paper. Sarah stood to watch. Before her fascinated eyes the brush dipped, touched, moved swiftly to form a misty scene that was like something seen in a daydream, a woodland glade on a rainy day, colors soft. There were no hard, definite lines, yet the impression was of some remembered landscape, summer-sweet and alive with soft breezes and birdsong.

"Ah, perfect!" breathed Sarah.

Betsy smiled. "You could have floral motifs, or even dimly seen figures for the romantic cards. But who would write the messages?"

"You will—wait, don't panic." Sarah laughed at the girl's tragic expression. "I'm not asking for poetry—at least not of the rhyming kind. No fancy phrasing, just quiet, warm sentiments. For example—" She paused and thought for a moment. "Suppose a girl has had a painful argument with her sweetheart or her husband, and she wants to try and open up lines of communication. What would you suggest she say? What would you like to hear from your sweetheart in such a situation?"

Betsy tilted her head, imagination caught by the question. "Well, maybe just—" She turned back to the drawing, caught up a pen, and under the scene deftly printed a few words: "I love you. I didn't mean the things I said. Can we try again?" She held it out to Sarah, diffident and obviously nervous of her reaction.

Sarah nodded happily. "It's exactly what I had in mind—simple, to the point, tenderly expressed. And maybe some of the messages could be humorous, if that's the mood the sender has in mind."

Sarah examined the little scene again, and gave a brisk, decisive nod. "Betsy, would you like to work for me as many hours per week as you can spare? I hope to have the card counter manned by a rotating staff.

Do you know another artist who could do something similar to this? If the idea doesn't catch on, the job may not last forever, but somehow I think people will love it. It would be such a nice alternative to mass-produced greetings."

Within two days Betsy and Charlie Smith, a young man who was working toward a degree in psychology with commercial art as his second love, were installed at their own counter in the shop, dividing the work time between themselves. A supply of blank, lightly textured cards and notes was ready. Sarah advertised the new greeting cards, and each of the artists created a representative group of sample sketches that were placed on a display rack. The displays were changed regularly, and no two drawings were alike. A customer might choose one of the display scenes or have a new one done on the spot.

The artists created landscapes with pastoral or mountain moods, some with figures. There were a few floral cards, even a sprinkling of comic greetings done by Charlie, who had a flair for cartooning. Before long his sad-eyed "Oscar" character was becoming a fad with the college crowd. Charlie used the brighter shades of acrylic paints for his humorous cards.

Sarah's customers quickly proved receptive to the idea of custom-designed greetings. To Sarah's satisfaction, the artists soon had almost more than they could do, and she promptly gave both a raise, though they had only worked a few days. It was well worth it; often someone stepped into the shop for one of the special cards and ended by buying other items. People seemed endlessly entranced by seeing their own feelings expressed spontaneously by the art and words of these talented young people.

It was soon evident that La Casa Encantada was going to thrive. Catering carefully to every age group and every price range and providing gift ideas that were charming and original kept the store busy with jeans and shorts-clad girls and boys as well as expensively dressed matrons, who purchased the more expensive paintings and jewelry and Sarah's original designs in sports or evening wear.

For a few days after the opening, Shirley faithfully presented herself promptly at nine, for work. Sarah had begun, cautiously, to believe her partner might become an asset to the business. Then Shirley fell from grace by beginning a hysterical argument with a student who came in looking for a bright pottery planter for her dorm room. Sarah never learned what the disagreement was about, and she managed to smooth it over by giving the girl a discount on her selection. Shirley, on the other hand, left the shop in a flaming rage because Sarah took pains to pacify the customer. After that day, Sarah's business partner came and went erratically. Secretly, Sarah could only feel relieved when Shirley was absent.

Maureen dropped into the shop several days after the opening. She looked around appreciatively.

"I see you've filled the shelves again."

"We have some great new items too. There are just dozens of talented people in this area, Maureen. The word is out that this is a good outlet for craft items, and new people bring their craftwork to show me, every day. And you wouldn't believe how well the sales are holding up."

"I heard about your greeting card idea," Maureen said. "I think I may buy a card myself."

"Wonderful. Come and meet Betsy, one of the artists. Maureen, she's fantastic. She does the loveliest little scenes in just minutes. Betsy's a darling. You'll love her."

She walked with Maureen to Betsy's corner, where she was just finishing a card for a middle-aged lady whose expensive clothing and fine jewelry made the ten-dollar bill she laid down seem very trivial. "Keep the change," she said. "You do beautiful work, my dear. I'll tell my friends about you."

Betsy slipped the card into an envelope. "Thank you, Mrs. Wilmott. Good luck," she murmured.

The blond Mrs. Wilmott blushed like a schoolgirl and glanced around as Sarah and Maureen approached.

"Maureen, how good to see you," she said. "I've just bought one of these wonderful original cards to send Jeff. It's—it's our anniversary next week."

After a few words of conversation, the woman left the shop and slid into a Lincoln Continental out front. Maureen shook her head.

"Poor Irene. Her husband left her months ago for a younger woman. I hear that his new romance has burned itself out. Do you suppose Irene's trying to win him back?"

"If so, I hope Betsy's card will help. Betsy, this is my aunt and my dear friend, Maureen Wright. Maureen, Betsy will make a card for you you'll hate to mail away."

Betsy laughed, her beautiful eyes full of fun. "We guarantee it! I'm happy to know you, Miss Dwight. You own Dwight Realty, don't you? Sarah's told me so much about you, and I see why she loves you."

"Maureen's my entire family." Sarah grinned. "It's an awful burden to her, I know, but she puts up with me, bless her."

Maureen patted Sarah on the shoulder. "I wish I had more burdens like Sarah. Now, Betsy, you must call me Maureen. I intend to bare my soul to you, so you can do a perfect card for me. It has to be—not in the least forward, but make a man sort of think of romance—ah, subliminally, if you see what I mean."

Sarah had turned to leave them, but she swung back. "What's this? You're sending a romantic card to a gentleman? Maybe I'd better hang around and hear all about this."

Maureen laughed, but the color rose charmingly in her pert face. She flapped her hand at her niece. "Shoo! Go away, Sarah. If you're a good girl, maybe I'll tell you all about it someday. For now, Betsy is my confidante. Lord, I'll bet she'll know half the lovelorn secrets of this entire town in a few months! Now if Betsy could just pass out some advice—"

"It comes with the card, free of extra charge," Betsy assured her. "Sit down, Maureen, and we'll design something extraspecial for this gentleman. He'll never know what hit him!"

"That's what I want to hear. Sarah, are you still here?" She turned a mock-reproachful face on her niece. "Darling, haven't you something better to do than to eavesdrop on an old lady's secrets?"

Sarah chuckled and bent to kiss her cheek. "Old lady, my eye! I'll bet your secrets would make my favorite soap opera pale by comparison."

"You may be right," Maureen admitted smugly.

Laughing, Sarah went to assist a customer who had just stepped in the door. As she crossed the bright, appealing shop, she felt again the delight of owning this business. Satisfaction gave her smile warmth enough to startle the young man who wanted to look around for a gift for his mother's birthday.

A few minutes later Maureen came into the office, where Sarah was bringing some records up to date and making notes of items to be ordered.

"How about some coffee?" Sarah offered, looking up.

"Now that's more like it." Maureen grinned. "At least observe the amenities before prying into my love life."

Sarah rose and crossed to the table that held a coffee maker and cups. She poured, glancing back at her aunt with an elaborately casual shrug. "What prying? I've decided not to ask you one single thing about the mysterious man you and Betsy have been giggling over."

Maureen's face fell. "Well, that's a fine, grateful attitude. Here I take time from work to come in and spend a fortune in this establishment of yours, and you refuse to let me tell you what I'm dying to tell you about Paul Cornelius."

"Paul—? Oh yes, I remember. The man who bought his granddaughter a Frontier Lady doll."

"That's not the memory tag I use, but yes, you're right." Maureen's sigh attempted to be comical, but there was real feeling in it.

Sarah caught it and glanced at her aunt intently. She handed her the cup of steaming black coffee. "What's this? Do I detect something serious afoot? I'm sorry if I teased you about a sensitive matter, love. Is there a problem?"

Maureen laughed, but unsteadily. "The question is, what constitutes a problem?"

"Apparently, something does, or I'm reading you all wrong," Sarah said quite soberly. She sat down and touched her aunt's hand where it rested on the desk. "If anyone's been unkind to you, he'll answer to me!"

Again Maureen laughed, got up from the chair she had just taken, walked rapidly about the room, then sat down again. She sighed, and looked at Sarah tragically, even though she smiled.

"Maureen, what is it?" Sarah studied her aunt with growing worry. This was not the Maureen Dwight she knew, the efficient, insouciant, 'with it' woman who radiated confidence. This Maureen was nervous, seemed unsure whether to smile or cry. "Is it something bad?" Sarah cried. "Tell me!"

"Honey, it's as bad as it can be. I've fallen in love, at my age!"

Sarah stared at her, lips parted. "But darling, that's wonderful, isn't it? What's got you so—so—"

"I know, I'm a wreck, aren't I? *All* the classic symptoms, Sarah. I'm ashamed of myself, believe me. I can't sleep, I start to eat and wander away and forget to finish—if this keeps up, I'll have to buy a dog just to keep from wasting food. I'm having trouble concentrating at work. I laugh at the wrong times, I find myself not listening to my clients—maybe it's senility instead of love!"

Sarah smiled widely. "No, I think you had the diagnosis right the first time. But what's so tragic about it? Unless the man—it's Mr. Cornelius, I gather? Unless he doesn't feel the same."

To her relief, Maureen shook her head. "No, I think it hit him first—as is only right and fair," she grinned, with a flash of her usual wit for a brief instant.

Sarah leaned forward. "Tell me all about it!"

"Well, I don't want to take up your time, dear, I know you're busy."

"Too busy for you? Never! Don't worry, Charlotte's here now, I just saw her come in. She'll take care of customers. Drink your coffee and tell me."

Maureen leaned back, sipped her coffee, and gave her niece a doubt-filled look.

"He took me out to dinner, remember? His daughter and son-in-law and little Kim were there. We went to the Double Eagle, in old Mesilla. Marvelous meal, Sarah, trout and salad and feathery rolls and a glass of Blue Nun. The dining room is gorgeous. You must see it, it's pure Victorian and has wonderful high ceilings, crystal chandeliers, velvet-upholstered chairs, velvet drapes, and deep, fringed valances. There are hurricane lamps on the tables, enormous paintings on the walls—"

"Yes, yes, but what about—"

"Paul's daughter and her husband? They're nice, maybe just a little standoffish, but only what you might expect. I was something of a shock, I fear, a sudden new friend invited into the family bosom."

"They—weren't especially cordial, then." Sarah read between the lines.

"No, it wasn't quite as clearcut as that. I think they were just honestly taken aback when Paul presented me, his date for the evening. Well, imagine it, Sarah. That morning their dear, widowed dad had no feminine interests, and that evening—I appear. Oh, he introduced me so proudly!" She blinked rapidly.

"Well, I should think he'd be proud," Sarah said. "He couldn't have found a lovelier friend, and if it had just happened that day, what difference?"

Maureen chewed her lower lip, and her gaze was directed toward the office wall where a bulletin board held some of Sarah's sketches.

"I don't know. Maybe I'm flinching at shadows. Maybe it was all in my imagination. I might have simply *expected* that kind of reaction. You know, daddy's grown-up girl sees the awful possibility that her mother might be replaced."

"It's not like you to imagine things. If you felt a coolness, it was probably there," Sarah said. "But after they get to know you, they won't feel anything less than grateful that you and Paul are friends. And—you are friends, aren't you?"

Maureen did not simply smile, she glowed. "Yes," she said simply. "We are, Sarah. Best of friends, even in so short a time. But—" The light dimmed behind her eyes. "But that has its worries too."

"I don't understand."

Maureen rose nervously and made another quick turn about the room, stopping to place a gentle fingertip on the desk edge, rubbing it back and forth thoughtfully. "Honey, I'm not a youngster anymore—" she began.

Sarah interrupted emphatically. "Nonsense! You're definitely one of the youngest people I know, and at the same time you have all that marvelous wisdom that living brings. You are a very special lady, Maureen."

Maureen sighed. "Thank you, love. You're so good for my spirits. What I'm trying to say is—my life style is—set. It's just the way I like it. I have my house, and I love it, and my work, and I couldn't consider giving that up, and—"

"And you're never *really* lonely," Sarah added softly.

The exposed self-knowledge in Maureen's eyes was painful to see. "I don't say that. I couldn't lie to you. You know exactly how it is."

Sarah drew a slow, deep breath and nodded. "Yes, and that's why I'm wondering—why are you afraid of your feelings for Paul Cornelius? He's free, and surely lonely. Even I could see that he admired you tremendously from those first moments."

"He—says he admires me," Maureen nodded.

"Well then?"

"Well, it's frightening to have a life you think is modeled exactly to your taste suddenly rocked by this kind of feeling!" Maureen exclaimed. "Maybe I'm about to make a fool of myself. I want to be sensible—"

"That's my watchword too," Sarah muttered, suddenly dispirited. "Sensible. Add to that, practical, ethical, controlled—"

"Oh, honey"—Maureen's distress was a shadow in her eyes—"I shouldn't have come in here and dumped my problems in your lap. I'm behaving like a teenager with a crush on a rock star."

"Nonsense! You're behaving like a wonderful, wise lady who tries to look before she leaps. That's got to be the right attitude. My mind insists that it is. I'm following that rule myself."

"Sarah, is there something wrong?" Maureen seemed to really see her niece for the first time today, and her eyes were entirely too penetrating.

Sarah made a determined effort, and her smile was so nearly genuine that it would have required an expert to detect the lack of pleasure behind it. "No, dear. You see before you a contented woman, luckier than she deserves. This place is working, Maureen. Beyond my most extravagant dreams. We're already making a profit. I think I'll be able to buy your ten percent sooner than planned."

Maureen tilted her head shrewdly. "Now, why do I seem to hear my own voice issuing from your lips?" she murmured.

Sarah laughed. "Well, perhaps our outlook on life is similar. But now you seem to have a chance to add something more, something precious, to your life. I wonder if you should let anything stand in your way?"

Maureen bent her gleaming head and looked up with a grin. "I do believe you may be right. I don't know if I can learn to suppress my caution. It took me a lot of years and a lot of bumps and bruises to get smart enough to protect this fragile heart. But maybe—well, we'll wait and see what the future brings."

"Only the best for you, because no one deserves it more," Sarah said.

Maureen straightened her shoulders. "It's lovely to have you nearby, Sarah. It helps to talk things over with someone who understands. Remember that I stand ready to return the favor."

"It's a deal," Sarah promised. She gazed thoughtfully after Maureen as the trim, white-haired woman moved gracefully out of the shop.

Would it help to accept Maureen's offer, to talk over the perplexities that chewed at the edges of her peace? But how could she? How admit that she had fallen in love with a man who already belonged to another woman? How explain that she had done what she knew to be right. She had short-circuited any chance of a further relationship with the man who would not stay out of her thoughts or out of her dreams, and now something within was desperately sorry. . . .

With a sigh, Sarah bent her head over the figures that required her attention, and it was probably only tiredness that made them blur for an instant before she fiercely blinked her eyes.

CHAPTER THIRTEEN

Sarah's social life was not totally neglected during this busy time. Larry Brandt called at least twice weekly, and Sarah accepted dates with him occasionally, finding him a companion dedicated to fun, and creative about it. He took her to dinner or to community theater productions or to El Paso to dine in the most popular and expensive places. Larry liked to dance, and he introduced Sarah to country music and western-style dancing. Doubtful about it at first, it became for Sarah an entertaining way to relax and helped her to shed the tensions and pressures of business.

She dated Max Gamble too. It was soon evident that Max would have liked to dominate all Sarah's free evenings. Uneasily, she wondered if he was reading something more serious into their relationship than she was ready for. One evening after a concert at the Pan American Center, Max walked Sarah to her door, silent until she fitted her key in the lock.

"Invite me in," he said softly, turning her and placing both arms about her to draw her close.

"It's late, Max. I have a busy day tomorrow, and I know you have to be in court early."

He kissed her gently, then with mounting urgency. For an aching moment Sarah wished with all her heart that she could respond. So many problems it might solve—

"Sarah, isn't it time we—got to know each other a lot better?" he murmured. "Let me stay here tonight."

She stiffened and drew sharply away. "Sorry," she said, with an attempt at lightness, "I'm not into one-night stands. I know that's a scandalous confession, but perhaps you'll regard it as privileged communication." She freed herself and opened her door.

He caught her hand tightly. "Wait, Sarah. What would be wrong with two people who respect and—"

She shook her head pleadingly. "I make it a rule never to argue with a lawyer, Max. I've said no, and I assure you I mean it. Now, I must say good-night. Thanks for a lovely evening."

She sighed at the look of chagrin which was the last glimpse she had of Max before closing the door.

Sarah fully expected that Max would not call her again. But he did, and though the same topic was broached with almost every date, Max remained almost determinedly good-natured about her reluctance to venture into a more intimate relationship. Sarah had the feeling that he did not believe she would remain reluctant. It made her wonder if it would be fairer not to see him again. Still, she liked Max and enjoyed his company. Perhaps another girl would have found him exciting; certainly, he was extremely attractive. So she continued to date him once or twice a week, trying to make it clear each time that all she felt was a warm friendship.

On a rare afternoon away from the shop, Sarah climbed from the pool at her apartment complex, caught up her terry robe, and rushed to answer the phone in her kitchen. It was Sam, nervously holding out an olive branch.

"Please don't hang up, Sarah. Surely we can still be friends. Can't we just have dinner and talk?"

She sighed, wishing she had ignored the phone and stayed in the water. "Sam, what's the point? We've each made our choices, and they took us in opposite directions. Let's not rake up old coals."

"Even if some of those coals might still be alive?" he asked softly. "Sarah darling, I can't tell you how I've felt, seeing you now and then, reading your ads in the paper, and that article they did on your shop as a promising new business. I realize now that I was wrong."

Sarah held the receiver silently, astonished that his pleading could still make her feel some remnant of affection and sympathy. It must be very hard for Sam to admit he'd made what he considered a mistake. Was she being too rigid, too unforgiving?

He seemed to sense the softening implicit in her hesitation. "Sarah, won't you let me take you out tonight? We can talk, clear the air. I've got reservations at—"

She quickly found her voice. "Sam, I can't tonight. I have a date I made weeks ago."

"Then you name the time," he said.

Reluctantly, Sarah agreed to a luncheon date two days later.

The next morning Charlotte stepped into the office, where Sarah was putting the finishing touches on a design for a pantsuit for evening wear, with a crystal beaded halter top under a little jacket. The suit was to be made in a blue, silky blend cloth.

"Hey, I like that," Charlotte said.

"Thanks." Sarah smiled at her friend. "I hope to have it ready by next week."

"Sarah—" Charlotte tilted her head in a way that meant she had an idea she was gathering courage to suggest. Sarah had learned to respect Charlotte's instincts. Many of her ideas had already been incorporated into the business. Often she had wished that Charlotte was her business partner instead of the elusive and unpredictable Shirley.

"You've thought of something. What is it?" Sarah laid the sketch aside and stood to pour coffee at the little table against the wall.

"Well—you've got all those sketches," Charlotte indicated the stack of new work Sarah had accumulated in the past week. Some would be discarded, or changed, some would be made into limited lots for sale in the shop. A few, like the pantsuit, would be one-of-a-kind garments with a much greater price. So far, Sarah had only to display these exclusive models in her windows, and they sold rapidly.

"Yes, I've really enjoyed working on these designs, and it's been going well. It's something to do on evenings at home."

Charlotte smiled. "If you accepted half the offers for dates you get, there wouldn't be any evenings at home. Anyway, it occurred to me— why don't you have a style show?"

"A style—" Sarah paused with her cup halfway to her lips. "Well, I hadn't thought—"

"It would be fantastic!" Charlotte's diffidence vanished in her eagerness. "The style section has been going well from the first. Your designs are so different, so bright and fun and appealing. And you've been mentioned in the paper. People stop in here out of curiosity. Now would be the perfect time to advertise a coming show of your originals. Sarah, you could expand into the fashion business, in a larger way. And with your talent I think you should."

Sarah stared at her. "Oh my, do you realize what that would mean? I don't think I could handle all the extra work—it would mean setting up a small garment factory, wouldn't it?"

"Well, you could simply hire more help to take care of this end of it— you'd have to have another shop, I guess, strictly for fashions. But you could do it—I know you could. Have a show, and see how popular your styles will be."

"Well"—Sarah was drawn by the suggestion in spite of a nervous awareness of the work involved—"we couldn't do it here—"

"Couldn't do what?"

Shirley danced into the office. Sarah suppressed a sigh. It had been days since her partner had bothered to come in—peaceful days.

"We're going to have a style show, featuring Sarah's designs," Charlotte said.

Shirley sprawled in a chair, interest in her pert, pretty face. "That's good. I'll model."

Sarah felt instant dismay. "That's sweet of you, but I'm sure you wouldn't want to be involved in anything so minor."

"Are you kidding?" Shirley grinned. "Whatever I may think of you personally, Sarah, your designs are terrific. I'd love to model them. I can get some of the girls I usually work with too. You can rent space for the show. Why not do a luncheon show in a dining room at one of the best hotels?"

"That's a good idea, Sarah," Charlotte agreed. "Then women who work can make it. And why not send out engraved invitations—something very simple and elegant."

"Right!" Shirley sat forward with excitement. "Make it classy. Now I know all the important names and addresses. Give me a few days and I'll have them for you. I can order the invitations, too—"

"Wait, wait!" Sarah felt her head spinning. "I don't know if I could have enough things ready for a fall showing. This is happening too fast. Shouldn't we wait until spring at least?"

"Well"—Shirley's contempt could not have been more obvious—"if you're going to chicken out now—"

Charlotte picked up the stack of new sketches and was glancing through them. "Most of these could be used, Sarah. The climate's so mild here that evening wear and sportswear won't be that different from season to season, except maybe in color and weight of fabric. You could add some cold-weather items, couldn't you?"

Sarah took the sketches from her friend and began to look over them, but Shirley snatched them from her. Sarah had to bite back a sharp protest.

"No, Charlotte—oh well, this great pantsuit, and this caftan, and this, and this—they'd be right for fall. The rest are too summery. The feeling's wrong."

Sarah was surprised to find that she agreed with Shirley's judgment. "The others should be used here in the shop as I first intended. If we do this, I want to really do it right. I'll design specifically for the show, for the season—" She found a warm excitement growing. "I think—Give me a few days, girls, and if I can come up with some kind of central idea, we'll try it."

"It will mean a rush, having the clothes made. We'll have to hire more seamstresses," Charlotte said. "And it will be expensive, Sarah. I wouldn't want you to go out on a limb financially for an idea that was mine."

Sarah made a quick mental survey of her financial situation. "I can manage it, I think. It would be an investment. But let's don't hire anyone else until I can be sure I can produce."

"Oh, don't be silly!" Shirley stood up and helped herself to coffee. "You'd better learn, Sarah dear, that in this world you either grab the brass ring when you get the chance or it moves along to someone else. Advertise for expert seamstresses, Charlotte," she gestured imperiously. "This could mean a lot of business for the shop."

Sarah was annoyed, but when Charlotte glanced at her for corroboration, she nodded. "While you're at it, better hire another clerk. I have a feeling I won't have more than spare moments to spend in the shop for a few weeks."

So the idea was born, and Sarah found herself with a project that was both challenging and frightening. Realizing that she would have to cut her social life to a minimum for a time, she canceled a date with Max Gamble and one with Larry Brandt, explaining the situation. Neither man was pleased in the least.

Every morning she woke with ideas percolating madly in her brain, to be added to the tentative list she'd begun the day Charlotte ventured her idea. She needed to shop for sample fabrics, make endless preliminary sketches—oh, it would be work! But on the whole it was a good feeling, perhaps the best feeling she had experienced since the night she had firmly pushed John Trist out of her life.

On a steamy evening, following a sudden hard rain that left the desert city washed dust-free, Sarah sat over her sketches in the office. The shop had closed hours ago, and it was very quiet and somehow mysterious with the showroom's night lighting now and then momentarily enhanced by carlights in the street.

She stood and stretched, and went to make fresh coffee before settling down to work once more. It was time to materialize some of the elusive ideas circling in her head. There was one in particular that she wanted to pin down, a hooded coat she visualized in a soft, sheer dove-gray wool, lined in a flame color. There would be a matching skirt to be worn with slender high-heeled boots in the softest, most flexible leather.

The phone broke her concentration. Startled, she blinked at it for a moment as it rang again. Why on earth did John's name fly to the forefront of her mind?

Impatient with herself, she lifted the receiver. "La Casa Encantada," she said.

"Is this Miss Wingate?" said a male voice that seemed vaguely familiar.

"It is," she said. "May I help you?"

"Yes, you may, if you'll let me buy you a drink."

"I'm sorry," she said stiffly. "You must have the wrong—"

"It's Brad Curtis, Miss Wingate. Remember? We met on the plane. I'm in town this week, and I especially wanted to see you. I saw the article about your shop. Sounds like you've got a real winner."

She thawed, but retained caution. "I hope so. We've been lucky so far."

"Well, how about that drink. May I pick you up? Say, have you had dinner?"

"No, Mr. Curtis, but I'm knee-deep in work, and I've ordered a sandwich sent in."

"You can't work while you eat—bad for the digestion. At least let me join you. I promise I won't stay over one hour."

Perhaps it was the surge of loneliness that had swept over Sarah when the phone rang, or the unusual quietness of the shop. She hesitated, but only for a moment. "On those terms, I'd be glad to have you. I'll order something for you to eat too. What would you like?"

"I'll bring the food. I'll be there in half an hour."

Sarah let Curtis in at the front entrance. She turned on the shop lights, and he toured the shop with approving interest.

"Lady," he shook his head appreciatively, "I think I'll hire you to rearrange the displays in my sporting goods shop. This is nice. I've seen a half dozen things I'd like to pick up for myself or my wife. Ex-wife," he amended, and Sarah thought she saw a shade of regret on his face. If so, it was quickly replaced as he turned, beaming at her. "And you tell me you designed the clothing you sell."

"Most of it. A good friend of mine did the beautiful handwoven vests and ponchos—Oh, that gives me a fabulous idea. Could you excuse me for a moment while I jot it down?"

She turned, caught up with the thought that had struck her. Poncho —great for fall, maybe a modified gaucho outfit—boots, divided skirt in suede, a bright, long-sleeved silk shirt, even the hat—

She was writing the idea down on her pad as Brad followed her into the office. He looked around quietly as she finished her notes.

"Forgive me." She turned back to him. "I've got to come up with some ideas for the fall style show we've tentatively decided to produce. I'm scared to death my imagination will dry up under pressure."

Brad tilted his head shrewdly. With his thick, sandy hair gone silver at the temples, his brown, lively eyes and square-jawed face, he was an attractive man. "Somehow I think you're the kind of gal who thrives on pressure."

She smiled. "I do hope you're right, because I'm going to know very soon."

There was a tap on the door that led outdoors from the office. "There's the food," Curtis said, and moved to open the door. A boy with a large box stood outside. Brad paid him, added a generous tip, and brought the box inside. Sarah cleared a space on her worktable and watched with amusement and a stirring appetite as he lifted out a variety of Mexican dishes.

"You've brought enough for five people!"

"Wanted to be sure I got something you'd like. I have burritos, and tacos, and—"

"My problem will be liking all of it," Sarah grieved in advance for the hazard to her figure.

Curtis pulled her desk chair to the table and found another for himself, then seated her with a flourish. He reached into the box and brought out containers of iced Coke.

"Hope this is all right with you. I have to stick with soft drinks. I'm an alcoholic," he said matter-of-factly.

Sarah's expression must have revealed her surprise at his bald statement for he grinned and sat down. "Well, I've learned that I better face facts, or kiss everything I cared about good-bye. I'd already lost my wife because of my drinking. You know, there was something about having to make appointments to see my own kids that had the effect of waking me up. I've been straightening myself out, been sober for months, and believe me, I'm never going back to the way it was."

During this frank speech, Sarah glimpsed a different man. She had thought Curtis brash, overconfident. Now she saw behind that facade for a moment, to a vulnerable, gallant human who was fighting a difficult battle.

But he was very quickly back in character, filling her thick paper plate with spicy food. "Now, sink your teeth into that, honey, and tell me ol' Brad doesn't know how to feed a lady!"

She obeyed and found the food delicious. Some of it was breathtakingly hot with jalapeño chilies, and Sarah learned to taste cautiously before taking a full bite.

"Thanks for letting me come by and bother you," Brad said. "I see you're swamped."

"It's good to take a break. I can work late."

He regarded her intently. "But not too late, I hope. It doesn't pay to exhaust yourself for business. Save some time for yourself."

"I know that's good advice." Sarah laid her fork down and wiped her lips with her napkin. "There just seems so much that has to be done. And truthfully, I love it."

"Delegate some of the work," was his terse advice. "You'd be surprised how many talented people are out there, willing and able to follow your direction—but not able to create the ideas and the leadership."

She regarded him with more attention. "I see your point, Brad. I think I'd already begun to see that it's easy to spread oneself too thin."

"For instance, what about your love life, pretty Sarah?" He rose and began energetically to clear away their feast, a glance at his watch showing that he had not forgotten his promise to let her get back to work within the hour.

"It's—" She laughed, embarrassed. "I admit it's a trifle sparse at the moment. This project is forcing me to clear the decks for a few weeks."

"That's all right, for a really important goal, I'm not saying you don't have to sacrifice to get somewhere." He nodded emphatically. "But don't let it run on too long, or—"

He was silent for a long moment, his face bent over the small task of repacking the box. Then he looked up with a rueful smile. "Or you might find yourself alone like me, wondering what ever happened to that companionship, that good feeling of coming home and finding someone there, somebody to talk to—"

Sarah could see his unhappiness plainly now. It was as if he'd grown tired of hiding it. "Is there a chance you might get back together with your wife, Brad? If you've conquered the drinking—"

He sat down on the corner of the table. "I've asked her to take another chance with me. Well, Annie really suffered back then, when I was drinking so much. I knew it, and I hated what I was doing to my family, but somehow I couldn't be deprived of what had become vital to me. Annie realizes that I was sick. If I can continue to stay sober, maybe someday she'll trust me again."

"I hope she does," Sarah said.

"Okay, enough of the soap opera." He grinned and stood, picking up the box. "It's time for me to go. You know, this has been a unique experience for me, Sarah. I came over here, frankly, with the idea of trying to make progress with a damned beautiful woman. I'm leaving with the feeling that I've found a good friend."

"That's the nicest compliment I've had in days," she said. "I enjoyed the evening."

"Now, don't get me wrong. I haven't given up the hope of—something warmer between us. Mind if I called you now and then?"

She hesitated. It was the old question: was it fair to encourage him when there was no real chance?

"Lady, I believe there's something making you unhappy," Curtis said, with a shrewd look. "You're missing someone, aren't you?"

She evaded the question. "As I explained, Brad, I've been too busy lately for anything but casual dating."

"But somebody already has the inside track, someone who isn't smart enough to appreciate it."

"Brad—" Sarah began helplessly.

He held up a hand, grinning. "I know, I know. I'm trespassing. Sorry, sugar. Well, you won't mind going out to dinner once in a while with an old friend, will you? Heck, you know more about Brad Curtis now than most people I've known for years."

"That would be very pleasant," she said.

"I like you, Sarah Wingate," he said. "You're nice people."

Smiling, Sarah let him out the door and locked it behind him, returning to her work. She found that the meal and the conversation had helped to release tension. She murmured aloud, "You're nice people too, Brad Curtis."

Sarah had been tempted to call Sam and break their luncheon date. Certainly, she had ample excuse. There was simply not enough time in the day to accomplish all that she had set for herself. She actually picked up the receiver and started to dial once, then changed her mind. If she broke the date, it would only seem a gesture contrived to exact a petty revenge.

Sarah met her former fiancé at the Sirloin Stockade promptly at one. He was already there, and he rose as she made her way to the table. She was wearing slim beige slacks and a brown, tan, and white print shirt in gauzy cotton. She had made no effort to dress specially for the occasion, but his look was one of admiration as he seated her. He slid into his chair and stared at her almost embarrassingly.

"Sarah, you've changed. I can't quite say what it is about you—"

"Nonsense." She gave him a friendly, but only friendly smile. "You just haven't seen me in a while."

"No!" He was vehement. "It's something in the way you hold your head, in the way you dress maybe. I like it. You seem more—I don't know—sophisticated, poised."

In spite of her herself, the compliment pleased her. "I'm the owner of a business now, and I try to dress the part."

"Whatever the reason, your new look suits you."

"Sam, would you mind if we order right away? I can't be away from the shop long. Charlotte has a class, and I have to interview a girl for clerk at two."

"You're already having to hire more help?" He seemed impressed.

"Business is good." She found herself relishing the understatement. "And we're planning a small style show this fall. So I'm in somewhat of a crash program to get the designs ready."

He signaled a waitress and glanced at her. "You mean you're designing fashions now?"

She felt a slight annoyance. Surely, in all the time they had dated she had often mentioned her interest in designing, had often worn clothing of her own creation. He had not retained that knowledge of her. That and what other knowledge had slipped his mind, she wondered cynically.

Shrugging off the small annoyance, Sarah explained about the show, and at least now he seemed interested in what she had to say. He betrayed no indifference or impatience, and he allowed her to keep the conversation completely impersonal until she had finished her salad, he his steak, and they were having coffee.

"Sarah, I don't quite know how to say this," he began hesitantly, his eyes begging her not to stop him. Tensely she waited, eyes fixed on the table.

CHAPTER FOURTEEN

"It's just—" he continued in a low voice, "I need to tell you how sorry I am about the way I behaved, sending you a note and running like a scared kid with the wedding only hours away. I'd do anything to prove to you how much I regret it."

She sighed and arranged her words precisely. "Of course I accept your apology, Sam. What's done is done. You made your choice, and I know now it was the right choice. However, I wish you'd had the courage to simply tell me face-to-face."

"But don't you see, I was under a lot of stress! I made a fool of myself. I wasn't thinking straight to give up a wonderful girl like you because of a little disagreement. I suppose you'll always hold it against me."

"For goodness sake, don't look so tragic. It wasn't a little disagreement. It was very basic. You had one idea of what our life—what my life with you should be like. I had another, completely different. And since I've tried my plans for the business, I'm more than ever convinced that what I'm doing is right for me. We'd have had to face our differences sooner or later, and the split might well have occurred later. That would have been far worse."

He looked up, and she thought how handsome he was, and how little it touched her now. "Then you aren't still angry at me? You've forgiven me?"

She hesitated. "That question has two parts and two different answers. Please don't push it, Sam. I'm only saying that I'm not sorry now about your—sudden decision, even though it was painful and humiliating at the time." She glanced at her watch and stood quickly. "I'm sorry, I really must get back to the shop."

He rose, blocking her way. "Then you'll let me call you? I want to take you out, introduce you to my family, my friends. They're terrifically curious about you. My mother dropped into your gift shop and bought a pottery bowl one day, hoping to catch a glimpse of you, but you were out."

Sarah caught a breath to speak, but he forestalled her.

"Sarah, listen, can't we just—start over? I know I've been a complete fool, but I'll make it up to you, I promise—"

"Sam, please!" she whispered, with a glance about them. "Of course you may call me. We're old friends, after all. But"—it was painful to say what she knew she must—"it's no more than that, Sam. Just friends. That's all."

"You're in love with someone else," he said, low and tense.

"Yes," she said, hoping it would end this useless and much too public conversation.

"Is it Brandt? Or that lawyer, what's his name? I know you've been seeing him, and the word is he's on his way up in politics. I guess that makes my credentials look pretty small!"

Impatient, Sarah shook her head. "No, Sam, it isn't Larry or Max Gamble. You don't know the man. All that matters between you and me now is that there is *nothing* between us."

She forced her way past him and did not look back as she left the cool restaurant and stepped back into the baking New Mexico heat.

Sliding into her car, she wondered what Sam would think if he knew that the man Sarah loved was going to marry someone else and that she had heard nothing from or about him for days.

Sarah had expected to use every evening after work to develop the ideas she was tentatively considering for the show collection. But on Friday Shirley changed her plans, in league with Ward and Charlotte.

Shirley could not honestly be blamed, however, for probably she would have much preferred to accept Sarah's courteous refusal of her carelessly issued invitation to an impromptu party Saturday night at White Sands. Ward was present at the time, placing several new bracelets in his jewelry display, and he immediately protested.

"Hey now, Sarah, you need a break. We want you to come to the party, right Charlotte?"

"Absolutely!" Charlotte came from behind a counter and caught Sarah's hand. "Ward's right, pal. You've slaved over those sketches every waking hour for days, and I bet you dream about them at night. You're coming, or else Ward and I won't go. You haven't seen the Sands, have you?"

"No, but really I should—" she began.

"Oh, for Pete's sake, don't beg her," Shirley broke in. "If it hadn't been my idea, she probably would have jumped at the chance."

"That's not true," Sarah protested. "It's just the work. You know I have to have some things ready to select fabrics for soon, or we won't have a chance of having them made in time. Some of the designs might have to be altered slightly—"

"There's plenty of time. Since we hired Marian"—Charlotte smiled at the eager, wide-eyed girl who was standing shyly on the fringe of the conversation—"you'll be able to leave the work in the shop to us. I know enough about bookkeeping to keep us up-to-date on that. You're coming to the party, and that's that. What should we bring, Shirley?"

Thus overruled, Sarah tried to redeem herself with Shirley by volunteering to furnish ground beef for the burgers. Shirley and Ward had charcoal grills, and Shirley had already arranged for a variety of beverages and most of the other necessary items for their feast.

"I've invited about thirty people," Shirley said. "Sarah, you can bring anyone you like."

"Oh, but I—"

"Well, surely you can twist someone's arm." Shirley frowned. "I don't like to have too many loose ends at my parties. Wives and girl friends get jealous if their men dance with an unattached girl."

Reflecting that Shirley was certainly an expert on jealousy, Sarah nodded.

But by midafternoon on Saturday, Sarah still hadn't brought herself to call anyone to invite to Shirley's party. Charlotte reminded her of it by asking who was coming with her.

Sarah laid down her pencil and glanced at her friend guiltily. "Charlotte, I know it's silly, but I hate calling a man for a date."

"I know you have at least two friends who would be delighted to get the invitation," Charlotte said. "Why don't you try Max? You know, I really think he's serious about you, Sarah. He called here twice yesterday when you were out looking at cloth for your gaucho ensemble."

"Max is out of town, something to do with that suit for damages—the Calt case, I think. He's in Albuquerque. One of the witnesses lives there. Besides, he's still upset with me for breaking our last date. He sounded a trifle cool when he called last night to tell me he was going out of town."

"I see. Then Larry Brandt?"

Sarah sighed, and wondered why she did. She liked Larry, and usually enjoyed his company. "Yes, I guess he's the obvious choice. It's awfully short notice though. He may be busy—"

But when Sarah reached him at the auto dealership, Larry's voice was warm and welcoming.

"Hey, Sarah! Good to hear from you, honey. Now don't tell me you want to buy a new car, trade in that junker I sold you?"

Larry always made her smile. "No, I wouldn't part with my car for love or money. I'm about to act the part of the liberated woman and ask you for a date. Do you think you can stand the shock?"

His voice went dramatically feeble. "Let me sit down, I feel faint." His laugh came warm and hearty over the wire. "Just name the time and place, honey, I'll be there."

"Pick me up at six this evening at my apartment. Shirley DeBrese is throwing a cookout at White Sands, and I'm invited, provided I can persuade some unwary male to escort me. Shirley doesn't like 'loose ends.' "

"Well, thank goodness for Shirley's good sense!" he said. "Shall I bring something? Beer or wine maybe?"

"I don't think she'll mind if you'd like to, but it isn't necessary. We can use my car—"

"Not on your life. I've got a new Ford Bronco demonstrator I've been dying to try out. See you at six, love. And Sarah"—he hesitated for a moment, then finished in a less jaunty tone—"thank you for thinking of me. 'Bye now."

Sarah hung up, feeling the familiar sense of guilt. She hadn't thought of Larry first, and she wasn't exactly yearning to see him, but perhaps he had gotten that impression. The sad fact was, she wasn't yearning to see anyone—except John Trist. And he was still in Africa, for all she knew. But it wouldn't matter if he were back in town. He was removed from Sarah by a distance that had nothing to do with geography.

Sarah had planned to work at least an hour after closing on Saturday, to lose as little time as possible to frivolity. Charlotte foresaw her intention and almost bodily hustled her out of the shop.

"Get home, have a long, relaxing bath, and put on your fanciest jeans and boots and a frilly feminine blouse, okay? Your friends like to see you looking as beautiful as you are. It lends class to the crowd."

Laughing at Charlotte's nonsense, Sarah nevertheless took her advice, only stopping off on the way home to buy ten pounds of the leanest ground beef at Albertson's.

When Larry rang her doorbell, she was ready, and looking more rested than the exhausting week should have allowed. Perhaps it was the rose pink blouse that lent color to her cheeks. She had braided her long, heavy hair in one braid, and she had a denim jacket that matched her jeans, both jeans and jacket pocket trimmed with an embroidered motif of daisies.

In the Bronco, Larry grinned at her. "You remind me tonight of the first girl I ever had a violent crush on. Come to think of it, I still think of her now and then. But don't feel shoved aside by a memory. Somehow I think you could even hold your own against the real thing."

Sarah gave him a smile, but her voice was doubtful. "I think that's a compliment, so thanks." She relaxed in the seat, and as they left the city behind them, she and Larry talked easily of the events of the week.

They retraced the route Sarah had taken from Alamogordo on her trip from St. Louis. As they roared over the crest of San Augustin Pass, Sarah tried not to see the stone pinnacles, or the memories the sight of them forced into her mind. As the Bronco nosed downhill, Shirley DeBrese passed them in her sports car at a speed that made Larry whistle.

"Lord, I hope that woman can handle that car!"

"She can. At least, she hasn't quite wrecked it yet, though I confess I don't like to ride with her."

"Who was that with her?"

"Charley Corbett. He's an artist, I understand."

"Charley?" Larry gave a hoot of laughter. "I know Charley. He's a checker-going-on-manager at Safeway, to hear him tell it. So he told you he's an artist? I guess he dresses the part at least."

"The evening I met him, he was extremely elegant."

"Was he? Usually he's the sandals, jeans, and tank-top type."

"Have you seen his work?" Sarah asked.

"Well, last week I bought a loaf of bread at Safeway and he checked me through."

She laughed. "Shame on you, Larry! I meant his artwork. Maybe the man really has talent and is only taking whatever employment he can find until he's noticed."

"Anyone who wouldn't notice Charley has to be color-blind," Larry snorted. "I did see one of his paintings once. He brought it to a party. The painting was about five feet by seven. Charley nearly gave himself a hernia carting the thing into the house."

"Was it good?"

"It looked like a close-up view of the interior of the Pizza Hut dumpster, and if that's what he meant to portray, I guess it was excellent art."

The talk turned to other things. Sarah's mind was already wandering to some problems she was encountering with the design of a fall suit. Perhaps some of her replies to Larry's remarks were a bit absent. He did not seem to notice.

They found several of the invited party guests waiting for them in their cars at the cluster of Spanish-style buildings at the entrance to the White Sands Monument. Shirley called to them that everything was arranged for the group to drive in and find a suitable spot for their party.

They followed the string of cars along sand-packed roads, curving in and out among the astonishing creamy dunes that had been sculptured by the wind into starkly beautiful shapes. Some of the outlying dunes supported cacti and other desert growths. Further into the vast gypsum beds the towering sand hills were clean and uncluttered by so much as a yucca stalk.

There were tables and overhead shades set up here and there within the park. A few groups of campers had already taken their pick of the widely spaced picnic facilities. Shirley led her string of followers for miles before she apparently decided on the perfect spot. There were no other visitors for a great distance, so they had the surrounding dunes to themselves.

Sarah found herself marveling at the surroundings. Seeing this area from the highway was nothing compared to being within this weird, moonscape world of white. Larry caught her hand as he helped her out of the four-wheel-drive vehicle, and began to pull her up the sloping side of a giant dune. He carried a saucer-shaped contraption made for playing in snow. At the top of the dune, he made her sit on the shallow, dish-shaped sled, gave her a push, and she found herself sliding faster and faster down the hissing side of the dune, to land rather awkwardly at the bottom.

Out of breath, she stood, dusted the clinging granules off, and looked up at Larry.

"Bring it back up!" he commanded.

"I'll send someone else. I want to help Shirley get the food under way," she called.

A young man she had not met called out that he would carry the toy up to Larry. Catching his girl friend's hand, they began to labor up the steep, sliding white hillside.

Sarah found Shirley taking amazingly competent charge of the supper preparations. She had cleaned the top of a nearby table and spread paper table covers weighted at the corners with catsup and mustard containers so that the light, playful breeze did not lift the cover away. Charley Corbett dressed this evening as Larry had predicted, in tank top and jeans, was ineptly trying to set up a hooded charcoal grill. Ward already had his grill lined with charcoal and burning. Sarah brought the ground meat she'd purchased and asked what she could do to help.

"Make the meat into patties," Shirley ordered crisply. "Here, I have a little mold that will make them all the same size. Try not to let the sand blow into the meat. Keep the containers covered."

Sarah began the task assigned to her, rather enjoying the moments of undemanding work, the happy voices all about her, the comical spills some of the men and women took trying to slide down the dunes. It was nice not to have to think much about what she was doing.

Someone had brought tapes, which soon were pouring music loudly from one of the cars, parked with doors open. A few of the couples—most of whom Sarah did not know and to whom Shirley did not bother to introduce her—began to dance.

As Sarah finished preparing the meat for cooking, Larry came down and demanded a dance. Since Shirley did not seem to need her help at the moment, she obliged.

Larry was a skilled and enthusiastic dancer. The rock music boomed over the desert air. Sarah wondered if someone would come and warn them to lower the volume. But no one did, and the hard-packed space between dunes was soon alive with dancers who had quickly grown tired of trudging up the very steep dunes.

Thanks mainly to Shirley's date, who could not manage to get his charcoal lighted and would not accept Ward's advice, it was after eight when the food was ready. Willingly, with appetites spurred by the fresh desert air and the exercise of dancing, everyone lined up to be served. Sarah volunteered to help fill plates with hamburgers or hot dogs, potato salad, and cole slaw. Charlotte was next to her, serving from a large container of baked beans, and she smiled at Sarah.

"Having a good time?"

"Yes, I'm glad you made me come," Sarah admitted. "This is a fabulous place, isn't it? Everyone should see it. And the party's fun."

"Larry acts as if he'd gotten a promotion, having brought you," Charlotte whispered.

"He's a good friend." Involuntarily, Sarah sighed.

"I think he wants to be more than a friend."

When Sarah was silent, Charlotte pressed the point. "I get the feeling he isn't your wildest fantasy though."

Sarah glanced quickly at her, distressed. "Oh, does it show, Charlotte? He's been so nice to me, I wouldn't want to treat him badly, or make him look small in front of—"

"No, no!" Charlotte hastily reassured her. "It's just that I know you well enough now to sense when something is—important to you. You have that special glow. Like the day John Trist helped us clean the shop."

Sarah was stunned at the knowing look her friend gave her. Thankfully, everyone had been served and there was no one to need her attention for the moment.

She sat down on the bench at the table, and Charlotte sat down nearby. "I'm sorry, I didn't mean to upset you," she said anxiously.

"It's—it's all right. I just wish you didn't read me so well. You're right. I was attracted to John Trist, but he's engaged to Shirley, and I don't believe in trespassing on someone else's territory."

"Funny, I had the distinct impression that John wouldn't consider it trespassing," Charlotte murmured.

"Charlotte, he's spoken for!" Sarah looked dully at the paper plate her friend placed before her, full of food that at the moment did not interest her in the least.

"Well, I can't help wondering about that," Charlotte persisted. "I mean—Shirley doesn't wear an engagement ring. And if there's been any notice of their engagement in the papers, I certainly missed it. You know, with Shirley's society background, it would have made quite a splash if her engagement had been announced. Ward wonders why we haven't read anything about it."

"I suppose they just aren't ready to announce it publicly," Sarah said. "Anyway—I discouraged John from calling me. He won't approach me again. And that's the way it has to be!" Her voice, low as it was, had a desperate ring.

The sun was setting gorgeously behind the mountains, turning the sky to brilliant pink and orange, streaked by thin clouds. In order to change the subject, Sarah pointed the panorama out to her friend, who took the hint. Sarah began to eat.

Perhaps she was overtired. Her appetite was nonexistent. Even her dislike of waste could not make her swallow half the food Charlotte had given her. She had just opened an iced Sprite, when Larry came and coaxed her out to the "dance floor." Sarah found herself following his spirited two-step as a country recording took the place of the rock tapes Shirley had brought.

Sarah fixed her mind on the rhythm, trying to slam a mental door on the emotions her talk with Charlotte had released.

"Why didn't you bring your plate and come sit with me?" Larry gave her an aggrieved look.

"You were finished eating by the time I could have joined you, and I thought you'd rather dance than sit and watch me eat."

"Aha! You saw me with Paulette, George's date." He sounded pleased, as if he'd caught her in a jealous reaction.

"I didn't, but I'm glad you found someone to dance with," she said.

Perhaps he wasn't as dense as he sometimes seemed, for he stopped dancing and led her away from the crowd, up the face of a towering dune, so intricately marked by the wind that Sarah hated to mar nature's gigantic work of art with their footsteps.

"I want to talk to you," was all he offered by way of explanation of their abrupt departure from the dancing.

She followed him to the top of the dune and sat in a spot where the last light of the sun still gilded the pale grains of sand all about them. Up here the breeze carried away the smell of charcoal smoke and food, and Sarah drew in a deep breath of air scented by sun-warmed gypsum and nameless provocative herbal essences of desert growths from beyond the Sands.

"What do you want to talk about?" she asked, not without some dread. She simply did not feel up to a heart-to-heart discussion, which was what she sensed he was preparing for. She was not mistaken.

He sat beside her. "Sarah, how much do I mean to you?" he asked abruptly.

She sighed. This was going to be difficult. If only she could keep from hurting his pride. "You're my good friend, Larry. Surely you know that."

He lifted a handful of sand and let it dribble through his fingers. His head was bent. "Would you care to spell that out? I mean—what kind of friend are you talking about? I was friends with my wife, even after the divorce, believe it or not. And I lived with a girl from Montana while she was studying at NMSU. We were lovers, but we were friends too. We decided not to make it permanent. When she went back home, there were no hard feelings, even though I missed her for a while. Somehow I don't think that's the kind of friendship you're talking about."

She had never seen Larry in such a serious mood. He had always seemed so lighthearted, so—untouched by anything with deeper meaning. Was it only a cover-up? She liked him better from this new viewpoint, but there was still only one answer she could, in conscience, give.

"No, that's not the kind of friendship I meant."

He said nothing for a moment, and she felt driven to continue. "I'm so grateful to you, Larry. You were one of my first acquaintances in Las Cruces. You made the first weeks easier, you and all the other great people who helped me—"

"Now you're lumping me in with 'all the others'!" He gave a bitter laugh.

Involuntarily, she touched his hand, then drew her fingers away, afraid her gesture might be resented. "No, I didn't mean it that way!"

"Didn't you realize that I was falling in love with you?" he asked, lifting his head to catch her gaze insistently. "Oh sure, I know you go out with that lawyer, and probably your ex-fiancé too—I never thought you were exclusively interested in good ol' Larry Brandt! I guess I just hoped—"

From their vantage point, a set of car lights came into view, curving swiftly among the dunes from the east, toward the party. Music floated up to them, and laughter. The coming night was cool and yet softly comfortable from the remembered heat of the day still stored in the sand beneath them. A passing breeze ruffled Sarah's hair and left a scattering of granules on her jeans. Absently, she brushed them away.

"Larry, I truly don't know what to say, except that I do value your friendship. I wish I could give you more than that, but I can't."

He was quiet. She searched for words but found none that seemed right. She felt tortured by questions. Had she behaved unfairly with Larry, accepting dates with him on a purely casual basis? But he had given little indication that those dates meant anything more to him. His light, humorous approach to everything had masked his feelings, yet perhaps she should have realized that she might be accused of leading him on, though she knew inwardly that it was not true.

The car on the road below pulled to a halt at the line of parked vehicles. It was full dark now. Someone had brought Coleman lanterns, and two of the cars had their headlights turned on the dancers. In the distorting shadows, Sarah could not identify any of the moving figures below except Shirley, who wore a scarlet shorts-and-halter set. Now she saw Shirley leave her dance partner and hurry into the shadows among the cars.

"Larry," Sarah faltered, "I can only apologize—"

Swiftly, he turned to her, his face a blur in the deepening darkness. "Hey, pretty lady"—the familiar light tone was back—"never think you owe me an apology. I knew from the beginning the odds against snaring a prize like you would be high. It was worth a try, honey, and I'm not sorry I tried."

He leaned to give her a quick hug. "Let's go down and show those amateurs how to dance!"

"I—I think I'd like to stay here for a few moments, if you don't mind. The moon's coming up. I've never seen anything so beautiful," she said, a trifle unsteadily.

"Well, watch out for sand sharks and polar bears, they're invisible in this stuff!" With a laugh that was very nearly the real thing, he slid away down the dune, and she watched his dark form against the pale landscape as he made his way back to the party.

Sighing, Sarah rested her face in her hands for a moment. It was so hard to know how she could have handled her relationship with Larry better, yet she felt accused. Common sense told her that there was always this hazard when people built a tentative relationship. How could it be otherwise? One accepted dates with a congenial person, perhaps hoping that something lasting might develop, perhaps seeking nothing more than entertainment for an evening, or a passing intimacy. It was impossible to know at the outset whether any of these hopes might be achieved, impossible to know if one risked a serious disappointment or might be about to inflict unavoidable hurt on the other.

Sarah ran it over in her mind, but the answers were always the same. She had hurt Larry, but the only way to prevent it would have been to refuse to date him at all. It *had* been a mistake to invite him tonight. She would not have done so if she had suspected his true feelings. But even as she felt sorry for his unhappiness, she cautioned herself not to label it a tragedy. An attractive man like Larry would certainly not languish in loneliness. He would accept the disappointment philosophically. Perhaps they might even remain friends. Sarah felt that she would be sorry if that could not be so.

She lifted her face, turned toward the rising moon, a glowing three-quarter moon that turned the dunes into a magical place. Sarah felt comforted by the glow, by the soft desert breeze. She gazed at the sky, drifting into more peaceful thoughts, knowing that she should rejoin the party, but loath to do so. Somehow the loud music and the loud laughter down there did not belong in this place.

She was so absorbed in her thoughts that she did not realize anyone was approaching until a hand was laid on her shoulder. She jerked around with a cry to find a tall form standing behind her.

She could not see her new companion's face, but she would have known him in a darkness that obscured even the silhouette of the well-shaped head, the broad shoulders. It was as if there was a revealing electricity in the air, a new sigh in the wind, an inner awareness that defied logical explanation.

"John!" she whispered.

"I looked for you in the crowd down there."

Sarah cleared her throat, took a deep breath in an effort to stop the trembling that began at her fingertips and spread to every part of her body. It was such a shock to see him here. There had been no chance to prepare her defenses.

He sank easily down beside her. She inched further away. "I didn't realize you were back. Shirley told us you were in Africa. How was your trip?" Sarah took hasty refuge in bright and inconsequential conversation.

"Very interesting. I had to stay longer than I expected. How are you?"

Was his voice not quite steady, or was it a trick of the rising wind?

"Fine!" she announced, her voice lifting a bit too much in emphasis. "Perfectly splendid, in fact. The shop is going beautifully. We're going to have a style show in the fall, and I've been working on that night and day—"

He picked up her hand. Some warm, intense vibration seemed to weld their fingers together. "I'm glad to hear you're doing so well. I missed you. Tried to call you a couple of times before I left. Someone said you were too busy to talk to me."

She swallowed, glad he could not see the guilty, hot surge of color in her face. "I—it's too bad I missed your call."

"Calls," he corrected dryly, and she could feel his eyes even though she knew he could not see her expression.

"Oh. Well, you know how it is, there's just so much going on. I've been spread pretty thin—"

He chuckled and released her hand, but only to slide a long arm about her shoulders. She stiffened and tried to draw away.

"I must go back down now," she said quickly. "They'll be wondering what happened to me."

"I doubt it. Most of them have had too much beer to worry about you or anything else. It's good to see you've kept up your social life, in the midst of all the crush of business."

"This is the first time I've been out in weeks—" She saw that she'd been neatly trapped and tried once more to slip away from his encircling arm. He seemed not to notice. If anything he held her effortlessly closer, and she began to feel silly squirming away like a recalcitrant child. It lacked dignity. Perhaps it was better simply to sit passively, pretending that his nearness did nothing to disturb her in any way.

"See those mountains?" he asked in a conversational tone, pointing to a dark line of ridges rising miles to the east.

"Yes," she said.

"The Sacramentos," he said. "Some of the prettiest, wildest country God ever made. I have cattle running in that area, on government land, U.S. Forest Service permit. It's the devil's own job, combing cattle out of there in the fall. Cattle can get wild as deer in a few months. But the grass up there grows knee-high. The streams are clear and sweet, running over sheer rock, fed by springs and rainfall."

"It sounds wonderful."

"I love the desert." His voice was slow, relaxed. "I was born here, and it's in my blood. But once in a while I feel the need to be up there, breathing that air that's never touched earth before."

She felt that he had forgotten her presence. He was silent, gazing across to that dark edge of mountain range. The images he had invoked in her mind of that beautiful mountain landscape caught her imagination. They sat in companionable quiet for long moments, as if there had never been strain between them.

He stirred, and at once Sarah remembered that she must not linger here with him alone. She pulled away and stood. "I really must go, John."

"There's something I have to say to you," he said, rising to tower over her. "I get the feeling—"

At that moment a panting voice sounded behind them.

"Well, so that's where you got to! Listen, that's a party down there, in case you hadn't noticed. It's rude—"

Shirley had to stop to catch her breath, but she took the least possible time to get her protest going again. "It's rude to ignore the rest of us this way, Sarah!"

"I was just coming down," Sarah said hastily, praying Shirley would not start a temper tantrum at having found them in private conversation.

Not waiting to see whether Shirley had more to say, Sarah moved quickly, hurrying past her business partner and down the steep, slanting surface of the dune. She went back down to the dancing and the gaiety with such a feeling of loss and emptiness that it made the music seem tinny and distant, the laughing dancers unreal.

"Sarah, is something wrong?" Charlotte paused by her side. Quickly, she forced a smile.

"Only that I have an awful headache. Do you see Larry anywhere? I'd like to go home if he doesn't mind."

"Sure, I saw him over there. I'll find him, you sit down."

Charlotte rushed away, and in a few minutes was back with Larry. Sarah was nervous about facing him after their earlier conversation, but he behaved as if that revealing scene had never taken place. With all his old friendliness and apparent cheer, he expressed his sympathy for her nonexistent headache and asked Charlotte to make their excuses. Shirley had not yet reappeared, nor had John. Perhaps they had a great deal to say to one another, in privacy.

Sarah climbed into Larry's Bronco, breathing a sigh of relief as he started the engine and drove rapidly back toward the highway.

She was grateful that he did not attempt to make more than sporadic conversation. Sarah's emotions were so confused that she did not trust herself to sound coherent. Running through her mind over and over was the thought, John's back, *John's back*. And however much she might ache over the impossibility of her feelings for him, she could not control the surge of joy that he was nearby again. She could not be with him. Somehow it did not matter. Sarah could not make herself wish that he was still far away, or that he had not come to find her tonight.

Larry walked Sarah to her door, though she protested. But he was about to turn away with a jaunty good-night when she caught his arm.

"Larry—" she hesitated. "Thank you for coming with me tonight. I'm so sorry—"

Quickly, he laid a finger across her lips. "Honey, if you're thinking of what I said to you tonight, you didn't take that seriously, did you? Heck, that was just Larry Brandt's best line. Hardly ever fails! Now, I've got to go. I'll keep in touch."

"Yes. Good night."

"Good night, sugar." He leaned to kissed her cheek and was gone.

Sarah worked doggedly, phone off the hook, all day Sunday, completing several designs, beginning others. Monday morning she fully expected Shirley to meet her at the shop, to take her to task for daring to exchange a private conversation with John at the cookout.

However, Shirley made herself conspicuously absent during the next weeks. Time flew, filled with so much activity, so much to think about, that it was only at odd moments that Sarah wondered about John, wondered why he had not tried to contact her. But, of course, that was hardly fair. She had given Charlotte and Marian instructions that if John Trist asked for her, they were to say she was not available, or out of the shop. And after a couple of distressing calls from Sam, Sarah had asked for an unlisted number at her home and requested that those to whom she gave the number give it to no one else. Thus her privacy—and her loneliness—was insured.

There was one small event that kept Sarah sleepless on a hot, still night. Coming home from the shop, she had found in her mailbox an envelope which she recognized at once as the creamy, thick paper Betsy Hobson used for her personalized greetings.

Opening it before entering her apartment, Sarah found a breathtaking scene, slightly more distinct, more detailed than the work Betsy usually did. It depicted a grassy glade near a sparkling deep pool. On three sides high stone cliffs enclosed the cool gem of the pool, where a doe and fawn stood. Trees graced the banks. It was unutterably lovely.

Wondering, Sarah opened the card to find who had sent it. Inside she found only Betsy's beautiful hand-lettering. The message read:

> When the heart remembers,
> How can the mind forget?

There was no signature, no name on the envelope, no clue to the sender behind this provocative missive.

Sarah stood for long moments that must have seemed odd to anyone watching, studying her card, heart pounding.

John? Could it have been John? Oh, if only—

She put the brakes of her mind on hard to stop the trend of that thought. More likely, Sam had sent the card, another attempt to break through her defenses, to rebuild what he had destroyed. Well, she would find out tomorrow by the simple expedient of asking Betsy.

But Betsy was no help. She smiled strangely when Sarah asked who had commissioned the card. "I can't tell you, Sarah dear. I had to give my solemn oath to the gentleman."

Sarah frowned, ridiculously disappointed. "He asked you not to give me his name? Well—but you can describe him to me, can't you? Betsy, I'm dying to know!"

Her young friend sighed, and gave her a quick hug. "I know. It's mean to leave you in suspense. But I did promise. I will tell you this much," she relented. "He came in just after you left for lunch one day. He had a color photo he wanted copied for the card—"

"Then it's an actual place!" Sarah exclaimed.

Betsy nodded. "And he insisted on paying me fifty dollars, and then he asked me to paint a large copy, and he's paying—well, enough to pay for a year at the University! But about the card—he had the message all ready. Those were his own words, not mine. And he even asked me to address and mail it."

"But who *is* he?" Sarah wailed.

Betsy chuckled. "Can't tell you, boss. One thing's for sure. That man's flat crazy about you."

She turned and went to her work, with one last teasing grin over her shoulder, and Sarah was left to wonder.

Daily, Sarah expected to learn who had sent the card. If it was Sam, he would call again at the shop, to find out if his offering had been accepted—or he would come in person. But he did not appear.

Nor was there further word of John, and Sarah's days kept their fast pace, undisturbed by further reminders of personal matters.

Not that she did not date occasionally. Max Gamble was the most frequent companion. Larry asked her to lunch a few times. She was relieved that he seemed still to be a good friend, and that he respected the limitations of that friendship without resentment. He was dating another girl also, and sometimes he talked to Sarah about her. It was pleasant, listening to him as she would to any friend, interested in what went on in his life, wishing him only good fortune.

There were other activities that increasingly demanded Sarah's attention. She had to limit these because of the upcoming show, but she did attend a few parties given by special customers who had become friends. She joined the Woman's Club, and she was invited to be one of the speakers during a two-day seminar the university was presenting, designed for people who were interested in starting a business. Flattered to be included on the list of speakers, Sarah accepted and did some earnest preparation on the remarks she gave on a July afternoon in a cool lecture room disconcertingly full of people and representing a variety of age groups.

After the initial nervousness Sarah began to enjoy the experience. The group seemed interested, even admiring, responding to bits of humor that found their way spontaneously into her talk.

Sarah described how her business had been conceived and begun, problems that had been encountered and solved along the way, problems and challenges yet to be faced. She was nearly finished with her talk when she was jolted by a familiar face in the back row: John Trist, his dark blue eyes intent on her face.

Quickly, Sarah concluded her remarks, endured the question-and-answer period, and slipped away. She returned to the shop and her work on the style show. Fifteen minutes later the office phone rang. She could have ignored it, or let it ring until Marian, busy with a customer, answered it in the shop.

Instead, her fingers caught it up after the first ring. She heard John's voice with a sense of inevitability. She had to swallow before speaking.

"Hello, John. I'm sorry, Shirley's not in today. You might be able to reach her at home."

"I called to talk to you. I enjoyed your lecture."

"Thank you. It was a new experience for me."

"You did a great job," he said warmly. "Those people went away encouraged to try their own ideas. I wanted to talk with you afterward, but I couldn't find you."

"I—I had to hurry back here. I'm working on my fashion designs, and I'm running a bit behind schedule because of the seminar."

"I know you're busy." Was there amusement in his voice? "Let me take you to dinner. No, don't turn me down, Sarah! There's something specific I need to talk to you about."

She was caught without an adequate excuse, and deep in her heart she was not sure she wanted to make an excuse. She sighed, wondering if the heartache that surrounded the constant thought of John Trist would ever go away. "All right. Eight o'clock?"

As Sarah laid the receiver in its cradle, she sensed that she had made some step, deep within her innermost being, a step from which there could be no turning back. She could not have said whether she was glad or sorry, or if she had ever really had a choice at all.

She did not work as late on her sketches as she had planned. Somehow she found it hard to concentrate.

As she dressed, a bit more carefully than usual, she told herself that it was more for self-defense than for allure. She needed the reassurance of looking her best. She took out a new outfit she had designed and liked so much she did not offer it among the sportswear at La Casa Encantada. The white peasant blouse and the blue skirt, with its richly embroidered border in an Indian design of white thunderbirds, were youthful and lighthearted in feeling. She experimented with her hair, finally allowing its freshly washed length to lie rich and satiny down her back, caught up at the sides with blue-beaded combs.

When the doorbell rang, Sarah had to give herself a moment to steady her breathing. Once more she asked herself if it had been wise to agree to this evening, knowing the effect John Trist had on her judgment. She had tried to push him out of her mind constantly since the night Shirley had shown her she was fooling herself about his interest, that it was nothing more than a casual chemistry for him. The work, the fullness of her life had helped. She had even tried to make herself believe it could make her forget him. Yet always in the quiet, unguarded moment, John Trist waited in the recesses of her mind.

The doorbell pealed once more. Nonsensically, she imagined that she could hear amusement in the sound, as if the man who requested entrance knew what she thought, what she feared—what she could not escape, no matter how she tried.

Sarah drew a deep breath and went to open the door. She had, guiltily, dreamed this moment so many times, finding John's tall body filling the doorframe, his dark head bent, blue eyes searching her own.

She found she could say nothing for a moment, and when he smiled, there was a sudden weakness in her knees.

"You're a treat for the eyes, ma'am," he said, with the exaggerated drawl of a western actor.

"Would you like to come in for a moment?" she asked.

"Yes. We've plenty of time, and I'd like to see your home."

Heart pounding, she stood back. John Trist walked in, making the spaces of her roomy apartment shrink with his size. He looked around, nodding with approval.

"You've made it yours. It speaks of you, Sarah."

She tried for a light note. "But is that good or bad?"

His eyes were instantly back on her face, probing, intent. He did not smile, and she regretted bringing his close attention upon herself. How much natural magnetism the man possessed! It made her long to simply walk into his arms, to touch his face, his hair, to trace the strong planes of cheek and jaw with her fingertips.

"It couldn't be anything but good, Sarah." He answered her question as if it had been meant seriously. "It's very good indeed. You have the knack of making living space into space that lives."

For a dismaying moment she felt overwhelmed by the warmth of his compliment. She cleared her throat. "Ah—should we go now? Or may I offer you something to drink?"

"We'll go. How do you feel about a picnic?" He grinned, and she could almost see the boy he'd been, and the eighteen-year-old whose life had once touched hers, a touch never to be forgotten.

She blinked. "A picnic? Tonight?"

"Certainly, what better time? The ants have gone to bed."

"Should I pack sandwiches?"

"I have everything."

Recklessly, she smiled and caught up the jacket that matched her skirt. "I love picnics. Lead on, Mr. Trist!"

He held out his hand. She placed hers within it, loving the strength of his fingers clasping her own.

CHAPTER FIFTEEN

John was driving his Jeep this evening. He drove fast out of town toward the Organ Mountains and turned onto the ranch road they had traveled before. He kept the conversation general.

Sarah assumed they were going to the ranch, but John left the road and sent the Jeep bouncing over the unmarked desert toward the mountains. There was absolutely no track at all. The vehicle slewed into dry washes and growled its way out at a nervous angle. The driver's strong hands twisted the wheel, finding a way through clumps of greasewood, mesquite, and cactus.

"Where are you taking me?" Sarah gasped, clutching at the back of the seat to hold herself in.

"You'll see. It's a favorite spot of mine."

They were climbing into the foothills now, toward a deep gash in the cliffs that now towered near. John drove into the narrow canyon and after a few moments braked the Jeep. He leaped to the ground, coming around to Sarah's side. "All right, weary traveler, get out."

Sarah did, accepting his help as he lifted her down. Her legs were a trifle unsteady and she was grateful for the solid earth under her sandals. John's driving through this tough terrain had been like nothing she had ever experienced.

Nevertheless, there was a sense of exhilaration that beat like a pulse in Sarah's throat. John was lifting a hamper out of the back of the Jeep, along with a blanket, which he spread in the sand at a little distance toward the cliffs, using a powerful flashlight and first making sure there were no uninvited guests at the party, such as rattlers or scorpions. With deft, experienced motions he built a fire from dry mesquite wood and dead yucca stalks. The crackling flames brightened the area near the blanket and somehow brought the falling night in about them, as if they were enclosed in a tent of black velvet. Moonless, the desert sky formed their ceiling, embroidered liberally with brilliant splashes of quicksilver. The dark cliffs stood guard at either side.

Sarah shoved all misgivings to the back of her mind. Her heart lifted, light as a child running toward new and exciting adventures. She breathed deeply of the fragant desert air. There had been an afternoon shower, and the mesquite had a heady aroma like no other scent. Sarah stood taking it all in, her emotions dancing like the shadows that flirted with the firelight.

"Are you hungry?" John asked, tossing pieces of mesquite root on the fire.

"Yes," she said promptly.

He grinned. "Well, you'll have to wait for your dinner. There's something I want to show you."

He took her hand, and she followed him into the deeper shadows of the steep, stone-enclosed canyon, climbing in the sandy earth, circling boulders that had tumbled down long ago from those frozen curtains of rock. It was dark in here, and Sarah was glad of John's flashlight and his reassuring hand on hers.

"I used to come up here and camp, when I could get away from the ranch work. There's no time for that now, but I like to come here as often as I can."

His voice echoed strangely off the cliffs, and the sound of their footsteps seemed an intrusion into the deep silence of the place.

And yet it was not entirely silent. Sarah could hear a very faint trickle of water now, and soon they stood by a pool fed by a miniature stream that over many years had carved its channel in the solid stone.

John's light, reflected off the surrounding walls, showed grass, fresh and green, around the edge of a pool hollowed out of the gigantic foot of the mountain.

As they approached, John warned Sarah to step quietly. "Sometimes you'll see a deer or fox watering here," he whispered, bending his head to hers, his breath moving against her ear. But there was no wild visitor at the pool tonight. Nothing moved but the grass, bending in the soft breeze, and the ripples of water shimmering in the glow of the light.

"It's—it's the place on my card!" Sarah gasped. She turned to him, smiling at her discovery. "It was you! You sent that lovely card. I've been wondering, ever since. Why didn't you sign it, John?"

He regarded her soberly. "Would you have welcomed anything you knew came from me?"

She caught her breath, seeking words that would not reveal too much. Finally, she settled for a slight shake of her head.

He smiled, touched her face, and turned to look at the pool, as if the subject were exhausted. Sarah felt relieved that he said nothing more. But the knowledge that her first instinct had been right, that John had sent that message, had a stunning impact. "When the heart remembers"

—she trembled, and tried to drive the intensity of feeling away with words.

"I've never seen a more beautiful place," she said breathlessly. "It's—magical."

He nodded. "That's the way I felt the first time my grandfather brought me here, when I was six or seven. I guess I still feel like that."

"I'm surprised people don't crowd in here to camp. That would be a shame."

"Almost no one knows the place exists, and that's the way we try to keep it. This is private land, and we discourage trespassers from leaving the established roads."

Sarah bent and touched the surface of the water, finding it cool, almost cold. The ripples spread gently away toward the center.

"It's a wonderful place, John. Thank you for bringing me here," she said softly, not wishing her voice to disturb the peace of the spot.

He said nothing, but their silence was as companionable as talk as they went back down the path to the campfire.

"I hope you've brought enough food for a crowd," Sarah said as John started to unpack the hamper.

"Perhaps you wish I'd brought the crowd as well?"

Sarah turned and tried to see his expression. But he was looking at her fragile sandals. He let out an exclamation. "I meant to tell you to wear sturdy shoes or boots. You'll have your toes full of thorns, and your feet will be cold."

"Nonsense. We walked to the pool without a single thorn, and the sand is warm."

"At least come and sit by the fire," he commanded. "We'll see if Melba gave me enough food for your voracious appetite."

He set out a crusty loaf of home-baked bread that must have left the oven that very day, thin slices of marvelously tender beef roast, crisp vegetable salad in small containers with a delicate dressing. There was a bottle of red wine, cheese, and chocolate chip cookies that made Sarah remember those her mother had baked.

She ate happily. At the edge of her mind she was uneasily aware that the joy of the moment could not last. She refused to face that knowledge for the time being.

John told her about his trip to Africa. Sarah was impressed with his knowledge, his deep concern about the problems of world production of food, his interest in new methods of farming suited to developing cultures.

As he talked, lying back on one elbow, staring into the fire, Sarah studied his face, liking the strength of the bone structure, the intensity of thought revealed in his expression.

He stirred abruptly and caught her gaze. She was grateful that the new warmth in her face would not be detectable in the red and gold flickers of light. "I've talked enough," he said. "Tell me about your business. How is it going? I gather you're off to a good start."

Here was something she could discuss comfortably. "It's been better than I could have hoped. We've been so lucky. The shop seems to have caught on as one of *the* places in town to find an unusual gift. The fashion department is popular—I told you that we're planning a style show for fall? And I've been approached by a businesswoman from Albuquerque who wants to start another Casa Encantada there. She has offered to handle all the financing. Her name is Jane Gray."

"Will you do it?" He regarded her with interest.

She traced an absentminded pattern on the blanket where she sat. "I think so. I've learned that she has other successful business ventures to her credit, and an excellent reputation. I'm going next week to look at commercial space available in Winrock Center. We'll follow the same formula there, find local artists and artisans to provide most of the stock. Mrs. Gray would manage the shop, under my direction. I like her. She's intelligent, and dynamic, and creative. I think she'd make a great success of it. And since I've done well enough here to risk borrowing a certain amount for investment, I'm seriously considering the expansion."

"It sounds like a good opportunity. You have an attorney to check out legal matters?"

"Yes, Max Gamble. Do you know him?"

He turned his face back to the fire and sat up abruptly. "Yes, I know Max. Nice guy. Great future ahead of him, or I miss my guess."

"Yes. I trust Max. He's pointed out several pitfalls already. He and the accountant he recommended have helped me grasp the finer points of running a business. He's already working on the expansion plan, making sure my interests are taken care of."

"And he's not bad on the dance floor either, I hear."

Startled, she stared at the unrevealing side of his face. "I take it you've heard that I date Max occasionally," she said at last.

He gave a short laugh that somehow lacked amusement. "Oh yes. You'd be surprised what remarkable reports come my way these days."

Indignant, Sarah sprang to her feet. Her brows drew sharply. "Reports? Are you saying that you have someone spy on my life and report to you?"

He grinned lazily up at her. "Sarah, you've been watching too much TV. That's silly."

He got up, staring at her across the fire, which had burned down to coals. "Does it make you angry that I'm interested in how things are going for you?"

"It's one thing to be interested and quite another to pry into my private life!" she snapped.

"No prying is needed where Gamble is concerned. There are always speculative eyes on him—and on his companions."

"That still doesn't explain how you know all about it."

"I didn't mean to—intrude in private matters," he said, rather unconvincingly. "It's just that when I mention your name to Maureen, her pride in you and everything you do comes out. She mentioned that you were seeing Max. She naturally feels that the thriving young attorney is extremely eligible and that he probably has the inside track with you. Is she right, Sarah?"

He stepped around the coals and caught her shoulders, turning her to face him squarely. He stared down at her with that unreadable expression that set her heart pounding.

"If you mean," she said firmly, "does Max want to marry me, I'm afraid I can't enlighten you. If he does, he hasn't mentioned it to me. We go out to dinner or to a party now and then. You may be right that Max is a conspicuous figure locally, and it's certainly no secret that we've dated, but it's hardly a front-page romance!"

"But he'd like it to be, wouldn't he? Though what he proposes might not necessarily be marriage, at least to begin with."

John was entirely too close to the truth. She tried to move away from him, but he put up a hand and stroked her cheek. It stopped her movement as if her feet were suddenly encased in solid stone.

"You needn't answer that," he said. "I'm well aware you haven't given me the right to ask such a question. But I want that right, Sarah. I want *you,* my darling."

The quiet words seemed to hang in the desert air, weaving themselves into the slow spirals of white smoke that rose from the dying fire.

Sarah felt that she could not breathe. For an instant she felt dizzy, disoriented. Desperately, she warned herself not to listen to John. Here was what she had dreaded, the illusion of the love she wanted becoming the trap Shirley had pointed out.

"Do you hear me, love?" he asked tenderly, and the warmth of his fingers on her cheek made her close her eyes for a moment. "I thought you—were beginning to understand how I felt the last time we talked, at the ranch. And then you started to avoid me."

She drew a deep, quivering breath, staring up at him, desperately confused. He did not seem the type of man Shirley had described. Yet it was John who had arranged the talk between her and Shirley, during which the red-haired girl had revealed her arrangement with John— their "open" relationship that apparently allowed either of them to become involved with others as they pleased, without severing the agreement between them. Shirley would be his wife, and there would be no mistake who was first in John's life.

Sarah couldn't bear to discuss it. She could not bring herself to ruin this lovely evening, to shatter the spell. She evaded the explanation he evidently meant to have.

"Hardly avoiding you," she said with determined lightness. "I'm here, and it's been a wonderful evening. But I didn't come to discuss my social life. It's the dullest subject imaginable."

He lifted his other hand and placed both palms along her face, fingertips sliding into her hair. Her senses quivered at his touch, and she made one last move to deny the power of his magnetism. She removed his hands and stumbled back from him. "I think we'd best go back now," she said unevenly.

"No," he muttered hoarsely, and caught her wrists to pull her close against him, the hard contact of his body sending vital, urgent messages throughout her own. His lips parted hers, and the kiss made the star-hung dark bowl of sky whirl and dip wildly about her.

His mouth lifted just when there was no breath left in her body. She breathed raggedly. "John!" she gasped, and it was a plea for things she knew she must forbid herself.

"Sarah, I love you," he said. "I knew it the moment you stepped through that door onto Maureen's patio and back into my life. But I think I've loved you forever."

With no will of her own, she lifted her face to his again, her arms sliding around his neck as he lifted her against him until her feet almost left the ground.

All taboos were swept away, all the resolutions that were so wise and well reasoned lost in the flood of desire. John Trist was promised to another woman, but Sarah could not deny her longings anymore, or the demands of her senses.

She had never known such a feeling, such delight in a man's nearness. Far back in the sanest corner of her mind she knew she would regret the reckless freeing of her heart, bound until now by chains of convention and honor. But it could not matter now. In this enchanted setting, there was a sense of being removed from ordinary rules and conventions. She and John were a part of the night and the desert, obeying instincts as old as creation.

Sarah knew later that in that moment she would have surrendered to John Trist completely. Astonishingly, it was his own restraint that drew rein on the situation.

He lifted his head, still holding her close, but more gently now. "Oh, Sarah, what you do to me! I think—I think I'd better take you back to town now."

It was like being dropped from a height without warning. "You— want to go back?" she whispered, head still whirling.

John's laugh was husky, and his hand tightened momentarily. *"Want* to? No, my little enchantress. It's the last thing I want. But when we— when our moment comes, I want it to be perfect. Nothing less is good enough for you. So—damn my unfortunate conscience! I'm taking you home. Just this once more I'll rescue you from the hazards of the desert."

On the drive back to town, John was silent, holding her hand warmly, strongly. Nor did Sarah wish to talk. She was trying to find her way, very tentatively, among the jumble of her emotions. She felt as if she'd stumbled into a fairy-tale forest, with moon-silvered paths tempting her in all directions, mocking her with the lure of delights just out of her reach. She had never known such an upheaval within her spirit, such a crumbling of resolution, a complete turnaround of her own solid, well-thought-out intentions.

She could not ignore the fact that John was to be married to Shirley DeBrese. And yet he said he loved Sarah, that he wanted her. . . .

She cringed mentally, knowing what Shirley would say to that. Of course he wanted her, just as he might often casually desire other attractive women not his wife. If Sarah accepted the brief pleasure this almost irresistible yearning demanded, she would deserve the unhappiness that surely would follow.

Yet her hand lay safe in John's at this moment, and the illusion of security she felt with him, driving through the night, was inescapable. The man at her side seemed to be glad of her presence, even though he had not followed through on their passionate embrace in the desert. And wasn't there some kind of paradox in that? It did not quite fit with Shirley's implications about his character.

Sarah sighed inwardly. She could not think it all out, could not reach a conclusion. The puzzle pieces kept shifting, altering shape. Perhaps if she had been willing to bluntly ask John how he could say he loved her when he intended to marry his financée—perhaps the truth would make itself evident. But then—then she could no longer hide from the truth and extend this precious time just a bit longer.

John parked the Jeep and came around to help Sarah out. He walked with her through the patio of the apartment complex to her door. Sarah found her key, wondering if he would ask to come in and what she would say if he did.

But he stood outside, touching only her hand, raising her fingers to his lips for a tiny moment. "When will you be back from Albuquerque?" he asked.

"Thursday afternoon or evening. I've hired a student to help Betsy and Marian. Charlotte will be in charge here."

"Can you get them to take care of things a week from Saturday? I'd like to take you to the mountains. How do you feel about horseback riding?"

"I used to ride a bit, but it's been several years."

"I'll bring a gentle horse for you. Then it's a date? I'll pick you up at five A.M. Saturday morning. Wear jeans and boots. If you get new ones, be sure they fit well, not too tight. Oh, and bring a warm jacket. Good night, darling." With a last smile he was gone.

Bewildered by the events of the evening, Sarah went into her apartment. Later, as she slid into her bed, she resigned herself to guilt about the time spent with John. But perhaps her conscience had taken a vacation. All she could seem to think about was the delight of being in John Trist's arms and the anticipation of seeing him again.

Early in the following week Sarah realized that some days had passed since she had talked with Maureen. Her conscience attacked her. Had she let business concerns and her own personal dilemma cause her to neglect her aunt? She remembered that Maureen had been struggling with problems when she had recently visited the shop. Sarah knew she should have kept in touch far more frequently.

She laid aside her work and dialed the realty office. Maureen was out showing a property. Sarah left a message, an invitation to dinner at her apartment.

As soon as she had locked the shop that evening, she visited a supermarket and bought chops, and vegetables for a salad. By the time Maureen rang the bell, at seven, the meal was almost ready. Soon the two were companionably enjoying their food with iced tea. Sarah had enjoyed cooking. It was relaxing after the stresses of the days past. And it was such a pleasure to have Maureen for the evening.

She observed her aunt surreptitiously as they ate the light dessert, a fruit mix with a dab of whipped topping. Her silver hair was cut a new way. She wore a rose and white pant suit. Maureen appeared serene, even happy, but she said nothing whatsoever about Paul Cornelius. Finally, Sarah cast caution aside and reached to touch Maureen's hand. "Well, for heaven's sake, tell me what's been going on since we talked! I've been dying to know if you've resolved your problems about Mr. Cornelius."

Maureen looked up, eyes sparkling mischievously. "I wondered how long it would take you to ask!"

"Don't keep me in suspense." Sarah poured more iced tea for Maureen and settled back to listen.

"To begin with, Paul asked me to go to Carlsbad with him last weekend. We toured the caverns, and went boating on the river, and ate at a western place where they serve a chuck-wagon meal and entertain with western ballads and trail songs. It was great fun."

"You spent the weekend with Paul? I didn't even realize you were out of town!" Sarah smiled. "I was working on sketches and I meant to call you, but—"

Maureen laughed. "And I was chiding myself for not telling you where I was going. You didn't even miss me!"

"Darling, I'm ashamed of myself. But go on. You went to Carlsbad, and—?"

Maureen blushed delicately. "And I found out that I'm not over the hill quite yet. I found out that love can begin at any time of life."

"And Paul?"

"He's asked me to marry him," Maureen said simply, her eyes glowing.

"Oh, Maureen! You said yes, of course!"

She nodded firmly. "I did. But not until after I told him that I thought his family might not welcome his decision to bring me into his life—and theirs."

"And what did he say?"

"He said he believed that he was old enough to be out of the family nest if need be, and that if they didn't accept me, he'd be obliged to run away from home"—she gave a delighted burst of laughter, remembering—"or the equivalent, since they live in Montana. He admitted that there might be some silent resistance to the idea at first, but he was not about to sacrifice his chance at happiness for someone else's reservations."

"Good for Paul! I love him already. Can he absorb a niece into his clan? And when's the wedding?"

"Next month. It will be a very simple ceremony, at my church, and you will be my only attendant."

Sarah got up and came around to hug Maureen. "I'm so happy for you I could burst!" she said. "No one deserves it more than you."

They discussed the upcoming wedding happily for a time, then Maureen held up her hand. "That's enough about me. I want to know how you are, Sarah. I can see you're working too hard. You've lost weight, my girl. It's becoming—you could never look anything but stunning, but I'm not so sure it's good for your health."

"I'm fine. I thrive on the work," Sarah assured her. "And I've got the fashion collection well along now. You knew, didn't you, that I'm thinking of starting another shop in Albuquerque? Oh, and I'm ready to buy your interest in this one, unless you want to keep it. Max Gamble is working out the details of incorporation for La Casa Encantada."

Maureen regarded her with a mixture of pride and worry. "Just as I thought. You're driving yourself to a frazzle. Don't misunderstand me dear, I applaud what you've accomplished. But when do you find time to rest, to play a little? Sarah, I hope you're not making the mistake of hiding yourself in your work."

"I think it would be safer if I did!" Sarah exclaimed involuntarily.

"What? Sarah, something's bothering you. Tell me what it is. Please let me help!"

CHAPTER SIXTEEN

For a moment Sarah longed to do just that, to lay the whole tangled tale before Maureen, to admit to her that she was hopelessly, insanely, in love with John Trist, that even his prior commitment to Shirley DeBrese was no longer a deterrent.

But somehow she could not bring herself to speak of her feelings just yet, even to Maureen. She found herself making a laughing remark to mislead her aunt.

Not that she was entirely successful. She knew that when Maureen left the apartment, she was still wondering what lay behind Sarah's studied and artificial pretense of ease. Sarah was grateful that Maureen respected her need to keep her anxieties to herself for the time being.

Sarah drove out of town on Interstate 25 Tuesday morning, bound for Albuquerque. She had the satisfaction of knowing that her work on the designs for the style show had progressed to the actual making of the garments, first on inexpensive fabrics, where any need for alteration of the patterns would show up. She knew her assistants and the skilled people she had hired would keep the project moving while she was away, as well as looking after the shop itself.

The time required by the trip was restful. She passed by exits to small towns with intriguing Spanish names, Magdalena, San Acacia, Socorro and Belen. The *bosques,* the wooded areas along the Rio Grande, were in sight to the west of the highway, while to the east lay dry, eroded terrain, and in the distance, hills.

Sarah registered at the Hilton Inn, then met Jane Gray at La Placita, in the Old Town Plaza, for lunch. The map Jane had given her proved easy to follow. Albuquerque was a lively city, sprawling up into the slopes of the Sandias, and it was exciting to think that soon Sarah would have a part in its business life.

Jane Gray was older than Sarah by some fifteen years, but one might not have guessed that from her energy and her blond, youthful looks. She was tall and slender, well dressed. She possessed an open, friendly face, and her personality matched.

They talked over a leisurely and excellent lunch, then set out to look at possible space for the new shop, finally settling upon the Winrock location.

"I like what you've done with the Las Cruces setting," Jane said. "I think we should follow that example closely in decor, choice of stock, and pricing."

Sarah spent the evening in Jane Gray's home, enjoying dinner with Jane and her husband, and an attractive single man Jane invited for Sarah. Afterward, as Sarah was thanking her hostess, Jane confided that Rob Wilton had been more than a little impressed by Sarah. Driving back to the Hilton, Sarah wished that Jane's revelation had possessed the power to excite her. It was pleasant, a compliment—and meaningless.

The next day saw most of the initial planning for the new Casa Encantada completed. Jane invited Sarah to a dinner theater for the evening.

"Rob could be talked into joining us," she grinned.

"Thank you, Jane, but I think I'll go to bed early tonight. I want to do some shopping tomorrow and then go back to Las Cruces and have my attorney work on our agreement."

As Sarah lay in bed that night, she felt a weariness that dimmed the pleasure in the accomplishments of the day. Her excitement with the new project had drained away, and suddenly she was eager for morning, so she could turn her car southward toward home.

Her fatigue betrayed her, however. Falling asleep very late, she overslept next morning. She had planned to enjoy some leisurely shopping, but her eagerness to get home made her skip that and hurry with her preparations for the drive back to Las Cruces.

She reached the city by two-thirty, stopped off at her apartment long enough to unpack and shower and change, then drove to the shop.

With a sinking feeling, she recognized Shirley's car in the parking lot. When Sarah stepped inside the shop, she found Shirley arguing with Charlotte about something, while Charley Corbett blinked diffidently in the background. Thankfully, there were only two customers to hear the argument, teenage girls who were yearning over the jewelry display.

Several enormous paintings were leaning against a counter, and Shirley was gesturing angrily toward them.

"I have a right to display Charley's work here if I want to. I promised him he could hang these and we'd sell them, and I'm not letting any *clerk* tell me what to do."

"I don't care if you promised him the crown jewels of Denmark,"

Charlotte said quietly. "We're not hanging those—those things until Sarah has a chance to approve."

"I'm part owner in this place, don't forget!" Shirley snapped. She turned and lifted the smallest of the canvases. She tossed her crinkly red mane. "Come on, Charley. We'll take some stuff off that wall, and put this up—"

Sarah strode up to the group. Shirley hesitated, eyes shifting nervously. "Oh, Sarah! I thought you were out of town. Wait until I show you the find I've made—"

But Sarah's eyes were rivited to the painting, a violent clashing of wildly incompatible colors that resembled nothing so much as an uncovered landfill.

"What are you planning to do with that?" she asked mildly, sensing the beginnings of a headache.

"You've met Charley, haven't you? Yes, of course, that night at John's ranch. Charley's a good friend of mine, and I promised him we'd set up a display of his paintings and sell them at enormous prices. Now where do you think we should hang this?"

In spite of herself, Sarah grinned. "I don't really think you want me to say where we should hang it. You won't hang it here, Shirley. Sorry, Charley." She spared him a glance. "Are the rest of the pictures similar to this?"

"They're worse," Charlotte said distinctly. "No, don't get your feelings hurt, Charley. You know yourself that you can't paint. You've been told by every art instructor on campus, and every gallery in town, I'll bet."

"Shirley thinks I can paint." Charley's chin, a rather tenderly shaped feature, quivered, and Sarah was terrified the man was going to cry. His pale eyelashes were blinking rapidly.

Sarah struggled to keep from laughing as she caught sight of the next painting on the stack, which appeared to be the portrait of a pink rubber monkey atop a gigantic bowl of salad. "I'm afraid these aren't for us, Charley," she said firmly. "Of course, you can talk to the other owner, Maureen Dwight, if you wish, but I think I can tell you in advance what she'll say."

Shirley's baby-blue eyes flamed with familiar temper. She slammed the painting she was holding onto the floor so hard it was wrenched out of its dime store, rococo frame. Charley let out a shriek of protest, to which Shirley paid no attention. "All right, Sarah! You and Maureen Dwight think you're clever, because you can overrule any of my ideas. I might as well not own a percentage of this shop at all, for any say I have."

"You chose the last lot of pottery and two of the posters," Sarah reminded her. "And you have to admit that you've had a good return on the money you invested. But anytime you want to sell out, I'll gladly buy your share of the business."

"Where would you get the money?" Shirley sneered.

"I think that's my own business—"

"Oh, I see! You intend to borrow it from John."

Sarah's unfortunate sense of humor was overwhelmed. "Well, you did," she said. "I would only be following your example."

Shirley made a sound like a kitten snarling, and turned her narrowed eyes on her white-faced friend Charley, who was trying to fit his cherished canvas into the broken frame. "Get those things out of here, Charley!" she shouted, as if he were the author of her woes.

Sarah went back to her office for a cup of coffee, hoping Shirley would depart with her disgruntled discovery and his surprising works of art before customers coming into the shop saw any of the paintings. They were enough to give the place a bad name.

But moments later Shirley slammed into the office and stood in front of the desk, chest heaving dramatically. "I suppose you're satisfied, now that you've humiliated me in front of Charley!"

"Shirley, you should have asked me first before bringing him and all those dreadful canvases here," Sarah said, sitting down and opening a ledger.

"How could I ask you, when you've been mysteriously out of town," the other girl flung at her. "You were out at John's ranch, weren't you? He sneaked you out there."

"Don't be silly," Sarah frowned up at her. "I was in Albuquerque."

"Oh, sure. That's what you told Charlotte and John to say, but I'm not fooled. You're all in this against me!"

"You asked John about this?" Sarah interrupted with deepening annoyance.

"I finally found him at his apartment here in town this morning." Shirley shrugged. "Isn't it a coincidence? You both were 'missing' until today!"

Sarah could almost feel sorry for the red-haired girl. There was something pathetic about such suspicion.

"Shirley, I was in Albuquerque, making plans to set up another shop there. You can believe me or not. I don't care. But I do wish you'd go now and let me work. I'm behind with all this paperwork."

"John told me about the little trip you two are planning for Saturday," Shirley blurted suddenly.

Sarah tried to cover her dismay. "Good. No one wants to keep anything from you," she managed. Inwardly, she was far from sure of herself. Probably she should never have agreed to go anywhere with John Trist. Her feelings for him had drawn her into frighteningly deep water. As long as he was engaged to this beautiful, volatile girl who now paced the small office space, Sarah had no business seeing John at all. Only how convince her heart of that? How deny the urgent need to be with John?

"Well, you needn't think you're getting away with anything." Shirley's mouth, very pretty when not pouting, spread in a triumphant smile. "He's invited me to go too."

Sarah struggled to keep her expression unrevealing. She reflected miserably that she must get a better grip on her emotions. These days they were like a ride on a roller coaster, and she seemed never to learn to anticipate this sudden swooping drop of spirits. Why should Shirley's announcement be so surprising? John had not really said the trip was to be for two only, and who had a better right to be included than the girl he intended to marry?

"You'll be happy to know," Shirley gave the familiar, contemptuous shake of her head, "that I've had John invite a date for you so you won't feel like a fifth wheel." She turned to the door, pausing to glance back over her shoulder with brilliant malice. "I explained to him how close you and Max Gamble are these days." She laughed. "Well, we'll both look forward to the weekend, shall we?"

She went out, but Sarah heard her mocking, triumphant laughter long after Shirley had gone.

Sarah hoped that John would call the shop and explain the change in plans. She even rescinded her former instructions to Charlotte and Marian concerning calls from John, in case one of them caught the phone first. She could not bring herself to try to contact him, though she was tempted to send a message that she could not go with him—correction —with the group Shirley had arranged.

That would seem a retreat, an admission of Shirley's accusations. Probably, it was better to pretend that nothing in the new arrangement disturbed her composure in the least. Yes, that was best. And after Saturday she simply would not see John again, no matter how difficult that might be.

On Saturday morning, just as the dawn was spreading behind the Organ Mountains, the doorbell rang. Sarah was ready, but her stomach was nervously threatening to object to the cup of coffee that had been her only attempt at breakfast. Expecting John, she opened the door to find Max Gamble outside. The attorney grinned widely, so apparently her surge of disappointment did not show.

"Wow! You do look the part, love," he said.

His remark sparked irritation. She'd deliberately worn her oldest jeans and a simple white cotton long-sleeved shirt with a quilted, lined flannel shirt over it. Her western boots were new, of necessity, but were very plain, and chosen for comfort, heavy leather with walking heels. Gamble's comment made her as self-conscious as if she'd made the mistake of appearing in fringed buckskin. She picked up her small nylon handbag and a linen hat with shady brim, and followed Max out to the street.

John had brought a Jeep, a Cherokee Chief with his ranch logo on the doors, with a four-horse trailer. The horses inside stamped on the rubber-matted floor nervously discontent at their confinement. Shirley was standing very close to John, who was adjusting something at the trailer tailgate. She gave Sarah a slow, meaningful grin, then hurried to climb into the front seat, leaving the back for Max and Sarah.

"Good morning, Sarah," John murmured, standing at the driver's door as she came down the walk to the curb. "It's good to see you."

The words were ordinary, yet somehow just for her. Her eyes wanted to cling to his, to read some kind of reassurance in his steady regard. She forced a smile, very indifferent, very bright indeed. "I wouldn't have missed an opportunity like this! I've been looking forward to seeing more of this wonderful country."

John's brows contracted just a bit, and he studied her for a long moment that made Max stir resentfully at her side. The lawyer took hold of her elbow with a possessive grip. Within the four-wheel-drive vehicle, Shirley was obviously growing impatient.

"Are we going to hang around here and talk all day?" she complained.

Unsmilingly, his look including both Sarah and Max, John indicated that they should climb in.

The trip was longer than Sarah had expected, eastward over San Augustin Pass, north through Alamogordo and Tularosa, then east once more, climbing into the Sacramento Mountains. She realized that John was taking them into the mountains he'd described to her that evening at White Sands. She felt a foolish twist of pain.

In spite of the almost juvenile chatter Shirley kept up, reinforced by Gamble's pleasant comments, the atmosphere within the Jeep was not festive. Yet it was interesting to be seeing an entirely new face of the state that Sarah had adopted and had grown to love. The differences here were astonishing. They drove through cedar- and juniper-forested hills, and then into the higher reaches of the mountains, into pine and spruce country, steep rocky slopes, and beautiful beckoning valleys that in this area belonged to the Mescalero Apaches.

They followed the curving mountain highway into the town of Ruidoso, known for its ski resort, Sierra Blanca, and Ruidoso Downs Race Track, where summer racing of quarter horses featured the world's richest horse race, the All American Futurity.

It was an attractive town, expensive summer homes perched as if by necromancy upon slopes so steep they looked virtually inaccessible. In the valleys and canyons, inviting stores and motels, churches, and schools lined the busy streets.

"Listen, can't we stop for breakfast? I'm starving," Shirley pleaded.

John turned his head to glance inquiringly at the back-seat passengers, asking Sarah's opinion as openly as if he'd uttered the words. She deplored the immediate racing of her heart as her eyes met his. More to end the taut moment than because of any appetite, she nodded.

But she was unable to eat more than a few bites of the ham and eggs Max forcefully ordered for her in the Holiday Inn coffee shop. They did not linger over the food but soon were on their way again.

"Where are you taking us, man?" Gamble asked almost nervously as they left the resort town on Highway 37, a curving scenic drive northward through the mountains.

"We'll start our ride from Argentina Canyon, above Bonito Lake. It's a beautiful area."

Sarah was content for the first time on the trip, just enjoying the wooded slopes that rose on either side of the highway, and then a blue jewel of lake that was surrounded by wonderful mountain scenery. The road curved around the end of the lake and along the length of it. Their destination was several miles farther. John parked in a cool, shady campground where a shallow, sparkling stream meandered.

Without conversation he unloaded the horses, handing reins to Max and Shirley, and then to Sarah. Sarah studied the mount John had chosen for her with interest. She was a quiet brown mare with white-blazed face and intelligent, placid eyes.

"Don't be afraid of her," Shirley reassured unnecessarily. "She's just a kid-pony."

"Don't make Sugar sound like a nag," John said. "She's steady, but she's no slug."

He came to tighten the cinch on the western saddle, then boosted Sarah up, adjusting stirrups to the correct length. She tried to remain unaware of the touches of his hands as he placed her boot firmly in the stirrup. But it was not possible to ignore his eyes as he gave her that disturbing, questioning look once more. She tried for the indifferent smile she'd been hiding behind all morning, but when his hand closed for an instant over hers as if he were helping her adjust the slack in her reins, Sarah's smile barricade crumpled and dissolved. She knew that he must be reading the deep uncertainty in her eyes—she was helpless to hide it from him. He held her gaze for a long moment. There was a certain painful relief in the silent, yet honest exchange that passed between them in that moment.

CHAPTER SEVENTEEN

Before John turned away, he smiled, quickly, reassuringly. Then he moved to assist the other members of the party. But Shirley was already in the saddle of a palomino gelding, and the attorney managed quite well to get on the bay he had been given to ride. Apparently, both Max and Shirley had considerable experience with riding, which made Sarah feel more out of place in the group than ever.

Shirley, with red hair streaming behind her, urged her horse into a gallop up the trail into the mouth of the canyon, and Max Gamble followed. Their laughter floated back on the fresh, cool morning air.

John swung onto his horse, also a bay, a beautiful, spirited animal, but effortlessly controlled by the tall man. He smiled at Sarah. "Don't mind them," he said. "Kids will play. It's not particularly smart to run a horse on these trails. You'll see what I mean soon."

Sarah nudged her mare into a walk, following John, and then of her own accord Sugar began an easy fox-trot that was smooth and ground-covering along the needle-cushioned forest floor.

The trail was wide and easy at first, and Sarah relaxed, entranced with the scenes about her, high, rocky, wooded canyon walls lifting steeply skyward, the stream nearby, musical in the still air, birds quarreling in the great evergreens, oaks, and maples. The air was fragrantly resinous.

"It's wonderful here," she said, and John smiled back at her.

They soon reached the other two members of the party, who were resting their horses where the trail became narrow and precarious, a mere ribbon of rock along the flank of the mountain. Max moved back to ride ahead of Sarah. Shirley kept the lead.

Thanks to the mare's quiet, steady gait, Sarah found that she was not made nervous by the often breathtaking drops at the trail's edge. Sugar was willing and surefooted, never hesitating at difficult points. Max's gelding now and then danced sideways at shadows or something he sensed or smelled in the dense brush on the slope slide of the trail. But the mare was too wise for such foolishness. She walked or trotted, almost without need for guidance from her rider.

The party gradually fell silent, each rider conscious perhaps, of the magnificence all about. The towering cliffs caused one to feel small, and aware of a sense of vulnerability. If someone had told Sarah there were spirits here, primeval entities who took as little notice of man as man might take of an ant crossing his path, she might not have wholly scorned the idea. It seemed to her, though she smiled at her fancy, that she and the others were only tolerated here.

As she glanced at the group, she felt that of them all only John Trist seemed at home in this wilderness setting. Easy and relaxed in his saddle, yet with an impression of constant alertness on his tall, lively mount. When the trail split, he spurred his bay ahead at Shirley's and led the way through the fastness of deserted canyon, his very quietness discouraging the reckless display Shirley and Max had indulged in earlier.

It was past noon when at last they rode their sweating horses up the last steep switchback and out upon a boulder-strewn spine of windswept ridge that stretched away on either side as far as Sarah could see. Long grass bent to the will of the wind. Few trees had survived the elements up here. They crossed the ridge to the far edge.

Sarah was surprised how cold that breeze was at this altitude, but her sensation of chill was swallowed up in delight at the panorama that unfolded beyond them, westward.

The ridge fell away almost at their horses' front hooves in tangled, rough, secretive canyons, miles down to the desert floor, the Tularosa Basin. The San Andres and Oscuro mountains rose in the blue distances. In the basin lay the wide, pale expanse of the White Sands. Sarah was reminded again of the evening when she and John sat atop a moon-silvered dune and he had pointed out this place to her. He glanced at her now and smiled. Was he thinking of that evening too? She looked back at the view, tracing a strange, inky swath stretching from the Sands northward, many miles along the basin.

"What is that?" she asked. "That dark area there?"

"Mal país," he replied. "It's a waste land. An ancient lava bed. See, you can just make out the crater, that low mound at the northern edge there. The *mal país* is an incredible jumble of cooled and hardened lava, hard and dangerous to get around in. It's full of deep cracks and crevasses, and hot as Hades from soaking up the sun's heat. Yet there's wild life there, deer, coyotes, rodents, snakes."

Sarah gazed across the miles. She felt that she could happily stay here for hours. It was like being at the top of the world. She could see a town haphazardly strewn like a child's abandoned toys down in the desert.

Here and there in the vast expanse stood a ranch house or windmill. Far over the San Andres Mountains thunderheads were building. From this great height, it was almost possible to believe that one might soar off this tip of the world like the eagle John pointed out to them, riding the winds in lazy circles over the tangled canyons. When she expressed this thought, Shirley grinned.

"I'll buy you a hang glider, dear, and meet you at the bottom!"

John reined his horse away from the drop and led them along the ridge at a faster pace. During the next hour, until Shirley demanded a rest and something to eat, they rode their horses at a ground-eating trot along this lofty mountain top, with deep forested canyons dropping off to either side of the ridge.

John halted the group in a clearing just off the heights and out of the freshening wind. It was becoming uncomfortably cool now, the thunderheads moving swiftly toward them, growing and darkening. Sarah noticed John watching the towering clouds as they grew and changed shape. She shivered, glad of her heavy shirt-jacket.

"We're going to have to cut the ride short if that gets closer," John said, taking the soft drinks and sandwiches he'd bought in Ruidoso from the saddlebags on his and Max's horses.

Predictably, Shirley pouted. "I don't want to go back yet."

Sarah caught a glimpse from the corner of her eye of a ragged streak of lightning, still far out on the desert. The clouds grumbled low, like an old dog disturbed from his nap. She turned her eyes worriedly to John.

"We have time," he said softly. "We'll start down as soon as we eat. This trail will take us back to the campground by another canyon. Max, pass these around, and I'll tie the horses a little farther down the trail."

Shirley waited until John had led the animals away, then she turned angry eyes on Sarah.

"That's what we get for coming with a quivering little blossom like you," she accused. "John knows you're scared of a little old shower, so he spoils the ride for all of us."

Max glanced at her sharply. "That's silly, Shirley. You should know it isn't safe to be on these ridges in a thunderstorm, particularly on horseback. And I can tell you a good hard summer rain can make you feel half-frozen at this altitude. I got caught by rain on a hike in August once, in the Gila Wilderness Area. Took the worst cold I ever had in my life."

Shirley said no more, but her looks at Sarah were anything but friendly. John returned, accepted the sandwich and drink Max handed him, and sat down on a log near the trail. Shirley immediately sat down close against him, smiling up at him so suggestively that Sarah had to turn her eyes away.

John gave a peculiar sigh and laid his sandwich aside. "Now that we have a chance to talk," he said, "there's something I want to get out in the open. I think Shirley can help me."

Wondering what he meant, Sarah lifted her eyes to his. She was startled to see Shirley spring to her feet. John caught her wrist and held her where she was. "First," he went on, smiling at them, "a word of explanation, since Max, at least, will wonder what the devil this is all about. I apologize to you, Max. This is going to get into some personal matters."

"What's going on?" Max frowned at him and glanced with puzzlement at Shirley, who stood with rigidly averted face.

"I'll explain," John said. "When Sarah moved to town, and began her business with Shirley as a partner, Shirley told Sarah that there was a wedding in the offing—Shirley's and mine. Isn't that right, Shirley?"

But Sarah answered quickly, determined not to let anyone see how this subject affected her. "Actually, my aunt mentioned it first, and of course later—"

"Later," John broke in, holding Shirley now only with the pressure of his eyes as she whirled to face him almost defensively, "later, Shirley encouraged Sarah to believe this was true."

Shirley spluttered into hasty speech. "John, wait, I can explain!"

"Yes, I know you can. That's why I asked you to do just that on the night you drove Sarah home from my ranch. But judging by Sarah's reactions to me afterward, I've had the distinct impression that you didn't tell her precisely what I had in mind. What did you tell her, Shirley? Answer me!"

Shirley remained stubbornly silent, her face red with temper. Bewildered, Sarah stared from one to the other of them. Max was no less confused.

"What are you talking about, Trist? If there's something between you and Sarah, no one has mentioned it to me! I heard that you and Shirley were to be married. Are you saying now that you and *Sarah* have been seeing each other?" Angrily, he got to his feet.

John's glance at Sarah was laughing and tender. "Will you answer Mr. Gamble's question, love? Is there—anything between us?"

But he must have taken pity at the stricken look in her eyes, for he turned back to the others and took command of the situation. "That really isn't the question at the moment. I just want to be sure Sarah is made aware of the truth about the so-called engagement between Shirley and me. Months ago I agreed to Shirley's request that she be the one to quash the rumors of that engagement. After Sarah came, I asked Shirley once more to put a stop to it, particularly to enlighten Sarah. I gave Shirley the opportunity, and trusted her to clear the record. But she—tried something quite different, I suspect. So it's up to me to set the record straight."

"John, don't you dare!" Shirley exploded. Predictably, she started to cry. "You promised me you wouldn't do this!"

He studied her soberly. "Shirley, when someone spread the word among your friends that I had asked you to become my wife, I promised I'd give you time to correct the impression, to make some excuse that would save face for you. But you didn't stop the rumor. You enlarged on the lie, my dear, and in doing so, you almost cost me something I couldn't afford to lose. I can't let the lie continue, so I am making the statement now. Shirley and I have never been engaged."

Sarah became aware that she had been holding her breath. Something inside was unfolding like a butterfly just out of a cocoon.

Shirley turned and ran down the trail, away from the group. Quickly, Sarah stood, with the idea of finding Shirley and trying to comfort her very real distress.

"Leave her alone for a little while," John advised. "She's angry and embarrassed. I'm sorry for that, but this had to be said. I made a mistake in waiting so long."

"I think I should have been told from the first that you and Sarah had a relationship!" Max put in angrily.

"Max, forgive me!" Sarah said. "Truly, there was nothing to tell," Sarah said.

John grinned. "Believe me, that's true, Gamble. This girl was determined not to trespass. There was no deceit involved."

Grudgingly, Max nodded. "Okay. I see how it was. Well"—he stuck out a hand to John—"my loss is certainly your gain, pal."

John sighed. "Don't be so sure. Sarah is not a girl a man can take for granted."

A low roll of thunder swelled and grew in intensity. Max gave the sky a worried look. "John, that storm's getting too close for comfort. Let's get out of here, okay?"

"Sure." He quickly gathered up the picnic debris and placed it in a paper bag. Then he held out a hand to Sarah. "Ready, honey? Let's get the horses."

A sudden cold gust of wind swept over the ridge, thrashing tree branches angrily. Sarah shivered and studied the clouds, alarmed to see thunderheads looming above the mountain, almost as if seeking them out. Hurriedly, she followed John as he started down the steep, rocky trail with long strides. Max scrambled along in the rear.

They turned a bend, and John stopped so suddenly that Sarah almost bumped into him. "Oh damn!" he muttered.

"What's wrong?" she asked.

"The horses are gone." John studied the ground for a moment, then pointed to a small boot track and hoof marks in a patch of damp soil. "Shirley's playing a little trick on us," he said. His face was anything but amused. The rain was beginning, slow, almost warm drops at first, and then faster and faster, pelting and cold. "Lord! When I catch her—" John muttered.

Sarah huddled in her inadequate jacket as the soaking rain began to wilt her hat brim and drip down her neck. "Why would she do a thing like that?"

Lightning flared shockingly, and thunder seemed to shake the mountain under their feet. John grabbed Sarah's hand and continued down the trail, which quickly became slippery with rain water. The downpour became harder, as if nature meant to literally wash the intruders off the slope. Lightning cracked blindingly upon the stony ridge back of them. Sarah's heart jumped and began to race with fright. She was wet to the skin, and so cold that it did not seem possible that this could be a midsummer day.

But the trip down that long, winding canyon might have been only an uncomfortable, if frightening adventure, had not one more mishap occurred.

In places the trail was nothing more than sheer rock, and it was very slick underfoot now, with water rushing across to fall over the edge and find its way to the stream that at this point was a perilous thirty feet below. Sarah's boots, leather-soled and new, found very little grip on the wet rock. She had been struggling to keep her footing, helped by John Trist's hand again and again. He had let go of her fingers for a moment at a narrow place. Just as he turned to assist her, her left foot slid. She gasped as he caught at her and missed her hand by a fraction of an inch.

Blinded by the rain, Sarah unbelievingly felt herself falling over the trail's edge. Her sensations seemed to become slow-motion as she struck and rolled, struck unyielding rock and soil again and slid, helpless to stop herself.

CHAPTER EIGHTEEN

One last painful blow to her hip, and Sarah came to rest against a slender pine trunk.

"Sarah!" John's voice was frantic.

She raised a shaking hand and wiped rain water and tears of pain from her eyes just in time to see him plunge over the side to come down to her. Dazedly, she saw that his rush to reach her side had dislodged a large boulder.

"John, look out!" she cried. It was too late. The stone rolled from its muddy bed and came down the slope at John's heels, catching his foot and making him sprawl headlong, his leg at an unnatural angle. Sarah threw out both hands as if she could somehow will the rock to stop.

It came to a halt upon John's leg. Sarah saw his grimace of pain, and he slumped, head down on the steep slope.

"Max!" Sarah screamed. "Max, help him—oh, please!"

"I'm coming!" he called, though his voice wobbled nervously.

He was more cautious in picking his way down than John had been. In the moments his descent required, Sarah moved her legs and arms experimentally, struggling to disengage herself from the tree and oak brush that had broken her fall. She was conscious of painful bruises, and the palm of one hand had a small cut. She managed to move, away from the tree and upward, crawling up the steep incline until she was near John. She touched his face, so frightened that she could scarcely breathe.

"John—oh, darling, are you hurt badly?" She bent over him trying to shield his face from the pouring rain. He had lost his hat in the fall.

Max made his cautious approach, careful not to dislodge anything more from the wet earth that might come down upon them. Halting beside the boulder that pinned John's leg, he examined the situation, his face strained and frightened.

"Can't you get it off?" Sarah's voice shook. "I'll help—we have to get him free, Max!"

"Stay where you are," he cautioned. "I can shift it, but then we'll have to move him. He can't stay there, head down. Listen, hold him still if he tries to move. I'll slide this thing over, and we'll see."

Sarah laid her arms about John's shoulders, pressing her face close to his, praying that he wouldn't feel anything. She heard a series of grunts as Max strained to lift the rock enough to push it to one side and expose the injured leg.

"All right. It's off," he panted. "Let me see how bad it is."

Sarah turned to see Max shake his head anxiously. "Max, what is it?"

"His leg's broken, I think." He paused for a long moment, thinking, then met her urgent eyes. "We'll have to go for help, Sarah. But first, we've got to find a place to put John. Give me a minute."

Biting her lip to keep from giving in to hysterics, Sarah watched as Max slid further down the slope. Now that the shock of the accident was wearing off, she felt nauseated with fear. John still had not stirred. Perhaps it was best that he was unconscious, since they must move him. Nevertheless, it added to her anxiety. Was something more than his leg injured? And oh, this awful thunderstorm, the rain pelting down so hard they were all drenched to the skin. Heart in her throat, she remembered what she had read about hypothermia and shock.

She found that she wanted to sob like a little child, but something warned her that she must not give way to her fears now. She must remain calm, for John's sake. The situation was very serious. She could not hide that from herself. They were miles from help. Max would go for help, but he did not know the area. On foot it would take hours at the very least. During that time, anything at all could happen to John, hurt as he was, and helpless.

"Sarah!" Max called, climbing laboriously up to them. "The only level spot is below us, under that bushy tree about ten feet above the creek. We'll have to get John down there and try to make him comfortable. We'd better do it quick, before he wakes."

"But won't it do further injury to his leg?" Sarah gulped wet air, trying to stop shaking.

"We've got to risk it. He can't stay head down in the mud and rain for hours." Max's voice became gentle, and he gripped her shoulder, hard. "Honey, if we wait longer, he'll come to and the pain will be bad. It's the only thing we can do for him, and we have to do it now. Now, Sarah!"

She nodded and rose to her knees. Max rose to grasp John's left arm as she grasped the right. Together, they eased down the muddy, rock-strewn slope, pulling John's limp body.

It took several long minutes, and it was soul-wrenching for Sarah to imagine what being dragged over the rough ground might be doing to John's leg.

When they had nearly reached the designated tree, John groaned and stirred, his eyes fluttering open to stare blankly. He mumbled something, and they stopped pulling him. Sarah laid her hand on his face.

"John, you're going to be all right." She said urgently. "You've been hurt, and we have to move you to a better place. I know it hurts. Can you hang on?"

As her voice faltered, Max broke in, firm and brisk. "John, your leg is broken. We're trying to get you off this slope and into some kind of shelter. Can you move? Can you shift around and maybe get up? If you could lean on me—"

John, rain streaming over the strong planes of his face, nodded and began to help. He managed to slide his long body around, face rigid with pain they could only imagine, until he was no longer lying head down. With their help, he made a gigantic effort and got to his one good leg, where he stood swaying, supported by Max on one side, Sarah on the other.

It seemed to Sarah to take hours before they managed to reach the small, relatively level spot Max had found. They eased John down to a sitting position, then Max broke away the lower branches of the thickly needled juniper tree to make more space.

"The ground's dryer under here," he called. "I'll make a place for John to lie down."

While he worked, clearing away rocks and dead branches in the thick, soft duff under the tree, Sarah anxiously studied John's face. It was white, but he clung to consciousness and managed to work a penknife out of his pocket. Grimly, he began to slit his left pants leg, ripping through the tough denim. Sarah swallowed a huge lump in her throat and stayed silent while he examined his leg. When Max slid out from under the tree, John's request was low-voiced, strained.

"Please find a couple of stout branches, as straight as possible. Cut the twigs off with my knife. You've got to splint this thing for me."

Max looked sick. "John—I don't know anything about first aid!"

"I'll tell you what to do."

Under his tight-lipped direction, Max and Sarah managed to do what he asked. It required Max's strong, ungentle effort to straighten the injured leg. They bound it quickly with strips of cloth torn from Max's shirt to the supporting limbs cut and smoothed for the purpose. When they were finished, John was very white, but he was still alert.

"You'll walk out for help, of course." His glance touched both Sarah and Max.

"Of course." Max said.

"Good. It should take you and Sarah a couple of hours to get to the campground."

"I'm not going!" Sarah was shocked. "I wouldn't leave you here alone, John."

John ignored her protest, but he reached for her hand and squeezed it. "Let's try to get a fire going before you go. Can you dig out some dry stuff from under the tree?"

"Yes. But first, let me pull you back under the branches out of the rain a little."

John nodded. As gently as possible they helped him move into the makeshift shelter. He was silent for a few moments, dealing with his anguish in his own way, while Sarah met Max's eyes fearfully. Max gave her a reassuring little nod and wink, and she felt relief. Surely he would not expect her to leave John, he was merely taking the wise course of nonargument while practical matters were settled.

In a moment John showed Max where the best place for a fire would be, in a rocky niche within arm's reach of his new position. Max gathered dry needles and twigs, and with his cigarette lighter quickly got a small fire going. Then Max and Sarah broke up dead limbs for a supply of wood as John gave careful instructions for finding the campground.

"Let me give you the keys to the jeep. You may find other campers there who will help. If not, you'll have to drive a few miles down to the first cabins."

Max nodded. "I'll tie something on a limb at the top of this bank along the trail so we can't miss you when we get back, and I'll be as quick as I can, John. You can count on it."

"You won't be able to start back here before dark, and I doubt if you can find anyone who would try coming back in at night. Don't worry if you can't. I'll be fine until morning. The rain's stopping."

John turned to Sarah. "Honey, don't worry." He touched her face with reassuring fingers. "For God's sake, be careful. You saw how treacherous these trails can be. Were you hurt when you fell?"

"Only a couple of bruises. John, I'm not going," she said firmly. "Max, go on, and hurry, please."

Max grinned, bent to touch her hair, and was gone before John could protest again. They could hear him scrambling back up the steep rise to find the trail again.

John looked alarmed. "Sarah, no! Go with him. You don't realize what you're letting yourself in for—"

"Oh, I'm an old hand at being lost in the mountains." She smiled. "Let me build up the fire. You're shivering. I can't believe it's summer!"

"The—altitude," he said with difficulty. "And being wet—"

"You're in pain, aren't you?" She tried to keep the quiver from her voice. "I have aspirin in my shirt pocket. Let me find something that will hold water, and I'll get some from the stream."

He mumbled something. She backed out of their small shelter, grateful to see that the downpour had eased to a drizzle and the sky was showing patches of blue. But every bush, every inch of ground was soggy with moisture, and mist rose now, carrying almost as much wetness as the rain.

Sarah looked about for anything that could hold water. She spotted an empty aluminum can some careless hiker had thrown away. She blessed that careless littering as she rinsed the can and filled it, straining the storm-muddied water through a scrap torn from her shirt.

John accepted the aspirin and the water, his eyes fixed blurrily on her face. She added wood to the fire. All the wood was wet, but as long as she kept the fire high enough, the damp sticks eventually caught. The warmth of the blaze was reassuring. Sarah was thankful to find that John was no longer shivering, though his face was still cold to the touch.

She tried to remember what she had read about what to do in an emergency like this. She knew that being wet was a bad circumstance. She slipped out of her jacket, wrung it out as best she could, and hung it where the fire would dry it. She saw that John was drifting into sleep. Surely that was not a good sign, until he was thoroughly warm.

She touched his face, relieved when he opened his eyes. With an effort he smiled. "Thank you for staying," he murmured. "You shouldn't have, but—I'm glad, love."

"I couldn't do anything else."

Suddenly, he reached up with both arms and pulled her down against his chest, kissing her cheek. "Sarah, I love you. I want you to marry me."

Sarah was chilled from the soaked clothing that clung to her body, yet a sweet warmth flooded her body, and even in these difficult circumstances, she knew a boundless happiness.

"John," she whispered, moving her lips against his cheek.

"Well, is that my answer?" His voice held a ghost of humor.

Her laugh was shaky. "Yes, I'll marry you, darling. There's nothing I want more. Except to have you where you can be taken care of—" Her voice broke.

"You're all the help I need." He kissed her hungrily. But as he shifted his position a bit, he gave an involuntary gasp, and she knew that his leg was paining him. Gently, she drew away and began to find more wood for the fire.

"What we need is a cup of coffee," he said. "All I can offer is a couple of candy bars in the pocket of my coat." He fumbled for a moment and drew out Hershey bars; that immediately gave her an idea.

"I'll heat them! Let me have your knife." Under his amused gaze, Sarah cut one bar of chocolate into small pieces in the soft-drink can. Then she went to the stream and filled the can with water. Back at the fire, she set the can carefully in the edge of the flames, and watched over it until she saw steam escaping. She tore another scrap of cloth off her shirt to use as a potholder. Taking the brew from the fire, she stirred it with a twig, then proudly offered it to John, who rewarded her with a smile.

"Sarah, you're a wonder." He tasted the chocolate-flavored water and nodded. "Not bad. And it's hot—just what I needed. You have some too."

"After you've finished, I'll fix the other one."

After he drank the last of it, he was visibly drowsy. At his suggestion she helped him out of his denim jacket and put it by the fire to dry. When he had dosed off, she laid her own partially dried shirt-jacket over him. She put the other Hershey aside for later and set herself to keeping the fire alive.

They day slid into evening, dusk settling in with the complacence of a tabby on a hearth. Shivering with cold and apprehension, Sarah turned and re-turned John's coat to dry it, carefully feeding the fire. When the coat was dry, she laid it over John's legs.

She gathered a new supply of wood for the fire, walking along the creek a hundred yards in either direction, finding branches under bushes and trees. She dared not stay away for more than a few minutes at a time, but she felt that she must have a large stack of wood.

As she brought the last armload, stumbling in the growing darkness, guided by the little campfire, she heard John mutter something and quickly fell to her knees beside him.

"John, are you in pain?"

His voice was slurred, not as strong as before. "Sarah, don't leave me—"

Her heart twisted. "I'm here, darling. Of course I won't leave you. Does your leg hurt? Are you cold?"

He did not answer. Hastily, she took the aluminum can and prepared another hot drink, and made him take more aspirin. He talked to her, almost as if he were not fully aware of his circumstances. Then he fell asleep.

She kept a vigil over him, pushing away her own nervousness at the loneliness, the miles of empty wilderness crowding around them. The stars glowed cold and bright, and the air was chill. Thankfully, there was no wind.

John woke again, sometime past midnight. He lay for a few moments as if gaining a grip on the situation. He turned his head toward her.

"My guardian angel. Sweetheart, you must be very tired."

"No, I've been resting, listening to the night."

"You aren't afraid?"

"Not with you here."

His hand tightened on hers, and suddenly he spoke of that night so long ago when he had found her lost and alone in the Organ Mountains. "You were so scared, just a thin, big-eyed little girl. But you were brave, riding in front of me in the dark, not crying."

"I wasn't afraid after you came. I never will be, as long as you're near," she said simply.

"Come closer." He pulled her down to lie next to him. "You're cold, Sarah. Where's your coat? You've put it over me!"

"I'm fine, John, I was near the fire. But I must find more wood."

"No, you can't go stumbling about in the dark. Stay next to me, and we'll be all right until sunup." He tried to turn toward her and let out a hiss of pain.

"Oh, darling, I can't bear for it to hurt you so!" Sarah's tears, long held in, spilled over.

His arm tightened. "Hey, no crying. Where's that brave girl I remember? We'll get out of this. There'll be help soon. Max is probably on his way even now, bringing help."

"I'm not worried about myself," she swallowed. "It's just—your leg! I'm so afraid—"

"We can't afford to be afraid." With an effort, he chuckled. "I've been fantasizing for weeks about having you next to me like this. The pleasure almost outweighs the pain."

But though she tried to regain her spirits and follow his example of courage, she knew that he was in pain, and it was dreadful to be helpless in the face of his need.

He asked her to talk to him. She obeyed, reaching past her anxiety and into memory for things that might amuse him and divert his mind. His occasional question showed her that he was listening intently.

And then, as the comfort and warmth of lying close to him were threatening to put her to sleep, she heard a noise and sat up.

"John, listen!"

Together they strained their senses to hear above a sigh of wind that sang through the pine tops. When the breeze died away, they were sure. Help was on the way. There were voices, and lights bouncing on the canyon walls, and hoofbeats, slow but sure.

Sarah sprang up, only pausing to re-place her jacket over John's chest. "Here!" she shouted, trembling with relief and joy. "We're down here. Please hurry!"

"All right, we hear you," someone called. "Stay right where you are. Don't try to come to us."

"Oh, hurry, *please.*" Sarah felt hysterical now that help was so near. "John has a broken leg!"

Her voice echoed off canyon walls. It was only moments until men had slid down the bank with blankets and a big thermos. Max was one of the first, and he shone a powerful flashlight on her face.

"God, Sarah, are you all right? I've been half crazy worrying about you and John."

She brushed away tears with hands that were mud-and-soot-stained and tried to smile. "We're all right, but if that's hot coffee you have, please let me take some to John."

Another man grasped her wrist, taking her pulse. "Where's Mr. Trist, Miss? I'm a doctor."

"Oh, thank God!" she cried, and grabbed his hand to take him to John.

After that it was a blur. Someone put a blanket about her and gave her a cup of coffee. Then a man helped her up to the trail, though she protested at leaving John. She was boosted onto a horse, the same one she'd been riding earlier in the day.

"These are John's horses!" she exclaimed.

Max was nearby, and he nodded grimly.

"Yeah, that brat Shirley tied all but the one she was riding in the campground. She didn't have keys to the Jeep, or I guess she'd have taken that. We found her horse at a summer cabin. Evidently, she caught a ride with someone and lit out—but not before she managed to ruin two tires so I couldn't use the Jeep either. I had to ride horseback down to the cabins and find one that was occupied. The people there took me to the nearest phone, then we had to wait for the doc to get out here from Ruidoso. We've got a helicopter standing by at the campground now."

Just then the rescuers brought John up on a stretcher and carried him down the trail, the others following on horseback. The ride was very difficult for Sarah. Her bruised body and deep fatigue made her wonder if she could stay on the gentle mare for the endless dark miles back to the campground. By sheer force of will she did, but the hands that helped her down when they arrived there, and assisted her into the helicopter were very welcome.

Almost immediately, they were airborne. John had been given an injection and was asleep. Sarah too fell asleep in the seat and hardly knew when she was taken into the small hospital and put to bed.

It was midafternoon on Sunday before Sarah woke. For a few moments she was disoriented, until she remembered what had happened. She sat up too quickly, gasping as bruised ribs and back and legs reminded her of the fall she had taken.

"Sarah?" a timid voice said. "H-how do you feel?"

Sarah turned with utter astonishment to see Shirley leaning forward in a bedside chair.

"What are you doing here?" Sarah gasped. "How *dare* you—"

Then she saw that Shirley had been crying, that she looked dreadful, eyes darkened underneath with fatigue, her pretty face twisted with genuine distress. Sarah bit back the angry words.

"Sarah, I know you must hate me! I have no excuse for what I did," Shirley mumbled, wiping her face. "But I am sorry, I want you to know that. When I heard what had happened to John—oh, I'll never forgive myself as long as I live."

"How is John?" Sarah cut ungently into what promised to be a long recitation of regrets and remorse. "Tell me if John is all right."

"Oh yes." Shirley paused to blow her nose. "He was asleep earlier when I looked in. The doctor says his leg will heal perfectly, though he'll be in a cast for a while. It was a simple break, not a very bad one—"

"Quite bad enough!" Sarah snapped. She leaned back on her pillows. "I never was so frightened in my life," she said, "wondering if his injury and the soaking from the rain would send him into shock!" She shuddered.

"I know, I know!" Shirley nodded eagerly, her blue eyes wide. Sarah could not doubt her distress. "When I heard it on the news in my motel room this morning, that John had been hurt, I felt so—so awful!"

"You should feel awful, Shirley," Sarah assured her. "I know you want me to say I forgive you, but—it's too soon, don't you see? All I can think of is John lying in the mud, hurt and wet and cold."

"But—I couldn't know all that would happen," Shirley wailed.

"That's a ridiculous excuse. You left us without a way out of that canyon. It was a spoiled child's trick. You were angry because John exposed your lie, so you tried to get even."

Shirley buried her face in her hands, so stricken that Sarah felt sorry for her in spite of herself.

Shirley looked up gravely, wiping her eyes. "Everything you say is true. But there's something I want you to know."

"Shirley, I really don't feel up to—"

"Please." She interrupted urgently. "Let me tell you why I did it all, pretending John was going to marry me, lying to you. After what happened yesterday, I'm ashamed. I know you can't forgive me, but maybe you could try to understand. I deceived you—because I love John. I really love him! Oh, I know it's you he wants. I knew that long ago. But —I just couldn't bear to let go somehow."

"But surely you didn't imagine he'd go along with your fake engagement forever!"

The girl gave a rueful grin, like a little girl caught at the cookie jar. "At first, I think I did believe he would. I had just sort of—hinted to a friend of mine that John and I were making plans, and the story spread all over town. And we *had* dated a lot—casually—but I hoped—Sarah, I adore him! And he's such a gentleman, you can't know the half of it! If he thinks something he wants to do will hurt or embarrass someone—"

"But his first reactions to the rumors of the marriage should have shown you it wouldn't work. He wouldn't go as far as marriage to prevent your embarrassment!"

"Well, I suppose you're right. He certainly was angry. He wormed it out of me that I started the rumor. I told him I loved him, and it only made him laugh. He said"—she sniffled, and a tear slid down her cheek —"he said I didn't really, and I had to stop the talk."

"Well, why didn't you?" Sarah was torn between exasperation and pity for her.

"Well"—she swallowed, and wiped her eyes again—"I know I should have. I just kept putting if off. You know, my friends were so impressed, and envious—"

"I see." Sarah's voice was dry.

"And then you came!" A flash of temper dried Shirley's tears. "You came, and all at once John was demanding I tell *you* the truth, and I—I just couldn't do that. I thought, if you backed away from him for some reason—"

"Yes. And I did, you know." Sarah sighed. "At least I tried to."

"Well, you might have tried harder!"

It was almost a relief to glimpse the old Shirley. "Oh well"—Shirley gave a long, shaky sigh—"I knew it was no good from the first. But if you hadn't come to town, I think I could eventually have won him over. I'll always believe that."

"Perhaps you're right."

She was relieved when a nurse stepped into the room and firmly ushered Shirley out of the room, coming back to check Sarah's blood pressure and pulse and to ask if she needed assistance to walk across the room to the bath.

Sarah managed without help, washing her face and brushing her hair. Someone had brought Sarah's handbag from the Jeep, so she was able to apply makeup and disguise her paleness and dark smudges under the eyes.

She returned to her bed reluctantly. The doctor came in, gave her a quick check, and released her. "Miss DeBrese bought some clothing for you," the smiling nurse said, unwrapping a sleek pair of black jeans and a silky blue shirt. "Yours were a ruin, believe me. I hope she knew your size."

"That was good of her." Sarah blinked with pleased surprise. "Yes, she knows what I wear."

"We had someone clean your boots. And here are underthings."

Happily, if stiffly, Sarah got dressed. She was just braiding her hair in a plait over her shoulder when the door swung open and a wheelchair was pushed inside.

"Thank you, Mrs. Killeen," John smiled at the aide who had brought him. She nodded, glanced curiously at Sarah, and withdrew, leaving them alone.

With a glad cry, Sarah ran to kneel beside John, who caught her as close as the chair would permit.

"John, you're all right?" She studied his face anxiously.

He grinned and pressed his lips to her hand. "Good as new. Almost. They're letting us go home, if you feel like driving us. Max caught a bus back, and I've rented a car for Shirley. We'll board the horses here until I can send someone for them."

Sarah smiled, warming herself at his vital strength, undiminished by the wheelchair and the cast. "Yes, of course I can drive."

"I'm eager to get back. We have some arrangements to make," he said softly, tracing the contours of her face with one finger. "Do you want a small wedding or the works?"

She was unable to speak over the sudden lump in her throat. She swallowed. "Do you feel you must make an honest woman of me because of one night alone with you in the wilderness?"

"Yes," he replied innocently, "but come to think of it, that wasn't our first night in the wilderness, so you can hardly claim that I've compromised your reputation, lady!"

"Aha. Already trying to wriggle out of it!" Sarah accused.

His sigh was exaggerated. "No, no. I know what's right. I'll stand by my word." He lifted her chin with one finger and bent to kiss her, long and tenderly. "How soon can we be married?" he asked, low and vibrant.

She stood, but he still clung to her hand. "As soon as we can arrange a small ceremony," she said, "just Aunt Maureen and Charlotte and Ward and my friend Kelly, and Max and your friends—I don't want to give you time to change your mind."

"Very wise of you," he nodded. "I'm glad I'll be marrying a woman of sense—as well as various other qualifications."

"John—" She hesitated, looking down at him seriously. "I haven't asked you, and I must. Will you object to my business activities? I'll— I'll give them up, if you want me to." But she gave an involuntary sigh at the last words.

He laughed. "Do I look stupid? Woman, you're a gold mine!"

"John, I'm serious. If the shop or my designing are going to come between us, please tell me now."

He regarded her with intent eyes, head tilted. "You'd actually give them up for me?"

"Yes."

He squeezed her hand. "I'll never ask that of you, darling. I want you to be exactly what you want to be. All I ask is that you let me share your life. If you can spare time to travel with me now and then, I'd like that."

She laughed, knowing she had never dreamed of such happiness. "Just try to leave me behind! I've learned that I can place good people in charge of things and have more freedom. I'll go anywhere with you, anytime, on a moment's notice."

Sarah bent to meet his lips. The door swished, and a nurse cleared her throat.

"Are you ready to go, Mr. Trist?"

"Mrs. Killeen, give us your best wishes. This conniving woman has made me promise to marry her!"

The nurse beamed. "That's marvelous. Congratulations, Mr. Trist. I'm happy for you, Miss Wingate."

"Mind you," John added, "I only agreed to sign on the dotted line because you never know when you might be stranded on a mountain with a broken leg and need some first aid."

"Pity me, Mrs. Killeen." Sarah's radiant smile did not match her words. "I'll have to put up with remarks like that the rest of my life."

Laughing, the trio made their way down the hall and out to the Jeep. The nurse helped John inside. Sarah climbed into the driver's seat.

John leaned to pull her close, his lips warm and demanding on hers. She was breathless when he relaxed his hold ever so slightly. "Did I mention that I love you?"

She thought. "I don't believe so. But it's never too late," she said, holding up her face to be kissed again.